WHEN BEOWULF MEETS KYLA

D.L. Narrol

WHEN BEOWULF MEETS KYLA

DOUBLE DRAGON

A DOUBLE DRAGON PAPERBACK

ISBN 978-1-78695-856-3

Double Dragon
is an imprint of
Fiction4All

This Edition Published 2023
Fiction4All
www.fiction4all.com

D.L. Narrol

WHEN BEOWULF MEETS KYLA

DOUBLE DRAGON

PROLOGUE

The beast dodged every vicious swing of the sword. The Viking warrior showed no fear as he charged closer to the monster. The beast moaned and howled where it focused its compounded hatred for the warrior. The Viking warrior continued to thrust in *longa* stance where he managed to cut the beast enough to draw blood. The beast moaned in agony with a thundering holler, enough to vibrate the earth beneath them.

The warrior was relentless, where he had to put the monster to rest so the Danes could live again. He had to prove to his native land of Geat that he was the strongest and the only warrior who could slay the troll.

They continued to duel along the craggy cliffs overlooking the thrashing Baltic Sea. The monster pulled back from the warrior feeling almost defeated. It noticed an undefined cave where it scurried into the cavity. The strong warrior followed with his menacing sword. The darkness of the crisp night and crystallized sleet caused the warrior to lose focus. He ran his strong hands along the damp walls of the cave realizing that without sight the troll may have its way. The warrior held his sword in *guard of the long tail* stance ready if the troll were to pounce. The warrior could hear the heavy grunts and coarse breath of the monster.

He stopped and remained still. He saw no image of the beast. The cave's stench was damp and musty, which overpowered the foul aroma of the troll. Long gnarly fingers hovered near the Viking warrior's throat. He couldn't see shadows or silhouettes, for the darkness was too blinding. He could, however, smell the troll's foul stench.

"Troll! I know you're here!" the warrior called out.

The troll was silent. The Viking could feel a dewy slime

drip onto his chain mail vest. He knew the troll was too close, but he couldn't see its image. The troll's rough claws took hold of the warrior's throat. The warrior yelped, while in the midst of suffocation. The long bony fingers had a tight grip over the warrior's broad neck. The warrior dropped his sword to the ground.

A swirl of colorful smoke manifested into the darkness. The warrior gasped, kicking and punching the monster, while its grip was locked around the warrior's neck. An image of a petite woman dressed in a whisking black garment formed behind the smoke.

"Beowulf, you are wishing for my presence?" she asked.

"Witch!" he managed to say, while he tried to pry off the troll's relentless pressure from his neck. "Grant me out of this place."

"You force the words from your collapsing throat. You wish to be rid of here?"

"Yes," he grunted.

"I will then remove you from this century and place you in yet another time. It will be a time of no trolls. It will not even be Daneland or Geatland. It will be of a civilized land that you will not understand. You will never understand it. Yes?" He tried to nod, but felt himself losing consciousness. "You are a powerful man, Beowulf. You may have the strength of 30 men, but you may perish in your new world."

"Please!" he blurted. "I will perish here, but not in this different time you speak of.

Please, grant me my wish and I will be forever grateful."

"You may very well perish in this different time."

She hovered above him. His hands had a tight grip around the troll's claws.

"A land of no trolls? Then I must be sent there," he gasped in his dripping sweat. "Grant me my wish."

"I will conjure your arrival near a dwelling, perhaps the inhabitants will take you in, yes?"

6

He could no longer speak or swallow. "Very well."

CHAPTER ONE

It was an unusually warm day for London. We sat outside the teashop discussing all sorts of disgusting things. Beth and I talked about our courses and the content that was being pounded into our brains. We're both majoring in English literature. I couldn't speak for her, but I sometimes don't know why I would punish myself with such a cumbersome degree. However, what has intrigued me most is the study of *Beowulf*.

"Beth, I have gathered quite the array of sources for the essay, and you?"

"Haven't even started."

"Are we getting a bit bored with our studies?"

"Who knows? What are we going to do with English lit anyway?"

I paused to think about her question. "Teach?" I knew she would give a sour face with that answer. I noticed she began to pick at her teeth. "I don't really mind writing about *Beowulf*."

"Of course you don't, Kyla. You think Beowulf is hot."

She continued to lodge her fingernail between her gums. I chuckled.

"Hot? Wouldn't you think he's hot? He's a mighty troll slayer with the strength of thirty men."

"I'd do him."

"I would too. I even think I'd marry the bloke."

"Kyla, you would never be able to marry Beowulf."

"Why not?"

She worked profusely at trying to locate her lipstick in her purse. "He's not husband material," she insisted.

"What do you know about husband material?" I asked. "Could you ever live in Scandinavia?"

"Of course I could."

"Could you ever live in sixth-century Scandinavia?"

I laughed. "Maybe I would as long as I was Beowulf's queen."

"He was no king, Kyla. Make sure you gather your seal skins for those long winters."

"King?" I thought to myself. "Of course he was a king, wasn't he?"

"You're not even sure. He was no king, Kyla. Check your notes. Looks like I study harder than you. He was a silly warrior and that's all."

"I think a warrior is quite good, wouldn't you agree?"

"As long as he didn't get attacked by a dragon."

"Dragon?"

"Oh, Kyla, don't you even know about the dragon? And, you claim that you would marry this man?"

"So, I'll read over my notes."

"Get yourself up to snuff with this bloke."

"Yes, I'll go over everything tonight and I'll be where I should be. He still interests me and if there ever was a bloke like him today, every woman would be chasing him."

Kyla gave a loud snort of laughter. She was very unfeminine at times.

9

CHAPTER TWO

It was yet another unusually warm evening in north London. I was at my desk trying to write a comparison essay on Beowulf's sensuality with King Arthur's sex appeal. Oh God. I hope I'm not spilling some of these thoughts onto my *Word* file. As I sat by my window I noticed the rain begin. It teemed where it cooled off the smog. How can I compare a king of Britain who defeated the Saxons and established an empire over the British Isles, Iceland, Norway and Gaul? Beowulf was no king or was he? King Arthur was so brave and remarkable. I kept my thoughts fixed on Beowulf, the great hero.

Then it happened. There was a powerful knock at my door. The dormitory shouldn't be taking visitors at such a late hour. I was hesitant, but thought that maybe Beth may want something. I gingerly made my way to the door and opened it. This is when I thought those diet pills I was taking were actually getting to me.

A man stood in my doorway. He was quite lovely, I must say. His hair was ill kept though, rather long with noticeable split ends. He also had an unruly beard. His hair was of a golden color.

"Greetings, m'lady," he said, as he took my hand and kissed it.

He bowed to me, still holding my hand close to his lips. I looked at my hand as he gave it back to me. I was speechless. I was on the verge of fainting due to the musty stench he brought with him.

I spun over to my purse and grabbed my bottle of diet pills. I threw them into the trashcan with conviction. I gave another look at the man. I must say he was absolutely gorgeous. I don't think I ever noticed biceps like that on

anyone around these campus grounds. But what was up with his attire?

He stepped into my tiny dorm and bowed to me. I blinked a few times, but he was still there. Was he going to a costume party? This man was dressed in what looked like sixth-century costume. He wore a tan colored tunic with a heavy vest of chain mail over top, a thick belt made of hide, and trousers of some kind – they were heavier than tights. He was holding a broad sword in his other hand. Did I need to panic?

"Do…" I sputtered, and tried again. "D-Do…" I watched him scan my dorm room. "Do I know you?"

He seemed to be amazed at my door. Was he a door salesman? He ran his hands along the walls. Was he in construction? What construction worker dresses like that?

"Perhaps not, but I have mysteriously been posted here. What strikes me so much as odd is that I'm not addressing you in my native language, Norse."

He then bowed to me again. I didn't know whether to laugh or cry. "You're first language is Norse?"

"Yes. It is the language of my native country."

I shook my head assuming this man was pulling a prank. "Norse? Do you mean Viking vernacular?"

"If you wish to put it that way…yes."

"Nobody speaks Scandinavian around here, and especially Norse."

"I suppose that isn't a problem, because you and myself are conversing quite well."

"Isn't that amazing? You do have a nice accent." He smiled, looking as if he didn't know quite how to respond. "Are you looking for someone in particular?"

"No."

"Are you lost?"

"As I previously mentioned, good lady, I was posted here. I don't really know where I am, but I was, however, posted here."

"Posted? Are you a soldier?"

"I'm a warrior, m'lady."

"You're a warrior. What exactly do you mean?"

"Surely, you understand what a mighty warrior like myself would do."

"So, you're a mighty warrior?" I said, and rolled my eyes back with a grin.

"Of course I am. I wouldn't be ordered by the king to slay mystical beings if I wasn't a mighty warrior, wouldn't you think, m'lady?"

"Mystical beings?" I let out a loud cackle. "Like goblins and trolls, perhaps?"

"Goblins? How outrageous that sounds. No, I have never encountered any goblins."

I folded my arms in front of me. "Then you're not a warrior, especially a mighty one."

"Oh, yes I am," he said. "I have had my fare share of trolls."

"Trolls? Then I think you're in the wrong century," I said, and tried to push him out the door.

"Of course I am in the wrong century."

"Well, yeah, your chain mail is not in fashion these days."

"Perhaps, but it is required when one is slaying a troll." He ran his hands over his chest and belly. I was starting to get nervous. "One must wear protective armor at all times, don't you think?"

I stepped closer to him. I scanned every inch of him, and then circled around him. "Who are you?"

"I am Beowulf."

I stared at him for a very long minute. I nervously primped myself. I tried to comb my greasy hair with my fingernails. I gazed at his brawny physique, his long un-kept golden hair, his bushy beard, his chain mail, and his sword. I tried to curtsy, but almost fell over.

"May I ask m'lady her gracious name?"

"My name?" I had to pause and think a minute. "Kyla!

Yes, Kyla Brookes is my name. Do you wish to call me Lady Brookes?"

"Is that how you are called here, in this time?"

"No. Nobody here in this time calls me Lady Brookes."

"Then why would you make this request of me?"

I fidgeted with my chipped nail polish. He smiled at me. His eyes seemed kind and warm. He stood in my dorm room with straight posture, looking strong and mighty.

"I really don't know. You're a fine actor."

"Actor? No, I am Geat. I am from Geatland. Where is this I am at now?"

"Ah, you see, you are a fine actor." I had almost completed the removal of my nail polish. What the hell was this gorgeous bloke going on about? "You are in England, the United Kingdom, the British Isles."

"I am among the Saxons? I am in Britannia?"

"Britannia? Oh, yes, of course. Yes, you're in Britannia," I said.

"Perhaps I have put you in grave danger. You are Saxon and I am Dane. Not a pleasant combination I'm afraid."

"Who are you?"

"Beowulf."

I stepped closer to him. I stared at him. "Beowulf? You're Beowulf?"

"Of course I am."

I threw my arms in the air. "Did your mother have some fixation with the poem or what? Who calls her son Beowulf?"

"Poem?"

"Yes, I'm writing a paper on it."

"I don't know what you mean."

He had a puzzled expression on his face. I got a bit fidgety.

"How can you not know about the poem, if you claim your name is Beowulf?"

"I'm the one and only, m'lady."

I felt awkward. This man who claimed he was Beowulf was standing in my flat. Maybe he wanted to rob me? Or,

13

even worse, maybe he wanted to kill me? What's he doing wandering about female dorms? He could be loose upstairs. I shouldn't let his good looks sway me. I slowly walked up to him and gawked without saying a word. He looked into my eyes and smiled. He lifted his head, and then wore a serious expression.

"I was in the middle of the bloodiest battle with Grendel. It appeared he was about to take me over. The rest of my men fled and left me cornered in a dark cave with the beast. Even my most fearless best man, Wiglaf, fled. I was surprised. Perhaps, he may have already taken me for dead."

"Yeah, yeah, right." I pretended that I understood. This poor man was obviously mentally ill. "Hey, Beowulf, didn't you say you had a train to catch?"

He was definitely in character. He could have been one of those eccentric method actors.

"Train?"

"Yeah, maybe you should be getting on your way, hmm?"

"I had been praying to the witch for days that she needed to cast a spell upon me, so I could leave my time and venture to yet another."

I backed away a few steps. "So, now there's a witch?"

"Oh, yes, most definitely. She cast me here."

"In my dorm?" I asked.

"Dorm? I thought you said this is Britannia?"

I wanted to laugh, but for some reason I believed him.

"My dorm is in Britannia. Oh, and stop calling it that. This is England, the U.K. Just accept it, okay; there was a name change."

"Name change?" He paced my tiny room. "Britannia changed to England? Did Geat also have a name change?"

"Where in the bloody the hell is Geat?" Then I thought of my English lit class. "Wait a minute." I stepped closer to him. "Geat is Sweden. You're Swedish."

"Swedish?" He gazed at me aghast. I couldn't help but light up when I saw the smile on his handsome face. "I'm Swedish."

14

He threw his arms in the air with delight. I got a little hysterical with emotion, so I leaped into his arms like a fool.

"Yes! Yes! Yes! You're Swedish."

We embraced each other. He swaddled me tightly in his strong arms. "Thank-you, m'lady."

"For what?"

Only one of my eyes peered through the cuddling of his arms. His arms tightened around me. He sighed with relief.

"For telling me I am Swedish, of course. Maybe now I will fit into this time period, now that I know Geatland is Swedish."

"Wait. Wait a minute. Geatland is not Swedish – it's Swed'en. Geatland is now Sweden." His arms slowly released me. I scratched my head and paced around the room. "You really don't get it, do you?"

"Get it?"

I rubbed my face with both my hands. "Shit," I said.

"Shit?"

He looked at me with a serious expression. His deep blue eyes almost pierced through my body. His cheekbones were high, with a straight bridge nose, his lips were full and luscious. The man was gorgeous, yet so innocent. I then noticed he was wounded, because he hobbled when he walked.

"Please, sit down. Can I get you anything?"

"Water, please, thank-you. My thirst has been raging for days."

I awkwardly exited for the dorm kitchen to fetch the man some cold water. When I returned I found him peeling his tunic off his body. I noticed several wounds on his chest. He glanced at me.

"Ah yes, you're noticing my wounds. Grendel, of course, is responsible for this.

Do you know of Grendel?"

"Of course," I said, as if I we were addressing an old foe.

"He terrorizes Daneland, and he is a troll." My lips were parted, but I was speechless. "How do you know of Grendel?" he asked, while he guzzled the water I gave him.

15

"I'm writing my English literature essay on him."

He nodded as if he knew what I meant, but how could he? "You are writing something on Grendel, the beast?"

"No. I'm writing about Beowulf. So, let me get this clear, you wished for life in a different time and the witch granted you your wish?"

"She did."

"I wish I was a millionaire, but that doesn't seem to be happening," I said, exposing my empty pockets.

He stood and shuffled his wounded leg around the room.

"One must remember that one must be careful of what one wishes for...chances are one may be granted," he preached to me, as if he had said this before.

"So, tell me, Beowulf, do you know what time period you're now in?" He looked around the room and made his way to the window.

"No, I don't know." He pulled away from the window. "Ah!"

"Oh." He was definitely shaken up. "Are you alright?"

He flopped on the floor.

"I need to understand this world I'm in."

"Here, why don't you sit down?" I offered.

"I am sitting, m'lady," he said, almost wheezing. "Are you alright? Did I do something to offend you?"

He sat crossed-legged on the floor with his head hung down.

"I don't understand where I am. Please, you've been so kind. I may be on my way. Thank-you," he said, and quickly stood up.

"When you looked out my window, you got frightened, didn't you?"

"I am a fearless warrior. I don't know fear as you speak about it. I don't smell fear. I don't feel fear, m'lady."

He turned to me and bowed. I followed him to the door. "What are you doing? You can't even think about leaving." He was still in his bowing position.

"What time period am I in, m'lady?"

"Time period? Well, you're in the twenty-first century," I answered.

I scanned the room trying to avoid eye contact with him. He sighed. "The twenty-first century? And, I'm from the sixth."

He approached the window again. I stood behind him.

"The twenty-first century is actually quite nice. We have television, cars, cellular phones, computers, and Mp3 players."

"Mp3 players?" he asked.

"Yes, they're little gadgets we don't really need in our lives in order to survive."

"I don't understand."

"You may never understand, Beowulf."

"You have instruments that are not so important for human survival – is that it?"

"The twenty-first century is loaded with that kind of crap."

"Crap?"

"In my century," I said, "We have crisps and pop."

"What is that?"

"Food...allegedly."

"Food? Food is vital for our survival, why would you say this?"

"I say this..." I hurried to my tiny bar fridge and pulled out a bottle of pop. Then I threw a large bag of crisps at him. "I say this, because this tastes good but it is quite terrible for a person's health."

He held the bag of crisps in his hands and noticed the text on the bag. "I see the scriptures."

"No, no scriptures," I said. He stood by the door and smiled at me, but I could see how uneasy he was. "Yes, you're far away from your time. And it would be beneficial for you to clean up and change your clothes if you plan on staying a while, that is."

"Yes, I may never be allowed back into my own time. The witch has developed a sincere love for Grendel that I don't understand. He's a troll."

"So, she took you up on your wish, so she could save

Grendel from you slaying him?"

"Of course."

He looked at me as if I should know this. He stared at me, as if I had a piece of snot hanging from my nose.

"Is something the matter?"

"Forgive me, m'lady, but I am enchanted by your fair beauty."

"Really?" My awkwardness was uncontrollable. "Well, I guess my diet has been working. I already shed a stone just in the past few months."

He moved very close to me and began to fondle with my hair.

"Such magnificent hair. So straight, so short, I have never seen anything like it."

"So, you like my blunt cut?"

I giggled and blushed like a little schoolgirl. He was silent, but stared at me almost as if he undressed me with his eyes. I could be thinner, but maybe sixth-century men appreciate my hourglass figure more than these modern types.

18

CHAPTER THREE

A few weeks had passed. The climate had turned to a continuous damp rain. I received an *A* on my essay, and Beowulf had been sharing my dorm room with me. He insisted on sleeping on the floor. I don't think beds were too comfy 1500 years ago. He had been a complete gentleman, despite his rugged, barbarian appearance. Since his arrival, I have taken him to a doctor for his wounds, and especially for his limp. Beowulf sat in the doctor's examining room wearing a surgical smock.

"Must I wear this tunic, m'lady?"

"It's comfortable, don't you think?"

"I don't understand how this can protect a warrior when in battle."

"You aren't going to need it for battle, my dear."

I took his hand and squeezed it. My family physician entered the examining room. She bent over the sink to wash her hands.

"So, Kyla, this is your new bloke?"

"This is a friend of mine," I said, with a smile.

"Hello, stand up, please." He slowly stood up. She searched his arms and legs and noticed several blade wounds. "My, you've been in some dreadful fights, haven't you?"

I stood up, and said, "Doctor, he walks with a limp."

"I need to see you walk." Beowulf paced several times in the examining room.

The doctor stared into his eyes. "How did you get this injury?"

"I fell down a cliff, m'lady."

"You can call me doctor." Beowulf looked at me, then her. "Doctor? A woman?" he asked. I let out a jittery laugh.

"You see, where he's from, there aren't a lot of female doctors," I explained. "Where's that?" the doctor asked.

19

He smiled, and said, "Sweden."

The doctor glanced at me with no response. She asked him to lie on the table.

She untied his gowned and placed her stethoscope along his chest.

"Your lungs sound absolutely fantastic. It's as if you've never been exposed to any pollution. You know, I've never visited Sweden in my life. Maybe I should."

"Pollution?"

"Maybe, after this doctor's visit, we'll talk, hmm?" I said, feeling awkward in front of my doctor.

"I must say, I'm so impressed with your tools, doctor," Beowulf said, whilst still lying on the table bare-chested.

The doctor glanced at me with a slight grin.

"Your injuries are brutal. You've been struck several times with a very large blade, almost like a sword," the doctor commented.

"Yes, Grendel has used some of my own weapons against me."

"Grendel? Who's Grendel?"

"Grendel is a head gang member, doctor," I said, standing up.

"Gangs? Maybe you need to notify the police," the doctor responded. She pulled me aside. "Kyla, I understand this bloke is drop-dead handsome, but are you really interested in pursuing a gang member?"

My face must have been beet red.

"He's not involved in that any more. That was in his younger days. He's just not one for doctors."

"Sweden is a very progressive country, especially in the medical field."

"I understand that. He's had a hard life."

"Is that Grendel bloke in prison?" she asked. "I-I think so."

We left the doctor's office as we headed downstairs to the tube station.

"These doctors, Kyla, I see are very much required. There really wasn't doctors in my sixth century."

20

"What did you people do when they needed medical attention?"

"Die," he said, simply.

We stood on the platform and waited for our train.

"Beowulf, the sixth century didn't really have much of anything did it?"

"That's where you are mistaken, m'lady. We have our own King Hrothgar, Grendel, and dragons."

I had to laugh as we entered the train.

"You didn't have the London Underground that's for sure."

We stood in the crowded train holding on to whatever poles or ceiling handles we could find. The train bumped and jigged. Beowulf smiled at me.

"You are right, fine lady, there was never anything like this." I buried myself in his arms and he held me tight. "Did you ever have to answer to and please a king?"

"Why the hell would I ever want to do that?"

"If I please my king, and most of the time I do, I would someday become king, myself."

"Shhh!" I looked around the crowded train to make sure nobody heard. "It wasn't too long ago England had a king."

"Really? When?"

"I guess before Elizabeth. It could have been George, maybe Edward. I learned this in secondary school."

"Elizabeth?"

"The queen."

"When did she rule Britannia?"

"She's the queen of England, and I wouldn't say she rules it. We have a prime minister to do that."

"Prime minister? How the world has changed, Kyla."

"Oh, yeah, the world has changed. I bet you never saw a fat person in the sixth century, either."

"Did this king hire great warriors to protect the people of England?"

"I think it was George, but don't quote me."

Beowulf laughed, and pressed, "Answer my question,

21

dear lady."

"I don't think so, because that's the prime minister's job."

"Oh, so now I see. Your king has lost his power as the absolute ruler?"

I noticed some of the passengers on the train grew interested in our conversation. I smiled at them and looked at Beowulf.

"Shhh!"

"Why, m'lady, do you stifle me so? What is there to hide?"

An elderly woman sitting down glanced at me. "Our last king was King George VI, you know."

"Was he a fat person?" asked Beowulf with true seriousness in his eyes.

The elderly woman looked at Beowulf with a confused expression. "Who? King George?"

"I don't think he was fat, but he was definitely the king of Britannia, I mean England," I was starting to feel a tad off beat.

Beowulf smiled at the woman and bowed. Not in a crowded train! He took her hand and kissed it. I heard some whistles in the background. The woman grinned and actually batted her eyelashes. The train finally arrived at our stop. I tugged on Beowulf's sleeve and we left.

"Maybe we can save the history lesson for later, eh?"

***

The days went by and I would attend class and then off I'd be with Beowulf. I found myself spending loads of time with only him. I sat in a very boring tutorial one late afternoon listening to my professor drone on in Anglo-Saxon. I glanced out the window and noticed Beowulf was waiting for me. Beth, who sat beside me, also noticed him.

"Kyla, who's the gorgeous bloke?" she said, hitting my arm.

"Shhh! We need to listen to the prof," I responded, with my finger to my lips.

"Bollocks! Who's the hottie out there?"

22

"Am I supposed to know every gorgeous bloke who walks about in London?"

"You are a little bitch these days, aren't you?"

I stood up and excused myself to the lavatory. I hurried through the hallway feeling guilty class wasn't yet over. I ran outside to find Beowulf sitting under a tree.

"What you doing out here?" I asked.

He immediately stood up and kissed my hand.

"I checked the sundial and realized you were soon to finish your day here at the university."

I was silent for a few seconds. I tried to figure out what it was he meant. Then it hit me.

"Clock? Sundials no longer exist, Beowulf. It's a clock." His expression appeared somewhat confused. "I took his arm and coaxed him to towards the exit. "Clocks have been around for a good while now. Just do me a favor, hmm? Don't ever mention sundials again, alright?"

***

I did manage my time where I could still complete my academic papers. One evening Beowulf sat on the sofa mesmerized with watching television. He watched tennis, then a few silly game shows. There was a program on how to lose weight. I worked feverishly at my computer trying to get my work done.

"Kyla, my dear lady? What is this obesity I keep seeing on this picture box?"

"Fat people. You see, people eat too much rubbish in the twenty-first century."

He nodded and pretended that he understood what I meant. He continued to watch television whilst I completed my paper. I sat beside him. He had already started a bottle of French wine. He poured me a glass. I held up the glass.

"Sauvignon blanc is this type of wine, Beowulf. It's French." I had to think a minute. "Or, it's Gaul. Does that make sense to you?"

"Gaul? This lovely wine is Gaul? My people have invaded the shores of Gaul."

"Look, you're doing well in Britannia, so Gaulish wine is also a good thing."

"It's lovely, m'lady."

"It's my favorite. Don't call France Gaul, though," I instructed. "It's France."

"France. Yes, France," He muttered. "Images in a box, how fascinating. Kyla, this television you have, do all people have them in their chambers?"

"Many have more than one, my dear." I sat beside him and played with his hair. "The world changed, didn't it?"

"In such short time."

"To me the sixth century seems like a really long time ago."

"But so much has changed over the centuries. It is so easy to eat and drink in this time."

"As long as there's quid."

"I see."

I smiled at him as he took my hand in his. He was definitely feeling lost and confused, but I could tell he was also relieved to be here.

CHAPTER FOUR

One afternoon I ran into Beth at the university bookstore. "Kyla, what's happening with you lately? I never see you."

"Essays, research, you know how it is."

"Bollocks! Something's up."

"Nothing is up," I responded, stepping away from her. "You have a bloke don't you?"

She pointed her finger in my face. I really hate when she does that. "Beth, I've been busy."

"Who is he?" Beth wouldn't even let me walk past her. "What's he look like?

What's he do?"

I sighed with frustration, and said, "I haven't the time for this. You always seem to have loads of time. You know what they say, idle hands are the devil's playground."

I pushed her aside.

"Rude! Where's your manners? Does your bloke know how rude you are?" I looked at her face to face.

"I do what I have to in order to survive."

"Ah, poor little struggling student. He must be rich."

"Beth, go fuck yourself," I snapped, and pushed her aside. "Did your mother ever wash your mouth out with soap?"

"What do you want?" I asked, with a sigh.

"There's a party this Thursday night for English Lit students. Shall I expect you?"

"I may be working on my paper."

I was anxious to pay for my books and leave. I threw my money at the cashier with angst. As I tried to exit the door, Beth took my arm.

"Where are you going in such a hurry?"

"Beth, let go of me, or I'll…"

"What? What'll you do to me?"

I took a deep breath and walked outside to the sidewalk.

25

"Beth, can you keep a secret? There is this man. He's not from here."

"I knew it. Where's he from?"

"Denmark maybe, somewhere in Scandinavia. He said something about Geatland."

"Where the hell is that?"

"Sweden maybe?"

She giggled like a teenager, as she said, "Ooh, sounds luscious."

"He is. And he's very gallant."

"Really? What's his name?"

I kept my eyes on the passing buses. "Wolfe. Yes, as in Wolfgang."

"Then, you'll bring him along to the party Thursday evening?"

"I don't think I can do that."

"Kyla, you must. Introduce him to everyone."

"No, he's too handsome. Yes, I think it would be difficult for me to keep the other women away. Yes, that's what it is."

She shoved my arm.

"Ah, you'll bring him. You have no choice. I'll have to blab to everyone Kyla's got herself a bloke."

"I think a party could be a bit sudden for him."

"Why? Has he been traumatized?"

"You could say that."

"What happened to him?"

It was obvious to her that I felt uncomfortable with the conversation, but she wouldn't stop pushing.

"Look, he's been through a lot. I don't know if it's a bit soon to do this to him?"

"What has he been through? A difficult divorce, maybe? Divorce can be devastating, Kyla."

"He's not going through a fucking divorce!"

She stepped back. Her eyes scanned around me. "My, aren't we edgy?"

"Look, he's a good man, but a party could be a bit trying for him."

"Oh, Kyla, you worry too much. Bring him."

"We'll see."

I forced a smile and gave a slight wave as I walked off. On my way home I was in a trance where I tried to figure out how I was going to bring Beowulf to this party. Would it be possible to get away with things? I've already dressed him as a modern man, what else could go wrong? I entered my flat and there he was trying to comb the knots out of his long golden hair. He stood in front of the mirror wincing with each pull and tug of the comb.

"You seem to be managing," I said, while I placed my books on the table.

"I can't imagine the length of my hair to be severed, which means I must undergo this torture," he said, showing the pain in his face.

"I think I'll have to take you to a hairdresser and let them deal with this mess."

"A doctor of hair is what you may mean?"

"Oh, yeah."

He set the comb down and hung himself over the window frame, which he has developed a routine of doing. He watched the traffic and people for hours. He wouldn't comment too often on his new world. I can't imagine what has been going through his head. I wonder what he thinks of me?

"Beowulf, perhaps you could sit yourself here with me. I think we need to chat."

"Yes, Kyla."

"Over the past few weeks you have grown comfortable in your new clothes and living here with me."

"Thank-you for all that you've done. I will be forever grateful. I hope to re-pay you someday."

"You don't need to do that," I assured him.

"My word is my honor, dear lady. I will, in fact, re-pay you for all that you've done. I'm so very thankful to you."

"I'm sure if I was posted in the sixth century you'd do the same for me," I said, with a slight chuckle.

"Oh, without doubt."

I sat closer to him, and said, "There's a party in a few days at the university pub, and you and I are invited. Would you feel comfortable attending?"

His eyes scanned the room.

"A party? You mean a festivity of such?"

"Yes, where many people gather together for food, drink, and conversation."

"Similar to the festivities at Hrothgar's mead hall. I'm sure it would be worth attending, thank-you. Heorot Palace is King Hrothgar's mead hall. We have had several celebrations with mead, wine, and boar head."

"Boar head? What on earth do you do with that?"

"It's a fine delicacy, m'lady. You should try it."

"I'm off pork. It's too fattening."

"It's all worth trying."

"So, it's settled. I'll bring you to the party. I guarantee there will be no boar head at this gathering."

He sprung up from the couch and dashed for his broad sword. He swung it around the room a few times.

"It will be grand to test my swordsmanship with the men of your time, Lady Kyla."

"What are you doing? My dorm flat doesn't have the space for a sword to be swung around. Nobody will have swords at this party, Beowulf." I gestured for him to put the thing down.

"I don't understand, dear Lady."

"Nobody in this time walks about with swords."

"But I am a warrior. I fight to my victory. I must bring my sword."

"No, you won't. If you were spotted with that thing, you'd be thrown in jail."

"Jail?"

I gestured him to put it somewhere safe and away. "The dungeon."

28

CHAPTER FIVE

It was Thursday evening. I had purchased an outfit for Beowulf to wear. His hair looked smashing after the hairdresser cut off his split ends. His beard was trimmed too, thank God. I had succeeded in playing down his Viking appearance. We were just about to leave when he decided to take his broad sword. I snatched it from his hand, where it plummeted me to the ground with its weight.

"No!" I shouted, like a mother angry at her child for taking too much candy. "Kyla, a warrior can't imagine spending much time without taking along his mighty sword," he said, as he gently picked me up in his arms. "You won't need it where we're going."

"There is such a place in your time?"

"Most places in this time do not require a sword."

"Has the human race grown so gentle, so tame? I'm pleased if this is the case."

"Not at all. We now use bombs." I snorted a cackle of laughter, and helped him slide on the tweed blazer I bought on sale. "You look gorgeous."

"A man cannot be gorgeous, only a woman," he said, gazing at himself in the mirror.

"Men are gorgeous as well."

"A man must prove his worth to his lady by displaying his great bravery. A man is never gorgeous, he is brave and fearless."

"In this day and age a man can be just as gorgeous as a woman, Beowulf."

I grabbed my purse and keys and headed for the door. He held the door open. "Now, you, on the other hand are completely…"

"Completely? Completely, what?"

"Gorgeous, of course."

29

He smiled and slid his arm around me. I almost melted. We walked to the party, which was only a few blocks from my residence. I noticed how tall he was for a man from his time. He must have been six-foot-one, which would have been giant-size for the sixth century. His shoulders were broad, and the snug t-shirt he wore really showed off his ripped stomach. He still had the limp, but he handled it elegantly.

"Beowulf, does it hurt when you walk?"

He sighed as he tightened his arm around my shoulder.

"I don't ever remember not feeling pain from a wound. Sometimes I pray to Odin to just let me die, so the pain will stop."

"Maybe this warrior lifestyle is not the best thing for you," I said, gently. He stopped and gazed at me.

"Pardon, m'lady? I am a warrior. I was born to serve my king and his people. My demise will be a great honor if I am in the midst of a bloody battle."

"Why did you pray to the witch to bring you here to this time?"

"I had undergone too many battles with the troll – and many more to come, I assume. I was tired of the troll playing his dirty tricks in the dark with me. I will slay him some day and he knows it. I just needed to rid him at that particular moment."

"Well, I'm glad the witch brought you here."

"Yes, to this time. It is so fascinating."

"It must me overwhelming for you."

"I am so much more fascinated by your beauty, m'lady."

He took my hand and brought it close to his lips. I felt uncomfortable, but in a wonderful way. I wasn't used to men treating me this way. He made me feel special. We were just about to enter the party. I stopped and stood in front of him.

"So, Wolfgang, how are you feeling this evening?"

"Wolfgang?"

"You will respond to the name Wolfgang."

"I see."

30

"Are you ready to submerge yourself in some festive twenty-first century chatter?"

He tilted his head toward me, and we entered the dormitory lounge. It's where we usually shared our academic festivities. Beth noticed me enter. She cut through the crowd and made her way to us.

"Kyla! You made it," she said, clinking the ice cubes in her gin and tonic. "Who's the handsome bloke?"

"Meet Wolfgang."

I smiled, and she glared at me. He took her hand and kissed her knuckles, whilst he gave a chivalric bow.

"I bid you good cheer, m'lady."

"Oh my." She giggled like a child and blushed at the same time. "Wolfgang, I hear you're from Denmark?"

"Daneland? I'm originally from Geatland. But I serve the Danes with my strength and bravery."

She slid her hands around the girth of his biceps.

"You must have tremendous strength. So, the Danish hired you to do a job?"

"Of course. To put an end to Grendel."

"Grendel? Is that a computer virus or something?" Beth asked, clinking the ice cubes in her drink. It appeared she really didn't care whether Beowulf was making sense to her or not. She couldn't get her eyes off him. "Do you miss your country?" she asked, standing a little too close to him.

"No!"

"My, he's quite adamant about his answers isn't he?" she said, looking at me.

"He didn't like Denmark very much," I interjected. "He had one of those dirty jobs. I guess he associates Denmark with that job-thing. Let's just say, Grendel was his employer. Computer virus? Not at all, Wolfgang is not a computer geek, that's for sure."

"Oh yes, but I am Geat not geek," he instilled.

Beth glanced at me with a confused expression on her face. "Geat? What the hell is that? Is it some cult or something?"

"Cult?" Beowulf asked, and smiled at Beth.

31

"I've never been to Scandinavia, but I've heard it's marvelous," she said, still clinking those irritating ice cubes.

"How can the sixth century be marvelous?" he asked us. She gave him a friendly pat on the chest.

"Aren't you a scream, Wolfgang? I'm sorry you're not homesick for your country. I'm sure it's not as primitive as you may think. Sometimes I look at the English lifestyle to be a rat-race as well," she said, bursting into a snort of laughter. He appeared confused but forced a smile. "Now, dear, what's so distasteful about where you come from?"

"Trolls," he said, and took a deep breath. "Oh my, he's so funny, Kyla!"

Her irritating cackle was starting to hurt my ears. She took the liberty of rubbing her hands along his chest. He was polite, but I don't know why. She was getting on my nerves. It was obvious she had one too many drinks. She fondled with his jacket lapel.

"Does London have trolls as well?" Her continuous cackle was enough for me to push her into the wall. So I did.

"Kyla, you boor. What's all this?"

"London, doesn't seem to have trolls," Beowulf answered seriously.

"Well, I suppose that's good, isn't it? London has its share of other rubbish, but no trolls," she said.

"But I've only been here a short time. One never knows when a troll could show itself," Beowulf said, with caution in his tone.

"Kyla, I like your friend. He appears a little stiff, though; maybe we need to loosen him up."

She took his hand and pulled him through the crowd. I went after them, but kept experiencing roadblocks where friends and acquaintances stopped me along the way. She brought him to the bar located in the corner of the room.

"What will you have, Wolfgang?" she asked, whilst topping off her gin. "Mead, if you have it."

"I'm sure we don't have that." He seemed uneasy, because I wasn't with him. "I hope ale will please you. Not too many request Mead."

"Whatever you have will be suitable I'm sure, m'lady."

"You can call me Beth, but I like m'lady as well," she said, handing him a bottle of ale.

"Thank-you, Beth. I can see that Kyla keeps fine company just as she is fine."

"You're mistaken; Kyla can be a real bitch sometimes. Don't get on her bad side."

"What a shame, she's so beautiful as you are as well, Beth."

"Flattery will get you everywhere," she said, primping her ponytail.

I finally cut through the crowd and made my way back to Beowulf. He was chatting up Beth quite nicely.

"Thanks so much for keeping Wolfgang company," I said, with a sarcastic smile. "He's lovely, Kyla. Where did you two meet?"

"I was in the midst of a bloody battle when I suddenly ended up at Kyla's door."

"Battle? With who?" Beth asked, still hanging all over him.

"The troll, of course."

I cut in, "He was having a scuffle with his ex-girlfriend."

"Oh, I see. She must be a shrew if you describe her as a troll."

"Trolls are never enchanting no matter how one looks at it," he said, with that serious expression he tends to wear on his face.

No matter what I did I could not pry Beth off him. I think she overdid it with the gin and tonic. She rubbed his chest, allowing her hands to travel south along his trousers.

"Tell me, Wolfgang, what is it that you do?"

At this point I noticed other females listening in. "I'm a warrior who slays trolls and dragons."

Beth giggled, and repeated, "Trolls and dragons? Well, you already gave us a run-down on your troll, but how about this dragon?"

33

I nudged Beowulf in the chest.

"I must please my king's request. Yes, dragons are part of the request."

Beth's irritating giggle got louder. I thought I was going to faint. I tugged on his arm so I could get him unstuck with Beth.

"Come on, Wolfgang, it's time to mingle with other people."

Something fell out of Beowulf's jacket pocket. Five coins hit the floor and made a sound so loud the background music stopped. Beth bent down to pick them up.

"Strange money you have in Denmark."

My friend, Duncan, noticed the coins and snatched them from Beth.

"These aren't Danish coins." Duncan held them to the light. "These are ancient. I know ancient when I see it. I collect ancient coins."

I nudged closer to Duncan in order to get a better glimpse. "You're obsessed with your coin collection, Duncan."

"I wouldn't poke fun at this. Ancient rare coins can be worth quite a fortune.

Where did you get these?" Duncan asked.

"I was given them after my last slaying."

Beowulf appeared confused. Suddenly, the party was in freeze-frame mode. Now the shit was going to hit the fan.

"Last slaying?" Duncan questioned. "Slaying of who?"

"I am a fearless warrior. I am a troll slayer."

Duncan glanced at me as if he was shaming me in his mind. You could have heard a pin drop. Everyone looked at each other in silence.

"These are rare; from an ancient time. They look like old Norse to me," Duncan pressed.

"I was rewarded them for my bravery." Beowulf bowed to us as if we hired him to do a job. "Of course they are Norse. What else could they be?"

"Have you tried the Mexican dip yet?" I interjected, nudging him in the ribs. Duncan slowly stood up holding the coins in his hand.

34

"Norse?" he asked.

"Of course they're Norse. I am Norse."

"So you're a Viking?" Beth asked, in a drunken slur.

"Beth, I think you've had your fill," I said, not looking too pleased with her. "Well, Kyla, Wolf has such a cute accent. He sounds like he's Swedish, but different Swedish."

Duncan took me aside. He'd always had a thing for me, however I wished he'd get lost.

"Who is this man? Do you really know him?" he pried.

"That's none of your business."

"I've never seen coins like this," Duncan insisted.

"Oh, yes you have. You found that Roman one once. That was much more ancient than these silly coins," I said, acting as if they were everyday currency.

"These coins are Norse. It's not easy to come across Viking currency."

"Stop making such a big deal out of this, Duncan."

"Who is this man? Where did he get these?"

"Scandinavians have these kinds of coins kicking around everywhere. This is not a big deal," I repeated.

"Who the hell walks around with ancient currency like this?"

"You do," Beth said, shoving Duncan.

Whilst Duncan was wasting my time, I caught a glimpse of Beth leaving the party with Beowulf. What may have been a wonderful evening turned into a living nightmare.

CHAPTER SIX

Beth tucked herself under Beowulf's arm, as they strolled down the street. "Wolfgang, you're such a mystery to me," she said, belching in his face.

"Perhaps you would like to see my broad sword?" he asked.

"Oh my, that's the best offer I've had all year."

I was close enough behind to see her face turn red. I tore through the streets like a mad woman contemplating all the ways I would slay Beth. Where would she take him?

"So, Wolfgang, I have a nice big bed. Would you like to see it?" she asked, leading him to the street.

"Oh, forgive me, fine lady. I thought you wanted to see my broad sword."

"Can't you show it to me at my place?"

"No, I cannot," he said.

"I suppose you really know how to whip that thing around."

"Of course. It's a means to my survival."

"You know, I'm surprised at Kyla for choosing you," she said, with a laugh. "Has she chosen me?"

"Why else would she be showing you off at the party? She thinks you're hot."

"Oh? Now that you say so, I am feeling slightly flushed. Yes, I do feel quite hot."

"Just look at you."

"But, I'm from Geatland. I am Norse. It isn't hot, in fact the chill never leaves one's bones." She laughed, not knowing how to respond. He wore a puzzled expression on his face. "Perhaps you need to venture to my time to see for yourself. It's a cold dark place."

They entered her flat. It was long before there was a knock at the door. Beth opened it to find me standing there soaked from the rain.

36

"Thank-God you're here, Wolfgang. I almost lost my mind looking for you!"

I tried to catch my breath, as I pushed Beth aside and ran to Beowulf's aid.

"I'm doing fine, Lady Kyla. I'm sure I'm in good hands with Lady Beth."

"Come along, Wolfgang, I think you've been out long enough tonight."

I tugged on Beowulf's arm. Beth waved at Beowulf.

"Cheers!" she said.

CHAPTER SEVEN

It was a rainy Monday morning. I sat in an exhausted state in the university library. Duncan took the liberty of sitting beside me at the next study carol.

"Kyla," he whispered. "Duncan? What?"

"I must see your friend's coins again," he said with angst. "And, I would like to get them appraised for their value."

"Kiss off, Duncan. I've got work to do."

"Are you not interested in finding out? If those coins are as ancient as I think, your friend could be in for a lot of quid."

"How much?"

"If they're older than five hundred years, there should be a considerable sum."

"What's in it for you?"

"Some recognition in the world of historic coins would be nice, and a small percentage."

"When do you want to do this?"

"Bring the coins to me this afternoon at around 2:00." I looked at my watch. "Where?"

"Here."

"Right. You better be here at two."

I scurried off to my dorm to find Beowulf practicing his broadsword moves. "Watch where you swing that thing. My place is very small."

"Forgive me, m'lady, but I miss using it."

I sighed. "Beowulf, do you wish you were back in the sixth century?"

"Not yet. I do find your world to be fascinating. I learn so many new things each day that I'm here. I never learned so much in such short time in the sixth century."

"I'm glad the twenty-first century has made you so happy."

"I'm not sure about that. It has filled me with wonder and

desire to learn more. But, happy? I feel very misplaced and awkward most of the time. I find many of the people in your time think there is something terribly wrong with me."

"That's not true," I said.

"Oh, yes it is. There is so much I am unfamiliar with, therefore, people treat me as if I am…well, dysfunctional in some way."

"Great! You learned the term *dysfunctional*. That's a very popular term in this time."

"Oh, yes, most definitely. Everyone seems to be dysfunctional. I don't understand this at all. The twenty-first century is a time of much. It has plenty," he said. "Not all nations, I'm sorry to say."

"Well, for what I can see, there is much. I activate your picture box…I mean television…and I hear people discussing dysfunction. I detect no dysfunction in this time, m'lady. I'm very confused."

"That's why almost the entire Western world is hooked on anti-depressants." He smiled at me with a low-toned chuckle.

"Yes, anti-depressants. I even learned about those. So many people with so much are very reliant on those…drugs, as you call them."

"I had a friend who was addicted to them."

"And, how did your friend fare, m'lady?"

"She got fat."

We were both silent for a while. He stared at me for a long time. Then he moved close to me and ran his hands through my blunt blond hair.

"You're so beautiful, Kyla. I don't think I could part from you this soon. In fact, I don't think I could ever be away from you. I have never felt this way for anyone."

I pulled away from him and stepped back. "Beowulf, I must discuss something with you."

"I'm certain that I am a burden to you. I won't waste another minute of your time. I can relocate."

"No! Let me finish. You're no burden to me." I tried to

stay focused. "I'm going to need your coins this afternoon. Do you mind?"

"They're the only value I have with me, besides my sword. Where are you going with them?"

"I'm supposed to meet Duncan in the library this afternoon. He's a coin-collecting historian. He thinks they're worth something. I'm sure he's expecting a handsome percentage out of this."

"May I be present when you meet with him?"

"No!"

He sat down and was silent.

"I'm sorry, Beowulf, but whenever I take you somewhere it's always a disaster."

"Is it because I'm a troll slayer?"

"That would do it," I said, then I changed my mind. Of course not! How would anyone at first glance detect that you're a troll slayer?"

"I suppose now that I'm wearing the clothes of your time, it would be impossible. I don't really know how anyone can tell."

"Exactly."

"But, I seem to cost you a bit of trouble whenever you are seen with me. Why is that, I wonder?"

"I think it's when people start to speak with you, they notice something is different."

"Perhaps, I shouldn't talk."

"No, don't do that. You need to express yourself."

"Perhaps, I'm dysfunctional?"

"No, you're not. You're a Viking."

He moved close to me and held me tightly in his arms. I felt almost sick with confusion. "I've been acting like a witch to you."

"No, not at all. I know witches, you bear no resemblance."

"That's good to know. I think it's only fair that you come along this afternoon. They are your coins."

He smiled as he tightened his hug around my waist. It felt safe in his arms. I took a few breaths of relief.

40

"Can I call you my wench?"

"What are you asking?"

"Can you be my lady in waiting?"

"I'm not from your time. This is getting too weird for me."

"You've been more than kind to me and I have developed strong feelings for you," he said, still holding me in his arms.

"I don't know, maybe it's the correct thing for you to go back to your witch in your time, because I don't know how you can survive here. You're a troll slayer, for God's sake. We're living in a time of terrorists, not trolls."

He tilted his head forward and stared at the floor.

"Perhaps I'm a fool. You're right. I could never survive here. I haven't an idea of what I could possibly do for a livelihood."

My heart started to beat a bit faster. My palms were starting to sweat.

"What are you saying, Beowulf?"

"I'm agreeing with you. You are correct in saying this is no place for me. Maybe the witch could hear my calls and grant me my wish to return to the sixth century. One does have to be careful what he wishes for, but in this case, I feel this is the right thing to do."

"You want to return to your time?"

"I'm afraid so, m'lady. You said it yourself: I'm a troll slayer. How many trolls are roaming around the streets of London?"

"Maybe you could put your sword to use and slay terrorists instead?"

"What are terrorists?"

"Forget it, you'll never understand."

"You see? I'm nothing but a burden to you." He scratched his head appearing confused. "You just said a second ago that I must return to my time. I quite agree with you, Lady Kyla, my wench, my lady, my jewel."

"Look, the twenty-first century is a dangerous time. I'm just warning you.

41

Mechanization has gone too far, perhaps too far for a fourteen hundred year-old troll slayer like you. However, I really enjoy having you around. I don't want you to go."

"You should wish me to leave you. It's only proper. You enjoy having me around, maybe for some good cheer every now and again."

"Please, stay."

"You're so kind, m'lady." He bowed to me, still holding hands. "If I should delay my time here, I would have to earn my keep and not be a burden to you, ever."

"Stop saying that. You're no burden to me."

"You have your studies to consider, not me, m'lady."

"I can do both."

"This has been a difficult time for you. I will live a quiet twenty-first century life, if I were to remain."

"This conversation is stressing me. Can we discuss this another time?"

"I don't understand your discomfort. I feel blessed to have spent this time with you, but I should return to my time. You need to venture into a new future in this exciting time period that you live in."

"Exciting? The twenty-first century isn't exciting. I find you exciting."

"You are too kind, m'lady." He gave a slight bow. He smiled and kissed my hands several times. "As you wish."

I glanced at my watch and bit my lip.

"If we're going to meet up with Duncan we should go now."

CHAPTER EIGHT

Duncan sat at the far end of the library on the main level. We joined him there. "Good to see you again, Wolfgang," Duncan said.

Beowulf nodded a friendly greeting to him. He pulled the five coins out of his jacket pocket and handed them to Duncan. "Please be kind with them. They are all I have," Beowulf said.

Duncan examined the coins with a magnified lens. "Fascinating," Duncan said. "What's so special about them?" I asked, feeling nervous.

"These coins could be more than five-hundred years old. As I examine them, they could be around a thousand years. I'm going to have to get them appraised. What doesn't add up here is...is..." Duncan mesmerized himself with the coins.

"What? What is it?" I asked, growing impatient with him.

"If they are as old as they appear, why is it they look as good as new?"

He glared at me then gave a blank stare at Beowulf. I couldn't look at Duncan. "There have been many findings of ancient artifacts that are completely intact, so what's the big deal here?"

"That's true, I guess," Duncan reluctantly agreed. "Where did you get these?"

"My last troll slaying I was rewarded with honor."

"Kyla, your friend is being a shit head. Where did he get these?" Duncan pressed me.

"Shit head? Is that what I am? What is a shit head?" Beowulf asked, with an alarmed expression. "What is this?"

"Where did you get these?"

"Did I not just tell you?"

"Duncan, stop the name calling. Act like an adult and do what you said you were going to do with these coins," I said with strength in my tone. I folded my arms in front of me.

43

Duncan glared at Beowulf then glanced at me. "I'll take these coins to the appraiser."

"We're coming with you, Duncan." I can only tolerate Duncan for so long. We took a lengthy bus ride to the appraiser's office. We waited for hours. Then the appraiser entered the waiting room. He was a tiny meek man, a close resemblance to Duncan.

"Please enter," he said, and gestured for us to enter his office. The three of us sat in a dim-looking room with a cheap desk and metal chairs. "Who is the owner of these coins?" the appraiser asked.

"They belong to me," Beowulf said, seeming a bit violated. The appraiser held them up in front of him.

"I've never seen anything like these. They look so, so...un-weathered." He slowly placed the coins on the desk and gave Beowulf a strong stare. "Where did you get these?"

Beowulf glided his tongue along his chapped lips. "I was granted them in honor of my bravery."

"Bravery? For what?"

The appraiser laughed. I suddenly planted a large wet kiss on Beowulf's lips.

Beowulf was taken by surprise. I think everyone else was startled from my behavior, as well. Beowulf placed his hands on my shoulders in order to control me. He bowed his head to me.

"I feel this is not the time nor the place, but I do appreciate your affection." Duncan sprung up from his chair.

"Tell me, are these coins worth what I think they're worth? As far as getting any information out of this bloke, it's impossible. He speaks like he's putting us on." The appraiser then looked at me.

"Who is this man to you, young lady?" he asked.

"A friend. He's a Norse friend. His background is Viking. His family tree goes back centuries. These coins have been in his family for a very long time."

The appraiser scratched his chin. "I see."

"I don't understand what my background has to do with

44

these coins," Beowulf blurted, fidgeting.

The appraiser stood up and paced around the room.

"You'll have to come back. It's impossible for me to give you an answer here on the spot. Come back tomorrow morning."

Beowulf stood up. "I'd like my coins back."

"Now, they must remain here so they can be appraised appropriately. Sorry, but that's the way it is."

I stepped toward the man.

"Give me a work order or some kind of paper work with a catalog number on it. We'll be back in the morning." I tried to coax Beowulf to leave with me. "It's alright, my dear. The coins will be fine."

That night Beowulf tossed and turned. I noticed him not experiencing a great night sleep as he moved about the floor beside my bed.

"Beowulf, what's wrong?"

He was buried in blankets, but then he poked his head through.

"Lady Kyla, forgive me, but I'm not at ease with a stranger holding the only value I own. I must say, I'm very concerned. I was awarded those coins for my bravery."

"No need to worry. All will be well. We'll go there in the morning to get the verdict."

I slid off the bed and slumped beside him on the floor. I pushed his long hair away from his handsome face.

"Lady Kyla, you're so very kind to me. I don't really understand why."

"Sometimes, Beowulf, I feel the gods sent you to me."

"Odin?"

"Yeah, sure, Odin did this," I agreed, with a shrug. "Perhaps, my fair one."

"Beowulf, would you like to climb into my bed? It's a lot more comfortable than the floor."

"I find your floor to give the best night rest ever, m'lady."

"I suppose it's better than that cold mud or rocky ground that you're used to."

He smiled at me. "I sleep on several hides, some fur pelts. It can be rather comfortable by the fire."

"I think you'd change your view if you were to share my bed with me tonight."

"As much as I am attracted to your beauty, I cannot impose on you. I refuse to do this to such a fine lady, such as yourself."

I slowly stood up.

"Shit," I muttered, and made my way back to bed.

The following morning we met Duncan and traveled to the appraiser's office. The three of us sat in the waiting room. I noticed Beowulf scanning the room again and again.

"It'll be fine, Wolfgang," I instilled.

Duncan glanced at me, and said, "For all I know some con artist did a great job with those coins. They do look like the real thing."

Beowulf turned to Duncan.

"They are the real thing. How could anyone, even in this twenty-first century, create such a duplicate?"

The appraiser entered the waiting room, and gestured to us as he had the day before. We sat in his ugly office once again.

"I must say these five ancient coins are definitely of great worth," the appraiser said to us. "They are over 1,400 years old, and look very well preserved in deed. You say they've been in your family for ages?"

"I was rewarded with great honor, sir," Beowulf answered.

"Great honor?" the appraiser questioned.

I interjected, "Wolfgang has a very risky occupation. He does things that you nor I would ever even think of doing."

"And, what's that?" the appraiser, asked with intrigue in his voice.

"It's top secret – something to do with Scotland Yard," I said, almost holding my breath.

"Scotland Yard?"

"Yes," I gasped, while Duncan gave me a menacing stare.

"What did you have them appraised at?" I asked, with

bated breath.

"They're a million pounds each, so that's five million pounds sterling for all five coins. They're fourteen hundred-year-old Norse coins. I've never seen anything like it. I mean I've appraised two thousand year-old Roman coins, but they looked their age."

"What does this all mean?" Beowulf so innocently asked.

"Well, sir, you are now quite wealthy."

"I'm wealthy? Five million pounds is a lot, is it?" Beowulf asked, still confused. "Wolfgang, with your looks and now this instant fortune – I'll have to buy a very short leash to put around you," I snickered, with a nudge.

"Leash? Why is that?"

Duncan glanced at the appraiser then leered at me.

"Is this bloke coming down from a lengthy heroin trip?" Duncan asked. "Piss-off, wanker!" I told him.

I can only take so much of Duncan. We stood up and made our way to the door. "Why does Wolfgang never seem to know much about anything? Who is he?"

Duncan pressed.

Beowulf stood directly in front of Duncan.

"There is so much I know that you will never know. I suggest you keep yourself at length from me."

I pushed Beowulf out the door and thanked the appraiser as we made our exit.

CHAPTER NINE

A few mornings later, I sat with Beth in local teashop. There was a copy of the daily newspaper sitting on the next table. The headline read, *Scandinavian Man Appraises Ancient Norse Coins And Becomes Millionaire*. I grabbed it.

"How would the press know about this?" I said.

"Maybe it's not about Wolfgang." Beth offered. "Some other Scandinavian man could have run into a great fortune with ancient coins."

"How many Scandinavian men do you know with ancient coins?"

"What's the worry? Wolfgang may become famous. He definitely has the looks and the charm."

"Beth, you don't really know who Wolfgang is."

"Is he an ex-con? How luscious..." she began. "Why on earth would you think that?"

"Is he a duke?"

"Duke? No, he's not a bleeding duke," I said.

"He's something hot. I just know it. A lion tamer? A fighter pilot? Is he a gigolo?"

"Beth, don't you feel things don't quite add up when it comes to Wolfgang?"

"Ah ha! He's an Olympic athlete?" she went on. I sighed with frustration.

"I sure hope he's not a member of parliament. How boring that would be.

Something is quite different 'bout that bloke, that's for sure."

"Beth! He's not from our time."

"That's obvious, he's too much of a gentleman to be one of ours." I took a deep breath and fiddled with my teacup.

"Did you ever ask him his age?"

"Yes, in fact, I did. He also asked me my age. He should

48

have known better to ask me that, naughty boy."

"What was his answer?" I pressed.

"He said he's fourteen hundred years old." Her foolish grin dissipated. "What a kidder. He looks maybe in his late thirties."

"He's not in his late thirties. He is fourteen hundred years old."

"I must say, he looks quite good for his age."

"How did you ever get accepted into university?" I slammed my teacup on its saucer. "His name isn't Wolfgang, you idiot."

"No need to be rude. Look, Kyla, if you're having doubts about him I'll take him off your hands."

"His name isn't Wolfgang and he was born several centuries ago."

"Look who's calling who an idiot. Age shouldn't matter anyway."

"He's been misplaced. He's not from our time. Those ancient coins are not ancient to him."

She appeared confused, but she started to giggle it off. "Kyla, you really do take your work far too serious. Does this have anything to do with our English lit course?"

"Please allow me to leave or I'll break your neck."

I stormed out of the teashop leaving her with that stupid expression on her face. When I returned to my dorm there was a crowd gathered at my residence floor common area. Photographers were snapping pictures of Beowulf. Reporters were asking him questions. I pushed through the crowd.

"What's all this?" I asked, with my stress levels rising to a new high.

Beowulf took my arm, and said, "I'm glad you're here. I don't understand why all these people are so interested in me."

"Let me deal with this," I said, gesturing for people to leave. However, nobody even flinched. They kept bombarding Beowulf with questions about the coins. "Excuse me, ladies and gentlemen, it's time you leave. If you don't, I'll ring the police." I tugged on Beowulf's arm and pulled him out of the building at almost a jog. "Beowulf, I'm so sorry this happened to you. I really don't know how all this happened."

"Why would these people be so interested in my coins?"

"It's not just the coins; it's you in general."

"This lady who would like to be my agent says she has big plans for me. I'm so confused. What's an agent? So much is happening around me, and yet I'm so unfamiliar with all. Perhaps, I need to return to my time."

"Just take a deep breath and relax. The twenty-first century gets this way sometimes; you'll have to learn to ignore it."

He unraveled a folded piece of paper from his pocket.

"Kyla, you need to look at this. Another agent gave me this information. It is a list of flats for sale on The Strand?" What is all this?"

"So, now you should be living downtown in a sprawling flat. I suppose I could help you with that. You should probably get your own place, anyways."

"If I do, will I still see you?"

I took his hand and held it close to me. "Of course, you'll never get rid of me."

"At Heorot, everyone stays together – all under the king, of course. Heorot Palace is King Hrothgar's mead hall."

"Heorot, the mead hall. I suppose you're all one big happy family."

"I suppose we are like one big family. Happy? I'm not too sure about that. We have so much to deal with like trolls and dragons."

He took a deep breath of relief.

"We'll have to get a banker to manage your money," I said.

"Banker? This is all so complicated. Forgive me for causing you so much trouble."

"This is no trouble. I want to guide you in the right direction."

"Perhaps, you care for me? I know I am developing strong feelings for you."

"Beowulf, I'm just a very nice person." I turned away from him. "Please, don't misunderstand me. I care about you."

"And I care about you."

"I just don't know how two people from two completely different times can be together."

"Oh, yes, that may be an impossibility."

"Let's just try and ride things out. That's what men in this century do. They're not too quick to commit."

"Why is that? You're telling me I must take my time in committing myself to you?"

"No, no I hope that's not what I'm conveying to you."

"Then what is it exactly you're trying to say?" I threw my hands in the air.

"I don't really know what the hell I'm saying."

CHAPTER TEN

Since Beowulf's coins were appraised at five million pounds, he purchased a beautiful flat on The Strand with a great view. He acquired a new wardrobe for his many photo shoots, because some of the artsy photography magazines used him as their main subject matter. He barely had any spare time. He was even asked to be a model for men's cologne. Beowulf's life in the twenty-first century definitely changed with the discovery of those coins. He insisted several times to pay my rent; he really didn't have to. He still won't sleep in a bed, no bed, not any bed, not my bed. He made a few friends. Occasionally, he'd go off to the pub with his mates and drink a few pints. He'd been doing well for himself, considering he's from the sixth century. I was happy for him.

One Saturday afternoon he rang me. I was delighted to hear his voice. He was such a fast learner; he came to use the telephone quite regularly.

"How are things?" I asked, praying he would want to see me.

"Well, my love, I've got some time this evening. Can I run a taxi over to your residence and bring you back here for tea?"

I almost burst with excitement.

"Beowulf, you will have to learn when living in this century that it's not polite to spring a date on a girl on a Saturday afternoon."

"Why is that?"

"It's not proper. You're supposed to phone her on a Monday evening, so you can book Saturday night."

"Perhaps I should write this down. I wouldn't want to forget."

"I'm going to have to ring you back, so I can make sure I'm free tonight."

"Oh, I see. When will you ring me back?"

"Beowulf, you're not supposed to ask that."

"Oh, I see. Forgive me, Kyla. Can you consider me your suitor, still?"

"Definitely."

"Just get off the phone, so I can ring you back."

He hung up. I sat on my bed to paint my toenails. By the time the nail polish would dry, it would give just the right amount of time. I painted my big toe. I shifted my eyes several times to the clock on my night table. The nail polish kept blobbing. It ran down the side of my toe. I had to hop around my room to fetch the remover. I was making such a mess. I was never very good at home pedicures. When I re-did my big toe for the third time I decided to phone Beowulf back.

The taxi brought me to his flat, and I entered dressed in a formal evening gowned. He opened the door and presented me with a bouquet of roses.

"You're so sweet. No wonder you're form another century."

He bowed and took my hand. He was dressed in a dark suit. His hair was long flowing and beautiful.

"Kyla, why don't you direct me to one of those restaurants? We can go there and have wine if you like."

"Sounds wonderful. How well you're adapting to your new lifestyle."

"The twenty-first century is great fun. I'm especially fond of your electricity and running water. This is what impresses me most about your time. Imagine having light whenever one desires it."

"People of this time take so much for granite. But I should correct myself; there are some countries in the twenty-first century that do not have such luxuries."

"They live like the sixth century?" Beowulf asked, appearing surprised.

"Well, I've never seen your century, but I can only imagine. Some less fortunate countries have a more primitive way of life."

"And why is that?"

"It would take too long for me to explain. We can discuss this another time if you like."

He kissed my hand and swept me off to the street. We walked to one of the trendiest restaurants in Leicester Square that I knew of, but had never been. The waiter sat us by the window so we could see London on a Saturday night. Large groups of people walked through the streets hopping from one club to another. Droves of tourists lit up the pedestrian walkways. Talented buskers were playing music from all ends.

The waiter came and poured our wine. It was a French white vintage and a very good year. We toasted to troll slaying and drank up. The candles were lit and the ambiance poured in. I was getting a bit tipsy in love with this unique man.

"The twenty-first century certainly looks good on you," I told him.

"I wonder how good the sixth century would look on you, my love."

"Sixth century? Well, that's not ever going to be a possibility," I said, as he topped up his glass. "Besides, you can't compare apples with oranges."

"Come again?"

"Lets just relax and enjoy the evening, Beowulf."

"Sometimes I dream at night about you becoming my queen in my time." I felt a brief moment of nausea come before me.

"Beowulf, can't you dream of something else?"

He bowed his head. "I'm sorry to hear you do not wish to be my queen."

"No, this all sounds like such a fairytale. It's the sixth century part that disturbs me."

"But," he said. "I'm from the sixth century, my love. It's hard not to dream of my time. I am not used to this fast time. Of course I dream of my time period every night."

"Forget about the sixth century."

"I don't think I can."

We sipped our wine and picked at our appetizers. We kept one eye on the London view from the window. We sat at a booth so he could change his seat and snuggle next to me. He brought my hand to his lips. He gave several soft, wet kisses.

"You're so beautiful, Kyla."

"Are all men in the sixth century like you?"

"Wiglaf is similar to me. He is my right arm man. I have a band of men, and he is the best. I trust him with my life."

I took a deep breath wondering when this fantasy would end. At this point I was falling in love with him. I gazed at our view noticing the touristy crowd outside running rather than strolling. Cars were driving every which way. Bottles of alcohol were flying through the streets. The crowds became chaotic. I almost choked on my wine.

"What's going on out there?" I asked.

"I don't know, but something has got everyone in a panic."

"I think there is a concert by St. Martin's. Maybe it's big name musicians."

A large figure spewed out of nowhere pulling coach lamps from the ground and throwing them at people.

"What is this?" I asked, pasted against the windowpane.

"It can't be," Beowulf said, growing pale. "Grendel; he's come for me."

"That thing out there is Grendel? Grendel, the troll, is terrorizing London?"

"It looks that way, Lady Kyla. I'm so embarrassed."

"I never pictured him to look that disgusting."

He was eight feet tall. His hands and feet were claws. His body was covered in brown hair and he resembled a sasquatch. His teeth were pointed and fang-like. His eyes were red and beady like a rat.

Beowulf stood up. "I need my broad sword."

He paid for the meal and we left. The streets rumbled with terror. Death and destruction was happening throughout the streets of London. We had a difficult time making it back to Beowulf's flat. He tore off his jacket and grabbed his sword.

"Kyla, promise me you'll remain here. I can't risk having you out there with Grendel. He's a very vindictive troll." He stood close to me and fiddled with my hair. "Grendel hates me with a vengeance. He will stop at nothing to bring me to my demise. It was me who helped King Hrothgar. The king murdered Grendel's father when he was a child. Since that day Grendel terrorized the Danes non-stop. I became one of the Danes, despite me being from Geatland. He would very much find pleasure in slaying you, because you're my wench."

"I am?"

He bent over to me and kissed my lips. I almost melted in his arms. But then he quickly changed.

"I must do what I was put on this earth to do."

"To slay Grendel?"

"Right!" He swung his sword with a vengeance. "I must complete the job I should have completed fourteen hundred years ago. I will do what I do best, and that is to slay trolls."

He scurried off. I ran to the window to watch him cut through the frantic crowd.

CHAPTER ELEVEN

I paced the flat several times where I allowed my nerves to get the best of me. There was no way I was going to sit around and wait for him to be destroyed by that thing. I felt confused and panicked at the same time. I didn't know if I should run out to the chaotic crowds to protect Beowulf. Could I really protect Beowulf? He's the warrior. There's a troll running through the streets of London and I've got to get a grip on things. Then the answer came to me.

I exited the building and immersed myself in the crowd. I followed the screams, troll roars, and crashing sounds. Journalists and photographers were everywhere. I came to an alleyway. Grendel was standing at the other end. Beowulf breezed past me, but he didn't notice me, thank goodness.

"Stop troll! Who sent you here?" Beowulf called out. Grendel grunted the sound, *'Witch'*.

"You've come for what reason? For me? You've come for me?"

Beowulf held up his sword and approached Grendel. He thrashed his sword in *woman's guard*. He thrust long and then short. Grendel let out a thundering cry. I remained behind the wall where I had a good view of the alleyway. The crowd fled with screams and panic. I remained still. I could see bold photographers snapping pictures.

Grendel approached Beowulf. He stood before him and grunted. He was absolutely hideous to look at. Beowulf appeared to be calm and in control. Grendel stepped closer to Beowulf and then closer. Beowulf didn't even flinch. Grendel pressed him to the wall of the building. He grabbed Beowulf's sword and yanked it from his hands. Beowulf didn't appear the least bit frightened; he must have experienced this before. Grendel clasped his long clawed fingers around Beowulf's neck. He pressed hard on his skin where I saw blood dribble down Beowulf's chest. I held in my screams.

I felt helpless. Grendel then flung Beowulf against the other building wall.

Whatever spectators remained were terrified. Beowulf picked himself up standing in his own blood. I couldn't imagine a man of my century ever surviving this. Beowulf kept one eye on his sword and the other eye on the troll. Grendel roared and stomped and pounded the road. Beowulf walked backwards in the direction of his sword. He picked it up and swung it at the monster. Beowulf thrust it at Grendel, making small cuts on the monster's arms and legs. Beowulf charged and lunged at the beast. The troll showed its fear of Beowulf.

I watched with baited breath where I made myself too visible. Grendel noticed me. He began to pound and claw at himself. He walked on all fours making his way closer to me. I didn't move. I could feel my sweat pour from my body. He pointed to me and then pointed to Beowulf. Beowulf noticed me as well, but said nothing.

Grendel got closer to me and watched Beowulf's reaction. Beowulf didn't react.

Grendel scooped me into his hairy smelly arms and began to squawk. He had fecal matter mixed in with his hairy body. I was so repulsed I almost vomited.

Finally, Beowulf reacted. He thrust his sword and charged at Grendel. The troll laughed it up, because now it knew I meant something to Beowulf.

"Kyla! I told you not to come!" Beowulf shouted, with both eyes focused on the beast.

I could see the distress on his face. I made a terrible mistake leaving the flat.

Grendel smothered me in his filth. Beowulf pressed the point of his sword against Grendel's arm. However, I was in the way for a perfect slaying of a troll to take place. I'm such an idiot. Grendel screamed at Beowulf and spewed sticky goo in his face. My screams of terror went on like an alarm.

Beowulf managed to cut off Grendel's toe with his sword. The monster went berserk. His jarring screams and howls pierced my ears, with me still engulfed in its filth. He even smacked me against the wall of the building.

Beowulf tossed his sword and leaped onto the troll with me still tucked under its smelly arm. Beowulf showed his strength by lifting the monster in the air, but I was still attached. Beowulf tried to shake me off, but I was too wedged in. The monster continued to scream. Beowulf lowered us to the ground for my sake.

"Release her, now," Beowulf demanded. Grendel grunted and snorted, and backed away. "It's me you want! Release her!"

Grendel left in an uncontrollable fury. His severed toe area continued to bleed, leaving a trail of blood. Beowulf tried to run after us. Grendel leaped through the air, like a chimpanzee, where Beowulf would have difficulty keeping up. Beowulf could no longer keep us in sight.

Grendel made his way to a sewer. He limped from the loss of his toe. The stench of the sewer and Grendel combined was outrageous. He was waist deep in sewage. I tried to be silent despite the horrific thoughts that ran through my mind. He let go of me and watched me squirm and splash in the sewage water. He laughed like an absolute nut. I was terrified. I didn't even feel the abrasive cold sewage water. The monster then grunted and snorted at me. Was he human? What was a troll anyway?

***

Back at the scene of Grendel's triumph Beowulf noticed Beth approaching. She wore a concerned expression on her face.

"Wolfgang, what's all the commotion? What was a sasquatch doing in downtown London?"

"Lady Beth, I've got to find Kyla. Please remain in your flat." Beowulf placed his hand on her shoulder. "The troll has taken Kyla."

"That thing is a troll? I never knew what a troll looked

like, yet, I don't think I ever gave it much thought."

"Isn't there some way I can find them in this day and age? You have police. Can the police help us?"

"You're looking for a troll, I don't really think calling the police would do much good."

"So then, the police would be of no help?"

"I don't think our London police force would even know where to begin. Where do trolls usually, you know, hang-out?"

"I suppose trolls gravitate to feces, perhaps if there is canine or equine dung lying around."

Beowulf scratched his chin.

Beth's facial expression changed. "I don't think there's anyone who can help you on this one."

"Then, I must find Kyla on my own with no authoritative help whatsoever." Beowulf gathered a crew and searched alleyways, the embankment of the Thames, south of the Thames, and a few of the roughest parts of London. The search went on for days. Beowulf's face was on the cover of every news magazine. Several journalists and *paparazzi* managed to spend a few minutes with him whenever they could get the chance. He wasn't bothered by the publicity, because he didn't know what it was or what it meant. The police fluttered around trying to gain clues of my whereabouts.

"I need your full name," the constable said. "Full name?" Beowulf asked.

"Your surname and Christian name, sir.

"My name is Wolfgang Beowulf Ecgtheow. Ecgtheow was my father's name." The constable tried to write it down on his notepad.

"You're the witness to your girlfriend's disappearance. We need to find her."

"You would have to know where to find her, and I'm not sure if you can do that.

I'm the only one who can find her. She's been kidnapped by a troll and I'm the only man who can do the job in finding her."

The constable tried to ignore Beowulf's response. His notepad was in front of him, but it was still blank.

"Did you get a good glimpse of who took her? You know who did this?"

"Of course I do. Grendel is the troll who took her, but I am unfamiliar with your surroundings so it may take a bit of time to find her."

"I'm sure the scum who ran off with your girlfriend is definitely a troll," the constable said with a grin.

"Only a troll would do such a thing," Beowulf said, raising his voice. The constable noticed Beth standing beside Beowulf.

"Excuse me. You're friends with the victim, as well? Did you see who took her?"

"I wasn't there for the whole thing. I just saw the last bit," Beth said.

"Who took her?"

"Grendel."

The constable grew frustrated and bit his lower lip.

Beowulf stepped closer to the constable. "Grendel, my good man, is an unforgiving troll. He must be stopped."

The constable glanced at Beth. "Who's Grendel?" he asked.

"He's the troll who ran off with Kyla Brookes." The constable placed his pen in his mouth.

"Grendel is a troll? We're talking about a troll and this troll has a name, and its name is Grendel."

The constable scratched the information onto his notepad.

Beth appeared slightly irritated. "Yes, Grendel is a fucking troll! Don't act so surprised, Constable."

***

My situation with Grendel was hell. I never felt so dirty in my life. Grendel was feral and fierce. He was beyond anything prehistoric. I came to understand that he had no intension of harming me. I think he just wanted to piss-off Beowulf.

I watched Grendel fetch us some food. He'd rob some of the street vendors' potato stands. Despite how vile he was there was something about him that made me think I felt sorry for him. He'd babble on about how King Hrothgar killed his father.

Sometimes he'd even shed a tear. I learned that trolls are misunderstood. Maybe Beowulf was too hard on Grendel. What was I saying? He's a fucking troll.

The few times he took me away from the sewers I would rest in the tunnels of the underground stations. Everything was disgusting with Grendel. The underground tunnels were a far cry from sewage water. I was at ease hearing the subways streak by the tracks every few minutes. It was still disgusting, but it beat the hell out of sewage.

One depressing evening in the tunnels I watched Grendel rip apart five baked spuds. The subway rats wanted to join him. Over time, it no longer disturbed me to watch the troll share its meal with a cluster of street rats. I was getting used to the ambiance of the dark dingy subway tunnels. I had been Grendel's prisoner for a week, and was surprised that I was still alive.

***

During those horrible days I spent with the troll, later Beth told me what her life was like with Beowulf. I think she wanted to make me jealous.

Beth would show up at Beowulf's flat bright and early each morning dressed in her clubbing attire. She would bring him fresh baked scones and tea. Her great acting performance had him convinced that she was concerned about my whereabouts.

Beowulf sat on the couch and hung his head down.

"I've looked everywhere. Grendel sunk to his lowest this time. He found my weak spot."

"You don't have a weak spot, Wolfgang," she said, pouring the tea.

"Yes, my weak spot is Kyla. She's my love."

That was not what Beth wanted to hear. She fumbled with her purse looking for her lipstick. Some of her belongings fell on the floor in front of him. He watched her try to gather her fallen sanitary napkin, lipstick, and a map of the Underground Route Ways.

He stared at her profusely. "What's that?"

"This?" Beth asked, holding the map in her hands.

"The underground stations could be a strong possibility." He took the map and studied it. "There are so many tunnels, I wouldn't know where to begin."

"You think they're hiding in the Underground tunnels?"

"One has to learn to think like the sick mind of Grendel. These tunnels would be too clean and cozy for a troll. He'd more likely prefer the sewers."

"I can't imagine Kyla would allow this."

"She has no choice; she's with a troll."

"What is this thing capable of?"

Beowulf stood up and took his sword in his hand.

"Grendel is a murderer. He hates me more than you can imagine. He's been trying to get rid of me for a long time now. I work for the king. The king killed Grendel's father. I need to find Kyla. I will search every Underground tunnel in London."

"Well, now that you put it that way, I guess Grendel has a point to be angry. Think about it. This king killed Grendel's father. The king sounds like a real wanker. Maybe Grendel has a point. Why would you work for that skuzzy king anyways? The king is a murderer, right?"

"I'm a warrior. I do what warriors do best."

"I think you need to think this through. Maybe you need a career change. Maybe you could become a computer programmer or something."

"Come again?"

"I guess you don't get it, do you?" She paced around the room a bit. "Your name isn't Wolfgang, is it?"

"No."

"You're not from this time, are you? You're a warrior and you fight trolls for a living, don't you?"

"Yes."

"What's your real name?"

"I am Beowulf."

Beth stood before him in silence. She stepped toward Beowulf.

"Yes, so you are Beowulf. You have the strength of thirty men, don't you?"

"I do."

She bit her upper lip and then gnawed at it.

"This does have something to do with our English-lit course."

"Come again?"

"So Kyla got herself an ancient warrior. Not bad. She did good."

CHAPTER TWELVE

The subways screeched along the tracks every few minutes. The dim subway tunnels were not only depressing, but they were doing something to my eyesight. I really had nothing positive to focus on. Whenever I had an urge to cry, I would just suck it up and pretend none of this was affecting me. Watching the troll at his daily routine was like being at a circus, but not fun. I grew used to the sounds and the smells of the troll.

"Grendel, don't you get tired of constantly trying to get back at Beowulf?" I asked, trying to strike up a conversation. Grendel leered at me and grunted. "I mean, aren't you getting rather bored of the same old thing over and over?" Grendel gazed at me in silence. "Don't you think it's time to move on?"

He growled. Then he stood up in a frantic fury grunting and salivating on himself.

I turned the other way. I hoped I didn't get him too upset; he tends to lose control. "Grendel, you have to learn to calm down. Did you ever practice deep breathing? Yoga would do wonders for you."

He choked out, "Naahh! Brathing! Yagga!"

I guess that meant he didn't do any deep breathing and yoga. It was simply out of the question. He stopped and looked at me. He understands me only too well.

"Yes, deep breathing; breathe in, count to ten, then slowly breathe out on a count of ten. It must be slow."

He actually did what I said. He liked that I took an interest in him, poor pathetic thing. He actually felt better, so much so he defecated in front of me.

***

It was the end of a long exhausting week. Beth brought dinner to Beowulf's flat.

He stared at his food in silence. Beth watched every move

65

he made.

"Wolfgang, uh, Beowulf, tomorrow's another day. Don't worry; you'll find Kyla."

"They could be anywhere. This time the beast has outsmarted me. The London Underground is absolutely endless. I have found no remnant of them. Nothing."

Beth stood behind Beowulf sitting in his chair. She ran her hands through his long hair. Then she rubbed his shoulders and his biceps. She massaged his upper back so much that he responded to it. He groaned whilst taking deep breaths.

"Thank you, Beth. This is very soothing what you're doing, but I don't think I can accept any more from you. I do thank you," he said, gently pushing her hands away from him. "I feel as if I'm failing Kyla."

She continued to massage his neck. "Failing? Why would you say such a thing?"

Her arms wrapped around his chest. He tried to hold her hands, but she wouldn't let him. She ran her hands along his chest.

"I'm worried. I can't sleep. I can't eat. I must find her."

"And you will." She tore away at his sweater, lifting it up and fondling with each rip of his well-cut stomach. He slowly stood up and faced her. "Oh, Beowulf, I think I'm developing feelings for you." She lifted his sweater and immersed her face in his pectoral muscles. She pulled off her t-shirt and removed her bra. "Are you attracted to me?" she asked, standing in front of him in her underwear.

"Of course."

She took his hand and led him to his bed. He slowly sat on his bed and watched her remove her underwear.

"Beowulf, I'm naked. What are you going to do about it?" He sat lifelessly, not focused on her.

"Beth, I could easily mount you here and now, but I would be pretending you are Kyla. I'm sorry. I have never felt the love I have for Kyla. You are a beautiful woman, but I'm sorry I can only imagine myself with her."

"What is it about Kyla?"

"She's my first love."

"You experienced your first love at fourteen hundred years old?" Beth shook her head, and put her clothes back on. "You're right. I feel like a cad. I shouldn't be doing this behind my friend's back. I know for a fact she would never do this to me."

"That's one of the reasons why I love her so much."

"Tell me, Beowulf, have you and Kyla done it yet? Have you ever given it to her?"

"Given her what?" he asked, frowning.

"Fucked her. Have you ever fucked her?"

"Not yet."

"Good.

CHAPTER THIRTEEN

It was early morning. Beowulf insisted on checking the subway tunnels. He started at Westminster, then to Victoria. He crept along the sides of the tracks with a flashlight in hand. Beth would stand on the platform announcing to him whenever a train was near. It was a cumbersome task, but he was determined to find me. Beowulf would almost lose himself in the tunnels, because he would stumble onto some of the ancient tunnels that had been forgotten. They didn't contain subway tracks, but they were half filled with water.

***

"Grendel, I really need to be outside this tunnel. I need to see daylight. I'm lacking vitamin D. Aren't you?" I said, hoping he would come to his senses. But trolls don't have senses. He grunted at me, while I witnessed him catch a rat and stuff it in his mouth. The rat's blood dripped from one side of his mouth and onto his furry chest.

I turned away, so I could survive this. He grabbed me and threw me over his shoulder. This was not a very comfortable method of transport. He made sure no subways were coming and scurried onto the tracks. There were people standing on the platforms. They screamed when they saw him jump up beside them with me hanging off his shoulder. I was feeling quite nauseous.

The people standing on the platform were in suits, holding their briefcases in hand. It must have been morning rush hour. They ran out of the station in a panic. Some were calling for the police on their cellular phones. Grendel didn't concern himself with what people thought of him – that was obvious. He flew me up the steep staircase and onto the busy street.

It was raining, of course. It felt so good. I was feeling rather stale for these past two weeks. He took me to

Trafalgar Square for some reason. I was glad, because we would definitely be noticed there. The flocks of tourists ran in multiple directions. I could hear police cars coming our way in a fury. With all this chaos, where was Beowulf? Had he forgotten me already?

Several police officers ran after us with taser guns. They tased Grendel and he fell to the ground. I crash-landed on the hard payment. A crowd formed around us. I looked, but Beowulf was nowhere in sight. Two police officers helped me up. Grendel was being carried off on a stretcher.

CHAPTER FOURTEEN

I lay quietly in a hospital room. I was attached to an I.V. Several doctors and nurses came in and out of my room. Then one of the police constables who carried off Grendel entered my room.

"Hello, Kyla Brooks. You seem to be doing well, so I hear from the doctors," the constable said.

"That's good news," I said.

"Tell me, what was that thing that had hold of you?"

"That thing is Grendel. A troll."

"A troll?"

"Yes, I was in the London underground tunnels for two weeks with Grendel." The police officer stared at me. He looked like he wanted to say more, but decided to keep silent. "Constable, where did you put Grendel?"

"Jail."

"He won't like that, I can tell you."

"I don't really care."

"Is he in a cell with other inmates?"

"Most likely not. We're not sure if we should put him in an animal shelter, but that might be harmful to the other animals. Maybe sasquatches are not myths.

"Okay, if it makes you feel better, he's a sasquatch."

"I don't think there's ever been sightings in Great Britain before. This could be a first. It's remarkable that you came out of this with just a few scratches and bruises."

"I suppose," I said. The constable looked like he was anxious to leave. "You know, if he is a sasquatch then he needs to be somewhere other than jail."

"It could go to a scientific lab for testing."

"Grendel would hate that more than jail. I feel sorry for him."

"What are you talking about? That thing abducted you."

"He's from another time."

"That's for sure," the constable agreed. "What happens next?"

"Grendel, the sasquatch, could be examined by zoologists. A sasquatch could be classified as an animal, don't you think?"

"Yes, but he's not really a sasquatch. He's a troll."

"Whatever that thing is, it needs to be examined."

"Examined for what?"

The constable glanced at me as if I were just as crazy as Grendel, and he exited my room. I stared at the ceiling and took a few big sighs. Then Beowulf walked in.

"Beowulf, what have you been doing? I was stuck with that troll for two weeks in the Underground!"

He took my hand and kissed it.

"I apologize. I searched the tunnels, but I failed in finding you."

"I don't know how I survived. Grendel is the most vile being I've ever seen. He's in jail, you know."

"A dungeon?"

"Yeah, you could say that. I guess this chapter is closed."

"Not at all. Grendel knows how to escape dungeons. In fact, it's what he's best at."

"Yes, but, this is the twenty-first century. He'll never get past the bars, the wardens, the electric shock, and barb wire. I just described a penitentiary. Oh, no, what if they place him in that?"

Beowulf lifted one eyebrow. "Penitentiary? Is it worse than jail?"

"You bet."

"Of course he will be able to escape this penitentiary you speak of, he's a troll," Beowulf said, as if he meant it.

"You know, I tried to explain this to the constable and he really didn't care." I forced a smile and tried to act as if I didn't care, but I did. "Beowulf, what do we do? If Grendel escapes prison?"

"I'll have to slay him of course," he said. "What if he slays you first?"

Beowulf sat beside be on the bed and rubbed his bearded chin. "Yes, that could happen."

"Can you ask the witch to send him back to the sixth century?"

"I ask her everyday. She has responded a few times. She loves Grendel, so I don't know why she doesn't send him back."

"This is getting confusing," I said. "You have to do something."

"I will try to contact the witch. But there's a problem."

"More problems?"

"The witch, she's attracted to me you see."

"So is everybody else."

"Well, she and I..." He paused, and I knew what he was about to say. He and that witch had been together.

"Beowulf! How could you?"

"I hadn't met you yet, M'lady."

"Ugh!

72

CHAPTER FIFTEEN

It was in the middle of winter. A light sprinkle of snow fell from time to time. I hadn't seen Beowulf in a few months. He insisted we stay apart in case Grendel was on the loose again. I've been miserable without him. Beth has been lying to me that she never saw Beowulf, but I know she's been spending time at his flat. I've never been with him the way the witch has been with him. I've never been with him in the way Beth has been with him. I'm assuming Beth and Beowulf have slept together. I'm sure by now they have. Everyone seems to get a piece of Beowulf except me.

One snowy Sunday afternoon I peered out my window as I sat at my computer desk. I watched the snowflakes trickle down to the busy streets. A love song came on the radio and I found myself in tears. I stood up to walk across the room to switch off the radio when a special report was broadcasted:

Late last night the creature that terrorized the center of London last autumn escaped prison. It is unknown how it did escape, but some damaged remains have shown up as evidence. There is a search party for its capture.

I had to sit down and get a grip. Beowulf was right. Grendel escaped, so he could destroy Beowulf. I grabbed the phone to ring him. The phone rang several times, but no answer. Beowulf never installed a message machine. I guess he's too old fashioned about that kind of technology. Of course he's old fashioned – he's from the sixth century.

I had to reach Beowulf. I got my coat and scurried to Beowulf's flat. I knocked on his door profusely, but no answer. I waited a few minutes. It was obvious he wasn't home. I decided to go outside and look for clues of his whereabouts. I walked down the street and noticed a strand of wool that latched onto a wrought-iron fence. That strand of wool belonged to his scarf. I continued to walk in that direction until I found myself at the Thames. I scanned the area and spotted Beowulf walking on the opposite side of the river. What was he doing? I crossed the bridge to get a little closer.

Beowulf walked along the southeast end of the Thames alone.

"Witch!" he called out. Nobody seemed to be around. "Witch!" He continued walking eastbound. "Witch, show yourself. Grendel has escaped prison. Return him to the sixth century and let me be in this time."

A circular smoke ring of bright light formed in front of him. A small figure appeared.

"Beowulf, you are a troll slayer and that's all you will ever be. If I return Grendel to your time then you must also return. He could finish you there. Remember, I know how you will die."

"You're wrong. I will finish Grendel here. He roams the streets. I will find him and slay him; that is not the problem. The problem is that I want to spare the lives of the innocent people of this time. Remove him of this time at once."

"And you wish to remain here? Oh, you are a silly man. Do you not see how you being here has burdened the people of this time?"

"You are the sorceress. You are to blame for the burden put upon these people."

She leaped into Beowulf's arms. She ran her long fingers through his hair. He stepped toward a cluster of trees. She pressed her tongue into his mouth.

"No!" he said, pulling away from her.

"You never stopped wanting me, Beowulf. I know you all too well."

"I've changed."

"You will never change," she said.

She jabbed her tongue into his throat. He pushed her aside. "I'm not the same man as you once knew."

"It was a mistake sending you to the twenty-first century."

"Go fuck yourself, witch."

She levitated around him with surprise. "Where did you get this kind of talk?" the witch asked.

"I will speak as I wish. You must return the troll to the sixth century. Stop playing with me, and do so."

"Ah, you have found a woman here. Who else would teach you such talk? Who is she?"

"You need not know," he said. "I want you, Beowulf."

"No longer can this be, witch. You love the troll, and he loves you. You're all he has, so take him back. I'm not for you. I am mortal."

"Yes, yes, you have changed." She floated about him. "Who are you now, I wonder."

"I will no longer engage in your silly games."

"Who do you think you are? Do you think for a minute you have the power of Odin? You are only a man."

Beowulf backed away from her.

"You raise your voice at me? Since when, witch?"

"Since you belong to her."

"Take Grendel back. This is the time you banished me to. I must remain here."

"For her?" the witch asked.

"Yes, for her. You take the troll and leave me be."

"First, you must give me a child."

"I cannot. We have discussed this before. You are immortal and I am a man.

You cannot bare a child of a mortal, but you can of a troll. Go to him!"

"You may be mortal, but you also carry the mystical power."

"I am still mortal with or without mystical strength," he said.

"You will never survive here, Beowulf. This world will finish you. You missed far too much of human progression. You are only a sixth-century man."

"But I still have the strength of thirty men."

"What will that get you in the twenty-first century?" She

continued to float around him. "This woman has definitely changed you."

"For the better. She has taught me much." He paused. "She loves me."

"Impossible. She is a product of her time. When she realizes you are an ancient relic of your time, she will tire of you."

"I guarantee that will never happen. She already knows everything about me."

"Guarantee? You belong in ancient Scandinavia. You are a Viking warrior who must accept his destiny."

"My destiny is with her."

"I see you standing before me wearing the clothes of a twenty-first century man. I see you using the colloquialisms of a twenty-first century man. Your magic sword will only have you arrested in this time. You will be deemed as a crazy man and not a great warrior. Here, you will never be king of the Danes."

The witch vanished into a colorful ring of smoke.

***

It was getting late. I needed to get to the university library before it closed. I rushed along the streets bundled in my warmest coat. I carried a pile of papers in my arms. I ran into someone and fell to the sidewalk. I watched my papers fly into the traffic. I looked and realized I ran into a hurried troll. I looked back and saw Grendel run off in the opposite direction. I froze from fright. I don't think Grendel realized it was me.

A man from the other side of the street wove through the traffic to gather my notes that flew about the road. The kind man handed them to me. It was Beowulf.

"Thank-you, you're so kind," I said.

He smiled at me. He couldn't stop looking at me. He was more handsome than ever. We stared at each other. It was one of the coldest nights in London, yet somehow it didn't seem to matter. I felt warmed by his smile.

The winds howled and icy powder gathered on our hair.

He took me into his arms and kissed me. He took my papers out of my hands and tucked them inside his big suede coat. He ran his large strong hands through my straight blunt hair. He kissed my lips several times. I thought I was going to lose consciousness. He placed his strong arm around me and led me to his flat.

We sat in his flat for hours just staring at each other. I knew I wasn't going to get my assignment finished - that was inevitable. How many opportunities will I get to spend the night with a great Viking warrior?

We sat on the couch. He seemed mesmerized by me. He continued to rub his hands up and down my shoulders. Then his hands ran along my breasts. He kissed me again and again. I thought I was going to orgasm just by his sensual touch. He removed his jacket and pressed his body onto mine. He pulled off his sweater and then pulled my sweater off. I lay under him in my bra. He fiddled with my trousers and managed to slip them off. His brawny physique lay on me. His trousers were still on. It was like having Adonis ravish me. I touched his face and body several times to make sure he was real. It was like a fantasy come true.

He scooped me into his arms and carried me to his bedroom. I felt encased in his hard-sculpted body. He gently laid me down to his bed. He stood off from the bed to undo his trousers. He could barely slide them off because of his hardened mass that protruded so explicitly. He stood there by the bed naked, this strong frame of a man. He sat beside where I lay and kissed my breasts. He rubbed them in his large square hands, giving me a sensation of great heights. His seductive brawn over-powered me as he rolled on top of me. He was gentle and worked on fitting it in. It took longer, but he was unbelievably patient.

The thrusting began. He gyrated his pelvis in and out with powered thrusts. I found myself screaming into an unconscious orgasm of lust. He brought his soft lips to mine, smothering me with wet kisses. He rubbed his big rough hands along the contours of my body. He seemed quite attracted to my childbearing hips.

"Kyla," he whispered, with a deep breath. "Be my wife, my queen?" I stopped reciprocating his sexual gestures.

"You're asking me to marry you? Oh. This is too much."

"Be the mother of my children? We can have eight, ten, even more if you like?" I sat up on the bed.

"You want me to be the mother of your endless amount of children?"

"Please."

"I don't want to have a family at this time in my life. I'm only twenty-three."

"You're old enough."

"I want a career, Beowulf."

"What's that again? I've heard this word before.'

"You know how you're a troll slayer? That's your career. You're a professional troll slayer."

"Are you saying you wish to slay trolls?" He lay on his side holding my hand over his penis. I pulled my hand back.

"No, but I may want to be a teacher of English literature some day."

"Will you not marry me?" he said.

"I will only marry someone if they love me and I love them."

"Kyla, I love you very much. Do you not love me?"

I sprung up from the bed and tied his robe around me.

"This is all too fast. How can I marry a man who's fourteen hundred years old?"

"Do I look my age?"

"No, not even close."

He remained sprawled on the bed naked. I tried not to look at him, because his beauty was too overpowering.

"What kind of life could we have together? What would our children be like?"

"I can't answer your questions."

"Then why are you proposing marriage to me, and expecting me to be your milkmaid with hundreds little bambinos?"

"I've offended you?"

"How could you possibly know what offends me? You're from the sixth century.

I'm sure being a pregnant maiden in the sixth century was ideal for any damsel."

"What if I made you with child just now? Would that offend you?"

"It would scare the crap out of me."

I paced around the room. He slid off the bed and held me from behind. "Why won't you look at me, Kyla? Am I that hideous?"

I turned toward him and buried myself in his arms. "Beowulf, you just don't get it."

"I will protect you always."

"I don't doubt that. You need to learn the social dynamics of this century. I'm not like the women you're used to. I'm especially no witch."

"I feel much love for you, Kyla."

We fell back into bed. He pulled me on top of him. My breasts fell in front of him, which made him wild with raging libido. He mounted me continuously for hours well into the night. I never loved like this before. We lay side-by-side touching and fondling each other. His hair was messed hanging in front of his face.

"Beowulf, what are we going to do about Grendel? He broke out of jail. He may seriously hurt someone."

"No, he won't do that. It's me he wants to finish – nobody else."

"Yes, but he's dangerous."

"Not to you he wasn't, nor to anyone. None of you have hurt him in any way. It's me who has hurt him. He wants my head on a pike."

I sat up in bed.

"What did you do to him?" I paused. "You've explained this one to me a few times already, haven't you?"

"I serve King Hrothgar, ruler of Daneland. The king killed Grendel's father when he was only a child. Since I serve the king I am very much wanted by Grendel. He and the witch have had several relations. Grendel would like to think of her as his wench, however, I have also been the witch's lover."

"He likes the witch?"

"She's his woman. He's had her, I've had her; he hates me for that."

"I don't know how much of this I can take," I said. "I can't imagine you as the witch's lover. I find that disgusting."

"I'm sorry."

"There's so much I don't understand about your time."

"In the sixth century one must be a great warrior in order to survive. Hrothgar knew of me in Geatland. He called for me to help his people slay Grendel, because he knows I have the strength of thirty men." I ran my hands around his biceps.

"I can row a Viking ship through the turbulent Baltic waters with just my own strength."

"You're not going to sleep with that witch again are you?"

"No."

CHAPTER SIXTEEN

I woke up beside Beowulf. He was still asleep. I was careful leaving the bed. I didn't want to wake him. I made my way to the kitchen to make coffee. The phone rang.

"Kyla?"

"Beth. I suppose you want to speak to Beowulf?"

"I thought you two weren't seeing each other anymore?" Beth said, hopefully. "Well, we are. In fact, he asked me to marry him last night."

"Was he drunk on that sticky sweet mead stuff?"

"He wasn't drinking."

"Well, tell your boyfriend, Grendel is terrorizing the streets of London again."

"He's aware Grendel is on the loose, but he feels Grendel won't hurt anybody."

"Wrong. Last night, Grendel tore through the London Underground and pushed several people into the subway tracks."

"Was a train coming?"

"No, they're doing well in hospital."

"Thank God," I said.

"Nobody knows how to deal with this troll. The strange thing is the victims in the Underground didn't describe Grendel as a troll. They said something that resembled a sasquatch pushed them into the tracks."

"Yeah, I guess he does resemble a sasquatch." I noticed Beowulf was up. He walked through the kitchen to fetch a cup of coffee. He was still naked. "Beth, Beowulf just got up. Can I ring you back another time?"

"I guess. Cheers."

Beowulf put down his coffee and took me in his arms. He kissed me several times steaming with passion. His heavy breathing was uncontrollable. This man certainly had a healthy libido. I hoped I could keep up with him.

He threw me over his shoulder and lowered me onto the couch in the sitting room. He continued to kiss me. I tried to get a word in by pushing him aside.

"Beowulf, I need to ask you something. You need to stop for a minute."

"I love thee."

"I love you too. What are we going to do about Grendel?"

"As you can see, it is not easy for one to get rid of such a beast."

"Did you ever get anywhere with the witch?"

"Ah, she is a stubborn one," he said.

"Is she considering that maybe it's time for her precious troll to return to the sixth century?"

Beowulf started to pace around the room. I knew something was up. "What's going on with this witch?"

He stopped pacing but wore a serious expression on his face. "She has in deed agreed to return Grendel to my time."

"That's good news."

"It's not, I'm afraid, my love. She will only return him if I also return to my time."

"That bitch!"

"She's a witch, Kyla."

Beowulf made a dash for the shower. I sat on the couch with my cup of coffee. I turned on the television. The news was reporting the Underground episode with Grendel. I felt a chill run down my spine. I started to blame myself for all this chaos. I looked at my own selfishness. I could hear Beowulf in the shower.

"Witch?" I called. "Do you hear me? I know you hear me. Beowulf speaks to you all the time. Come here now!"

A circle of smoke and bright light formed in front of me. I remained sitting with my coffee; however, I was terrified of what was before me. A petite woman with strange colored hair, heavy make-up, and long painted nails levitated in front of me. The more I stared at her the more I couldn't

82

understand what Beowulf and the troll saw in her.

"I don't usually answer the calls of common mortals like yourself," said the witch. "Is Beowulf not a common mortal?" I asked, trying not to appear afraid.

"Of course not. He's a sixth century Viking warrior. You are not."

"Big deal. He's still mortal."

"He's an sixth century Viking with the strength of thirty men. What don't you understand?" She whisked around the room like an apparition noticing little things here and there. "What is this? The twenty-first century? Mortals have become belligerent abusers. They have already lost their bravery and instinct at this time. Why did you call me here?"

"It's about Beowulf and Grendel…" She laughed with a haunting cackle.

"I can see that Beowulf is faring well in your time. Grendel is not."

"Can't you send Grendel back to the sixth century? He's making an awful mess over here."

"If Grendel returns to his time Beowulf must also return."

"No. Why are you doing this?'

"I'm a witch aren't I?"

"You certainly are," I said. "I love Beowulf. He asked me to marry him."

"He asks every woman he mounts to marry him. He's from the sixth century, what do you expect?"

"Are you saying I'm not special to him?"

"You're a novelty to him now. He never slept with a wench from the twenty-first century. You're like a trophy to him."

"Trophy? I don't think so."

"That's what I thought, too. Remember, all he cares about is revenge over Grendel."

The bathroom door opened and Beowulf entered dripping wet with a towel around his lower half.

"Witch! What brings you here?"

"I'm getting acquainted with your little damsel here."

83

He stepped very close to her. She ran her long fingers up and down his chest. He didn't seem put-off by it, which worried me. He stood there with long wet hair. She took the towel from around his waist and began to dry his wet naked body. He looked embarrassed. It was obvious they had been together before. I felt like I was going to explode with anger and tears. I stood up and approached them.

"Okay, what's all this, eh?" I said. She glared at me. "Beowulf, I don't like her touching you."

The witch floated away from him. She stood so close to me that she was in my personal space.

"Look, he's from the sixth century, and he's a troll slayer – what else do you want?"

I began to cry. He wanted to come to me, but the witch wouldn't let him. I've been with blokes with personal baggage before, but this might be over the top for me to handle. He took the witch into his bedroom. I heard them shouting at each other. Good. It was as if she was his ex-wife. They were in there for over an hour. He stormed out of the room and what a relief it was that he was dressed. He took his sword into his hands.

"I'm going after Grendel to finish him at once."

My head spun with confusion. He took me in his arms and plunged his tongue down my throat. He kissed me and ravished me for a good ten minutes. I thought his penis was going to bust through his trousers.

"I love you, so don't leave this flat. Let me take care of Grendel."

He made his exit. The witch came out of the bedroom looking a bit worked over.

I could have strangled her.

"What are you looking at, wench? He claims he loves you."

"What did you just do with him in the bedroom?" I asked the witch. She began to cackle again. "I think I hate you."

"I hate you, too. Now, if you want to let your warrior do his job, he must not be worried about you roaming the streets."

"I know all this already."

"I must help guide Grendel, so I'll be off."

"Why don't you guide Grendel back to the sixth century?"

"All will happen in good time, wench."

A spiral of smoke spun from nowhere. She vanished into nothing and I poured myself a hard drink.

CHAPTER SEVENTEEN

Beowulf dressed in his sixth century attire to make sure his chain mail was placed on his body for protection. He decided not to bring along his sword for it would look too menacing to the public. He tucked his dagger into his leather belt instead. He made his way to the nearest Underground station. I trailed behind in a continuous jog.

"Wait up!" I called to him, out of breath.

"Not again! You need to return to the flat!" he shouted, with his arm extended and pointing in the direction of his flat.

"You're not going anywhere without me." He took me in his arms and kissed me. "I love you, you know."

"I know."

"I have a feeling about that monster's whereabouts. The witch is guiding me to him."

"I'm glad she's so helpful," I commented, sarcastically.

"The witch has guided me to a very popular place; a very special place of wealth and beauty. A place that you would like very much."

"Where?"

"A market of some kind, I think."

"A store? I guess we better get there. Which store?"

"Harrolds?"

"The witch has guided you to *Harrolds?* Grendel, the troll, is roaming about *Harrolds?"*

"Yes, I'm afraid. That isn't good is it, M'lady?"

"No, it's not."

We arrived at *Harrolds.* The main foyer had been severely roughed over. Wall sconces were torn off, hanging advertisements were torn up, and puddles of feces were everywhere on the floor. Grendel had been there. Several police officers were roaming about in search of whoever was responsible for this.

We entered the china section. Thousands, maybe millions of dollars, of *Royal Dalton* lay shattered on the floor. It was heart breaking. We got a glimpse of some of the sales staff, who were traumatized. I approached one of the ladies.

"Excuse me, but could you tell me what you just saw?"

The woman took a few deep breaths and tried to primp herself a bit.

"Some awful creature tore through this store level, and busted all our china to bits," she said, trying to hold back tears.

I glanced at Beowulf; he looked outraged. I smiled at the woman. "Can you describe this creature?"

"It all happened so fast. But it was definitely not human." Beowulf gently pushed me aside.

"Dear lady, do you know what direction this creature went? "I don't really know. As I said, it all happened so fast." Beowulf smiled at the woman with a slight bow.

"I'm so sorry about the china, good lady. Perhaps I can replace it for you."

"Sure, if you would like to do so. It will most likely cost you several millions in pound sterling of course."

The woman laughed. Beowulf's expression changed.

"Oh. I didn't think plates, cups, and saucers would be so costly. A hollowed out deer antler should work just as well."

The woman continued to laugh.

"There is such a thing as insurance," I said.

"Oh, I see." Beowulf turned to me. "Kyla," he whispered, in my ear. "What is insurance?"

"I'll explain it to you later. Right now there's a raging troll rampaging through this store."

We left that department of the store. As we paced through some of the damaged rooms, the atmosphere changed. We saw fewer customers, and many more police. We followed the police to the men's lavatory. Four well-armed constables stood outside the door. I tapped one of the officer's shoulders.

"Is that beast in the men's loo?" The constable glanced at me.

"Beast? I suppose. I don't know what the hell it is. Yes, it seems to have gone in the men's lavatory. Did you have an encounter with that thing?"

"Not this very second, but I did have an episode with it."

"What is it?"

"It's a troll."

Then a burst of madness exploded from behind the door. Grendel appeared carrying a slain customer in his arms. The officers fired their guns, but missed since the cubicle door swung off its hinges and into their faces.

"Beowulf!" I screamed, tears pouring down my face. "Grendel killed someone!"

Beowulf ran in front of the constables. The troll dashed through the different store departments pushing people over and running over them. He ran to the section of fine wines. Grendel backed into a display of French wines, causing them to crash to the floor.

"Excuse me? I'm going to call the police!" a male shopkeeper boldly screamed.

Grendel charged at the poor man and tore opened his throat. Beowulf saw the end of that incident.

"Troll! Stop!" Beowulf shouted.

Grendel was covered in the innocent man's blood. He glanced at Beowulf and continued to run. Beowulf grabbed a large intact bottle of wine and ran after him. He was two meters behind the monster when he threw the bottle at Grendel's head.

Grendel dropped to the floor. Beowulf leaped onto the monster.

I arrived with two constables. We stood and watched Beowulf grapple with the troll on the floor. Beowulf threw a few punches to the troll's face. Grendel managed to roll onto Beowulf with his hands locked around his neck.

"We must shoot this thing," one of the constables said to me. "No! This is their battle!" I shouted.

I knew if anyone intervened Beowulf wouldn't be pleased. Beowulf managed to buck his knees into Grendel's back. Grendel fell off of Beowulf, but sank his teeth into

Beowulf's arm. Beowulf was silent as he withheld his expression from the excruciating pain. I could see in his face that the pain was unbearable. Beowulf drew his dagger and stabbed Grendel in the leg several times. They both were saturated in blood. Grendel managed to pull away. The troll turned to Beowulf and kicked him brutally hard in the groin. Beowulf fell to the floor. The troll ran off leaving a trail of blood.

"Beowulf!" I shouted, and ran to his side.

He was out cold. The constable kneeled beside me. "His name is Beowulf?" he asked.

I glanced at the police officer, but kept my focus on my warrior. "Quite a nice name, don't you think?"

"I suppose," the constable said, with a smile. "Your boyfriend should come to shortly. He hasn't received any life threatening injuries. That thing is still roaming somewhere in this department store."

"That thing, constable, is a troll," I said. "Whatever it is, it's a nasty bugger." Beowulf opened his eyes.

"M'lady, Kyla? Where's Grendel?" he asked.

I took a deep breath, but had no answer for him. "I have to catch him."

The police officer looked at Beowulf. "You should see a doctor," the constable insisted.

"Oh, no, there's no time. Grendel will continue to kill and eat his victims. He has to be stopped."

The constable glared at me. "That thing eats people?"

"He's a troll, constable. That's what trolls do."

The two police officers pulled out their phones and made a report to the police station. Beowulf stood up and found himself with a limp.

"That monster kicked me hard didn't he, M'lady?"

"I'm surprised you're still standing," I said, trying to comfort him.

"It's not quite that same leg, but rather it's my you know. It really aches."

"Yes, a blow like that in the *crown jewels* would definitely

89

have you limping." Beowulf winced a few times and tried to straighten up.

"That troll, is getting its way here in modern London. This is making me furious."

I rummaged through my handbag and found a kerchief. I wrapped it snuggly around Beowulf's bleeding arm. "This should work until we get you home," I said.

"You're so kind."

I latched onto Beowulf's arm and tried to help him walk.

"It'll take some time for the pain to dissipate," I said, pointing to his crotch. "How would you know, M'lady? You're a wench. How would you know the pain I'm feeling just now?"

"I care about you."

"And I you. However, I need to call for the witch. I need advice. I'm not sure what to do. Grendel is on the loose in your time and in your town, my love. He's taken two peoples' lives, which would be very usual in my time."

My eyes dropped to the floor with remorse. "I wish Grendel didn't come with you."

"What a mess I've created here for you and your people, M'lady."

"You didn't create this mess; that thing did, that witch did. You have nothing to do with it."

"I have everything to do with it," he said, wincing in pain.

We exited the department store. He gently placed his finger over my lips. "Now, let me call for the witch."

I nodded.

"Witch? Come before me! Come now, as I beg of you!"

I didn't see or hear from her, but she seems to be everywhere. In that case, she must always see Beowulf naked.

"Witch! Hear my call! What's the troll saying to you?"

We slowly moved to a dim alleyway. A circular glitter of smoke formed beside Beowulf. The witch appeared.

"He's saying he will not play dirty like you who uses a sword, dagger, and or a bottle of wine. He says, you should act like a true warrior and fight like a man – with your bare

90

hands."

Beowulf stood still holding his dagger in hand. "But he's not a man? He's a troll."

The witch stepped very close to Beowulf – too close for my liking. She began to fiddle with his chain mail.

"Yes, you are a man. I know this most of all, because you are a good man, you will toss your weapons and fight with your bare hands. No more wine bottles, either."

"He's a troll. I am but a man."

"You will follow his request, because he is a troll and you are a man." He looked down at her tiny frame.

"You want me slain by the beast, do you not?"

She jumped up and pulled his face to hers and kissed him.

"I want you to follow what I say. You are a stubborn warrior, Beowulf." He kissed her back and handed me his dagger.

"Fine. I will surely slay that beast with my bare hands."

"Of course you will, Beowulf."

We could hear a sound, as if someone was munching quite loudly. Beowulf slowly shifted his body toward the direction of the sound. He walked to the other opening of the alleyway on the opposite side. There he spotted Grendel sitting beside several trashcans. Grendel was chewing on old food remains. I stayed back, because I wasn't in the mood to vomit.

"Stand up and fight me, troll!" shouted Beowulf.

Grendel stood up. His hairy body was immersed in food particles. Grendel let out a few grunting sounds. They faced each other. Grendel made the first move by pouncing onto Beowulf. Beowulf grabbed Grendel by the torso and threw him to the ground. Beowulf then leaped onto the monster. They locked onto each other, grappling and applying each other's weight and pressure. I stood by the alleyway exit and watched. The witch appeared beside me, but acted as if I wasn't there.

"Allow Beowulf to use his sword," I demanded of her. She slowly turned to me, and shook her head.

91

"He will die if he doesn't have his sword." I shoved her. She looked at me as if looks could kill.

"Beowulf will survive. He has the strength of thirty men. I am not worried for him.

I am more worried for Grendel."

"I'm not worried about a disgusting troll. Beowulf is still made of flesh and bones. I have no idea what trolls are made of."

"This is why he is the only man in all of Geatland and Daneland who can fight Grendel."

"We're not in Geatland or Daneland."

Beowulf thrashed Grendel to the ground. Beowulf jumped onto Grendel and locked his hands around his fury neck. The beast struggled and rolled over Beowulf like a crocodile death roll. Beowulf's hands were still around Grendel neck, but the troll was on top of him. I stood there and watched. I don't know how I could. The witch hovered slightly above me and made a loud cackle.

"You see, Beowulf can conquer this battle. He is a mighty warrior."

I tuned the witch out. The sound of her voice repulsed me. Grendel head butted Beowulf. I watched Beowulf's nose gush with blood, which didn't seem to faze him.

Grendel stepped over to Beowulf to make sure he wouldn't get up. He vigilantly scanned the alleyway and he was gone. I ran to Beowulf's side.

"Beowulf, please answer me, are you alright?" He painfully turned his head to me.

"Yes, yes, I'm fine, M'lady. That beast has got away once again."

"He's a slippery troll isn't he?"

"Of course he is. He's a troll. This is what trolls do best."

The witch pushed me aside to render aid.

"Beowulf, now you are fighting Grendel on his terms, not yours." I wanted to slug her.

"Where is it written that this battle must be on the beast's terms?" I asked her.

92

She looked at me with venomous eyes. "If it isn't on the beast's terms, then there is no battle, and when there is no battle there is no victory."

"And if Grendel kills Beowulf, there's still no victory," I said, smugly. "If Grendel kills Beowulf it is Grendel's victory."

Beowulf tried to hoist himself up. "Kyla, please, I know what I'm doing."

"I don't want to see you in battle anymore. This has to stop. The hell with the sixth century."

"Oh, my love, I'm sorry. This is too surreal for you. It most likely isn't wise for a woman of the twenty-first century to get involved with a warrior from such a primitive time."

"It's this troll thing that's getting on my nerves. I didn't realize that trolls eat people."

"Oh, yes. They quite enjoy the human delicacy."

"So, why didn't Grendel eat me when he hid me away in the subway?" The witch jammed herself between us.

"It is so apparent that Grendel fears no one as much as Beowulf. He knew stealing you, Kyla, would anger Beowulf, but to eat you would mean Beowulf's utter revenge."

"This is getting ridiculous. Aren't you two at each other's throats anyway?"

The witch's image started to fade. Several police officers and security guards approached us. I recognized the same constable from when I was in the hospital.

"Hello," he said to me.

"Could you get my friend, Wolfgang, to a doctor? He's hurt," I said. I felt the witch nudge me. *"Wolfgang?"*

"I will heal naturally on my own, thank-you," Beowulf instilled. I looked at the officer.

"He's the rugged type. He doesn't care for doctors much," I said. "Please, Kyla, allow me to heal in due time."

Two of the security guards placed a cold compress on his eye and cleaned up his face. I noticed the witch had vanished. Good.

CHAPTER EIGHTEEN

That evening Beowulf lay in bed resting. I put antiseptic on his wounds. He wasn't being a very co-operative patient. I sat beside him on the bed.

"Why do you resist me?" I asked, with my nerves overreacting. "Kyla, it is settled. I have brought burden and grief to your life."

"That's not true. I kissed him several times on the lips. There was a knock at the door. I tried to ignore it. "Beowulf, please rest. I'll fetch the door." It was Beth. "I suppose you heard what happened today," I said, as she forced herself into Beowulf's flat.

"As soon as I heard it on the news, I raced over here. Beowulf needs me."

"Why would he need you if he has me taking care of him?" I asked her. "Where is he? I must help him."

She carried on acting busy about the flat as if she owned it. I stepped in front of her just before she was about to enter his bedroom.

"He's resting."

"Of course, the poor man must build up his strength for the next troll escapade." I sat down to rub my tired eyes.

"Beth, you're making me dizzy. I love Beowulf and he loves me, so don't try to get in between. I have to deal with that witch, and she definitely has a strong hold on him."

"There's a witch?" Beth asked.

"Yes, there's a witch – *the* witch. She and Beowulf have been an on-off item."

"Beowulf has been banging a witch?"

"Shhh! Can you hush up? He's asleep in the next room."

"This is getting too weird."

"It gets worse," I assured her. "The witch and the troll have also been an on-off item. What's even weirder is

94

Grendel is insanely jealous of Beowulf having this fling with the witch."

"Who's Grendel?" she asked, looking stupid.

"The troll. The troll is named Grendel. Did you fail *English Lit 101*?" Beowulf limped out of the bedroom and tilted his head at Beth. "Greetings, Beth."

She ran to him and tucked herself under his arm. "I heard what happened, love.

Can I get you anything?"

"As you can see, I'm thriving well thanks to Kyla."

I tugged on Beth's arm and managed to get her off of Beowulf. "Beth, I think it's best you leave now."

"Can't you see he needs me?"

He tried to sit on the sofa whilst wincing in pain.

"Yes, Beth, perhaps you should leave. There is something I must discuss with Kyla. Please come again soon. We would like very much to engage in your company."

"You're asking me to go?" she asked. Beowulf and I both nodded at the same time. She sulked like a child as she made her way to the door. "I guess I'll be going then."

I gave a sarcastic wave and watched her exit my dorm. I glanced at Beowulf. He didn't appear to be himself. Was he angry with me?

"Can I get you some tea or coffee, love?"

"Kyla, we must discuss matters."

"Are you upset with me?"

"Not at all. I feel it is important for me to express how much I have grown to love you. You see, my love, I no longer feel it is to your benefit that I remain here in your time. I have been conversing with the witch. She has prepared a potion that will send me back to the sixth century where I belong – and yes, Grendel comes, too."

"No!" I screamed, and I found myself in his arms.

He stroked my head like a father would to his daughter.

"I will depart from here tomorrow morning. I want you to have my flat. I will leave you some money to pay expenses for the next year. That should take care of things. I have caused too much disruption for you. You must find yourself a fine gentleman who is of this time, not a fourteen-hundred year old troll-slaying Viking from Daneland."

"What's wrong with that? You should see some of the blokes Beth shags." He tried to pry me off him.

"Kyla, I think it's best you leave now. Here's the key to my flat. Please take it."

I took the key and threw it across the room. "No! Don't do this to me, you bastard!"

"Kyla, please go!"

His face changed; his eyes grew cold. His voice was like thunder. Nevertheless, I planted myself on his sofa. "I won't budge."

He recklessly picked me up in his arms, threw me over his shoulder, and opened the door. I wouldn't allow him to fit me through the doorframe for I held on like a spider would to a branch. He grew more frustrated. He could really force me out if he chose to, but that would mean physically harming me.

"Why are you doing this? Please respect my wishes. You've got to go." His voice was getting louder.

I kept crying and crying.

"I'm warning you!" As he tried to plunge me through the doorframe I could feel his rage. "I don't love you; I love the witch."

I fell out of his arms crash landing onto the floor. "You're a bleeding liar. I hate you for that statement, because I hate the witch."

"I meant every word," he said, and grimaced. "You meant nothing. You love me, not the witch."

"I love her and she will soon bear my child."

"Bullocks!" I shouted. I felt myself shake and tremble. "You can't do this. I will take my chances with you, Beowulf."

"I would destroy your life. You have so much to look forward to. Leave, leave now."

I pushed him away and made my way to the hallway. He slammed the door on me. I stood in the hall and tried to get a grip. I stormed outside the building and noticed Beth standing there holding a take-away coffee in her hand.

"Howyeh, Kyla, have you been crying?"

"Do you always loiter around buildings in the late afternoon?"

"Don't get snitty with me. You two had a fight?" she asked.

I kept my head hung low hoping it didn't look too noticeable that I was crying. "He's going back tomorrow."

"Going where?"

"You really are dumb. Has it not occurred to you that this Viking warrior named Beowulf is from the sixth century?"

"He's going back to the sixth century?"

"Yes, you putz! Yes! And Grendel is going with him."

"Grendel the troll is going with him?" she pressed.

I was so irritable and broken I could have killed her just then. "What are you going to do?"

"Do? What can I do? I can't build a time machine to follow him to sixth-century Daneland."

"Oh, I'm sorry, Kyla. That's just awful."

"He asked me to respect his wishes and to go on with my life. He said I should meet a nice bloke who isn't a fourteen-hundred year old Viking warrior."

"Yeah," Beth said, with a sigh, "but he looks so damn good for his age."

CHAPTER NINETEEN

Two months went by. I was finishing off my undergraduate degree and all was very well. I must say it was brilliant not to constantly be dealing with a filthy troll and a conniving witch. Beowulf was right: a normal life is what I needed. I really did enjoy being by myself. I would run into some nice blokes from time to time. They took me to a pub or we'd go out to the clubs. All was very well, I must say.

Not really. Nothing was very well. I was getting fat. I no longer cared about my appearance. I felt empty. I cried myself to sleep every night.

One chilly Friday night I got into my flat after drinking far too many gins with some of the girls from my classes. I entered the dorm lavatory and looked at myself in the mirror. I looked bloated. I stared at my smeared eye make-up and gazed at the chipped sink. I began to wash my face. I had to wash that pesky make-up off. I gazed at my image again in the mirror. I looked like a raccoon. My make-up was even more smeared. It was an absolute bitch to remove.

As I looked into the mirror again an odd colored tuft of light appeared behind me. I ignored it. Finally, I was looking clean and somewhat refreshed. Another image of a woman's face appeared behind me. I turned to see the witch standing before me.

"Kyla, I have come for you," she said. "Well, I have come on behalf of Beowulf." I jolted with panic.

"Is he alright? Is he ill?"

"He ails for you," the witch said. I folded my arms in front of me and sighed with relief. "I have come to ask something of you."

"What?"

"Do you wish to join him in his time?" I didn't know whether to laugh or cry. "What's the sixth century like?"

"You will surely loathe it," she said. She left the lavatory and entered the hallway, which led to my room. I followed, of course. The witch looked like it was difficult to be nice to me. "Let me put it to you this way: sixth century Norse territory will be cold, damp, no flush toilets, inadequate medicine, if any at all, and no civil law. How does that suit you?"

"Sounds like I'll die there," I said.

"No, you will not. If you love Beowulf then you will surely survive."

"I do love him. I feel so empty without him."

"Of course you do." We entered my bedroom. I sat while she continued to hover. "Tell me your answer."

"Does he love me?"

"Why do you think I'm here? He sent me here for you."

"Do I need to bring anything? Shampoo? How about sanitary napkins?"

"Fine, bring them."

"What do I do with my cellular phone?"

"It's useless in the sixth century, Kyla."

"Of course it is. Who would I ring?" I began to bite my nails.

The witch grew frustrated with me. She appeared as if she was anxious to leave. "Kyla, are you interested in Beowulf's invitation or not?"

"Yes!"

"It will not happen just as yet. It will be in the next few days. There will be a glow of light surrounding you. It could last for days even. Make sure you are prepared. Then you will vanish into sixth century Scandinavia."

"Sounds easy enough."

"Not so fast. First you must adhere to the Norse rules. If you do not you will not be granted this journey. Do you understand me?"

A haze of seriousness filled the room.

"What are these rules? What do I have to do?"

"Rule number one: you must wear the clothes of a Viking

99

woman."

"No worries – I'll download some images of what they wore."

"Rule number two: you must cook a Viking feast."

"I don't cook," I said. "At all. I haven't a clue." My hands were sweating so I rubbed them on my t-shirt. "Do you consider warming baked beans from a can cooking?"

"What is this silliness? I find it difficult to understand what Beowulf sees in you."

I rolled my eyes back. "Of all the witches in the world, why did Beowulf have to come across you?" I said, wondering if she'd cast an evil spell on me.

"Rule number three: you must be able to sew a leather tunic that would fit a man Beowulf's size."

"Sew? I don't sew."

"I suggest you learn, fast. Rule number four: you must slay a wild boar and bring it with you to the sixth century."

"How many wild boars have you seen running about London?" I asked. "Don't be smug, Kyla. Just do it."

"Look, I'll do the first three, but rule four is ridiculous. I'm not killing a wild pig" She positioned herself to leave.

"I will tell Beowulf your answer."

"Wait! I have to think about this. Where am I going to find a wild boar?"

"That's your problem. You have four days to fulfill the Norse rules and when you complete your task you will be re-united with Beowulf the Viking warrior."

I blinked and she was gone. I found myself swearing profusely.

CHAPTER TWENTY

I lingered at the university library until I was actually kicked out. I had found several downloaded images of Viking clothing. I also roamed about the stacks looking for books that contained images of Viking clothing. This was definitely a mission. My own studies had been ignored. I just had to fulfill those Norse Rules.

Also, I had spent some time in a garment shop, where I purchased a role of leather, which was very costly. It's hide, after all. I tried to find the cheapest leather, but it still cost an arm and a leg.

I sat up all night, studying what Viking warriors wore. After several glasses of wine, I realized I had to ring my mother.

"Kyla? What a pleasant surprise. What time is it, love?" my mother said half asleep.

"It's about half past five."

"You woke me and your father. What's wrong?"

"I need you to get over here now."

"Dear, what's so urgent that it can't wait 'till eight?" my mother asked. "You can sew, right?"

"Yes, I used to be a seamstress in my day."

"Can you sew leather?" I asked.

"What type of leather, love? Is it soft?"

"Its like thick cow hide. Bring your sewing basket. You have to help me sew a man's tunic tonight. We must use leather."

"Men don't wear tunics anymore. And leather, you say? That's not the easiest fabric to work with."

"Vikings wore tunics, Mum. Can you get here, please?"

"Now?"

"It's an emergency."

"Oh, my. I'll get there as soon as I'm dressed."

"Thanks."

I hung up. I book-marked the pages that showed detailed illustrations of how these tunics looked. I paced my dorm room while chomping on a gigantic bag of crisps. My diet is mud. In just a half hour Mum was at my door. What a reliable mum. She brought all her sewing materials. We worked until noon the next day. I had a man's tunic that would fit a broad shouldered man like Beowulf.

"Who will be wearing this tunic?" Mum asked. "A special man."

"Now, I see where all this hysteria is coming from." She smiled. "What does he do? Does he come from a respectable family?"

"He has an extraordinary position," I said, being cryptic. "Ah, so he's a professional."

"That he is. Very few people are qualified to do what he does."

Mum wore a grin on her face. She appeared relieved. She hadn't forgotten the last man I spoke to her about who was a professional drug dealer.

"I assume you will be attending quite the elaborate costume party?"

"Yeah, so it is. I now have to get working on my costume."

"What are you going as?"

"A Viking maiden, of course."

"How sweet. You'll both be attending as Vikings. Any reason for this historic time period?"

"He's from Scandinavia."

"He's not English? He sounds interesting."

"That he is."

Mum chuckled as if I was fibbing her. It was grand of her to help me. I would never have been able to come this far without her. We worked for hours on the costumes. But, then I tried to coax her to leave. I had to get on the web and search for Viking recipes. I finally got her out the door. I had no time to chat.

It was late morning. I sat at my computer with a bottle of wine beside me. I searched and I searched. I finally found a site titled *Viking Feasts*. I printed it out and ran outside my room to the common area where the kitchen was. I found Beth sitting there with some of the other female residents.

"Beth," I said, flustered as I pulled groceries out of the fridge. "What's up with the culinary attitude? Since when do you cook?"

"I have to prepare something, okay? Let's see. I need to prepare salted fish, salted pork, and horsemeat."

I stared at my printout. Beth and the other residents burst into a jarring cackle. "You're going to salt a horse?" Beth asked, still laughing.

"Horsemeat can roast on a spit like kebab," I explained. Their laughter transformed into snorts. "Beth, can you fetch me some mead?"

"Mead? Where the hell I'm I going to get that? I'll have to search for it."

"Then can you start? I don't have a lot of time. Also, can you also get some fresh bread?"

"Are you preparing something for a special Viking?"

The others continued to laugh, despite they didn't really know why they were laughing.

"Yes. When I can get you in private I will need your help with something big."

The other women understood, and made their exit. I continued to cut and salt meat. I placed it in plastic containers.

Beth approached me. "Kyla, what the hell are you doing? Beowulf isn't here anymore."

"I'm going there."

"You're what? You can't go there. This is too surreal."

"I'm going to the sixth century A.D. The witch has granted me this wish." She kissed her teeth at me as if I were an idiot.

"This is ridiculous, Kyla. You can't live in the sixth century."

"Why not?"

"Because you're from the twenty-first century, that's why

not, you goof."

"I love him and he loves me. He sent the witch for me. I'm going there in the next few days."

"Are you mad?"

"Madly in love, Beth."

"So, what are you doing with this salted meat? Are you fixing him a midnight snack?"

"The witch said I can only go if I follow the four Norse rules." She smacked her hand over her eyes.

"I had the same reaction as you. I have to prepare a Viking feast; make a tunic that fits him; have my own Viking attire, and last and the very least…" I held my breath, unable to say it out loud. It really was a ridiculous notion. Beth's eyes bulged out of her head.

"You what?"

"Will you help me with the fourth rule?"

"That depends what it is?"

"I have to slay a wild boar," I said, biting my fingernails. She gazed at me with her teeth parted. I continued to pack the meat in the containers. "Don't make me repeat myself. You heard me."

"Where the hell are you going to find a wild boar in London?"

"I don't friggen know!"

My eyes glazed with tears. Beth's facial expression suddenly brightened. "I have just the place," she said, with a grin. "The zoo."

"We can't walk into a zoo and murder an exotic animal. Have you lost it?" I said. "But, it's quite alright for you to salt horse meat? Have you lost it? You and I have always ridden horses, have you forgotten?"

"Don't make me cry. I'm doing this for Beowulf."

"How can you love a man who eats horse?"

"I don't know what the fuck he eats! I downloaded some information on the web, which stated that ancient Viking cuisine consisted of horsemeat."

"Then, he may even loath horsemeat, right?"

"How the fuck do I know!

"You're raising your voice, Kyla."

"What other alternatives do you have?"

"I guess, it's horsemeat, then. You need to teach him that it's cruel to eat horse."

"Of course I will. Do you think I want to eat horsemeat?"

"Kyla, who knows what you're capable of."

"I was going to search the web for a list of countries that have wild boars."

"Three hundred years ago Britain had wild boars. Now they're extinct."

I sat at my computer and began my search.

"It appears the northern countries in Africa have wild boars. Wait! They're also in the U.K.!"

"Where?" Beth asked with a soft tone.

"There's about 100-200 in Kent/East Sussex, and about 20 in west Dorset. In both these areas they are known to breed in the wild."

"Oooh…sounds dangerous, Kyla."

"Do I have a choice?" I asked, whilst shutting down my computer.

"Find another man. You know, the kind that aren't hundreds of years old."

"C'mon, we need to get ready to take the rail to Kent."

"I'm trying to understand this. We're going to steal a wild boar so you can kill it? I know you, you'll never get the nerve to do it."

"Are you going to help me with this?" I asked her. "Let's get to Victoria Station."

Despite the short train ride I slept the entire way. When we arrived, the first place we stopped was the Tourist Board.

"Excuse me," I said, to a mature woman behind a desk.

The woman was holding several maps in her hands and waved them around as if they were gold.

"Yes, do you need help planning a trip? A hike; perhaps sight seeing? This is the right place."

Beth stood a few feet behind me pretending she didn't

know me.

"Not exactly, but I do need your help," I said, to the lady. "I'm looking for wild and not so domestic pig farms. I need to find wild boars." The woman's eyebrows lifted from her eyes. Beth was pretending to be interested in one of the wall maps. "Yes, could you direct me to a wild swine farm?"

"Good heavens. I suppose I could check my agricultural pamphlets. I reckon you're looking to start up a farm?"

"No, not at all. I just need one wild boar."

The woman forced a smile and held out several pamphlets on swine farms in the area.

"There's a map you can follow. You could call for a taxi. It shouldn't be more than 10 kilometers. I think some of them even have guided tours, but that would pertain more to school visits."

"Tours? No, I won't be needing a tour. Thank you," I said.

We took a taxi and ended up in some vast agricultural area. There wasn't any human activity for what we could see. We made our way along the cow paths and then it hit us; the pungent aroma of swine. As we continued to walk, we noticed there were no more barriers separating the livestock. We made our way through the spongy pastures trying not to step on dung. There was a light rain earlier, so everything was wet and smelly.

"The smell is getting to be too much," Beth said, with her sleeve over her nose. "There's some trees over there, as well as rugged land. They could be roaming about."

"And if we find them, what then?" Beth asked looking a bit nervous. "Well, then we'll slay one."

"With what?"

"I dunno. We could throw rocks at it."

"Oh, you are so silly. Throwing rocks to kill an animal is inhumane. And it's against the law."

"How do you know?"

"I know it, everyone knows it. You'd go to jail."

"Jail? I think not."

"These pigs belong to somebody. You're also stealing. You're definitely going to go to jail."

"Who's going to know?" I asked. "The swine owner."

"He's got so many; he won't miss just one little piggy."

"Yes, he will. I bet they're all branded."

"Shit, I never thought of that."

We continued to walk where we met an area of rougher terrain. We sat down on the mossy rocks and searched the bottoms of our shoes for dung.

"So, I suppose we should be gathering rocks?" Beth asked.

"Yes, because the boars could be watching us even as we sit here."

I had almost dozed off with exhaustion when Beth heard a sound in the trees. We both sprung up, each holding two sharp rocks in our hands. Two wild pigs bolted across the bushes.

I pointed. "There! Don't let them get away!"

Beth was a much faster runner than me, so she went ahead. Then I saw her run toward me. She ran to the nearest tree and grabbed the easiest branch to hang off of.

"They're vicious!" she yelled. "Get out of the way!"

I ran to the same tree as Beth. She tried to hoist me up. I was hanging on a sharp branch close to the ground, but they're hogs and they're agility is limited – thank God. The boars kept running until we didn't see them anymore.

"Kyla, this just isn't going to work. You better tell that witch you can only fulfill three of the Norse rules."

"What? I can't do that."

"I don't see this panning out for you," Beth said.

"We've just begun our hunt."

"If you ask me, we've just concluded our hunt."

We had a rough landing getting down from the tree. We sat in mud and pig dung. I thought I was going to die.

"The witch was firm on this. She didn't make any exceptions."

"Wait 'till Beowulf finds out. He won't be pleased."

"About me not bringing him a slain pig, or the witch

demanding me to bring him a slain pig?"

"Both, I expect," she said, with a shrug. Then I got a bit agitated.

"Don't you think Beowulf, being the mighty warrior he is, can slay his own fucking pig, Kyla?"

"I don't really know if there were loads of wild boars available for slaying back in his sixth century."

"Well, we've made it this far. We might as well give it a good try."

Beth pointed at something coming our way in the distance. The boars had returned. They were running toward us in a fury. We sprang up sliding in the slippery feces and up the tree we went. We were both screaming and howling. I was hanging off an unworthy branch. The boars circled below us snorting and grunting. It was at this point I urinated my jeans. A puff of light appeared, and there was the witch. The pigs seemed frightened of her and they dashed off. I didn't blame them.

"Having a difficult time?" the witch asked. We fumbled to hold onto the tree branches. The witch encircled us, realizing we looked like hell. She gave a loud cackle. "You both look dreadful. It is obvious you are not able to fulfill the fourth Norse rule."

"We're just getting warmed up," Beth said. "Wow, she's a real witch."

"I'm not killing a wild boar," I told the witch. "Beowulf wouldn't expect me to, however, he would be angry at you for causing me so much grief."

"Beowulf has his hands full trying to find Grendel, so he can slay him once and for all for the sake of King Hrothgar's people."

"How's it going?" I asked, timidly. "Not well."

"You see, he needs me there with him."

"I will go and assess your situation. You will know the verdict in due course," she said, as she dissipated into smoke and was gone.

Beth looked at me. "What a bitch."

"She's a witch, she's supposed to be a bitch."

"No, she's a bitch, because she's a bitch."

My ass hurt. I somehow slid down the tree and fell flat. I limped a bit. We started to walk in the direction we came from. We were covered in mud and sow dung.

"I feel like hell, Kyla. This Norse rule bit isn't quite working."

We walked until I noticed the two wild boars were heading straight for us. "Beth! Run!"

We ran like sons of bitches, but those creatures were fast little buggers. The larger of the two sneaked up behind Beth and butted her hard from behind. She went flying into the mud. I knew I was next. I picked up a large stick and shook it at the little monsters. They squealed and snorted. I pretended to act like the dominant one of the three. They backed off and ran. I panted with fright and exhaustion. I helped Beth up. She wasn't doing too well.

"Kyla, I'm not helping you with this anymore. For now on, you're on your own."

"I don't really blame you. If you, however, were in desperate need of something I would help you no mater what."

"Ah, that's so sweet of you. But even though you're such a good friend I'm still done with this fucking fourth Norse rule."

We both hobbled to the main road.

CHAPTER TWENTY-ONE

We arrived at the train station. I sat on the bench and cried.

"Surely you can't be crying because I told you I'm not going to take this anymore," Beth said, chomping on a chocolate bar.

"No, it's not that at all. Now that I blew it with the pig the witch won't grant me my wish to be with Beowulf."

"Yes, she will. Beowulf would never let that happen. He loves you, doesn't he?"

"Yes, he does," I slobbered, like a baby.

I think I was making Beth sick. I stared at the ground and felt a chill run through me. A flash of light and smoke appeared. The witch returned. Beth stepped back.

"What's this? She's back."

"Of course I am."

"Blyme," Beth expressed.

"So, I see you have no intension of fulfilling the fourth Norse rule. Then, you will remain here in your time, and that is all."

"You little bitch!" Beth called out. I took Beth's arm.

"Stay out of this. Please excuse my friend, she doesn't understand."

"That's obvious. She better watch her step."

"Beth, you need to hush up," I cautioned. I stood up and moved closer to the witch. "Please honor the third Norse rule and not the fourth. You said you were going to inquire about this."

"Yes. I have spoken with Beowulf."

"You have? What did he say?" I was so anxious I could have shook the witch into a tailspin.

"He says he wants you with him."

I began to cry. Beth tried to comfort me, but seemed

confused. "Kyla, didn't you hear what she said?"

"These are tears of joy," I blubbered, with sniffles and tears.

CHAPTER TWENTY-TWO

I was back in London staying up late every night to catch up on my academic assignments. I had several bags of crisps by my side, just in case. Then one night a voice came to me, loud and clear.

"Kyla!" I looked about the room and saw nothing. It was definitely the witch's voice. "Kyla, get ready. You are about to leave your time and enter Beowulf's time."

"Shit!"

I ran about my room pulling out that silly Viking woman's get-up that I created with my mother. I quickly pulled off my jeans and sweatshirt. The witch then appeared in front of me.

"Why are you wearing your undergarments?" she asked.

"I'm about to put this peasant skirt on and ugly blouse. What's wrong now?"

"You're wearing your bra?" She walked behind me and pulled the back strap of my bra. "40D, Kyla?"

"Has Beowulf asked for my bra size?" I asked.

"You're not to bring your undergarments. You're going to the sixth century. What don't you understand?"

"Nobody will know I wear a bra, but if I don't wear it everyone will wonder why I'm not."

She stood close to me, face to face.

"Women didn't wear bras and undergarment briefs in the sixth century. That will have to remain here. Either you do what I say or you will not be granted your wish."

I grudgingly began to unfasten my bra. I glared at the witch with hateful eyes.

She was loving every second of this. I pulled off my briefs while trying not to let her see me naked. I draped the peasant Viking clothes over by body. I tied a leather vest under my bosoms.

"This is not my idea of support," I said, with regret. "You are to do as the women did of that time."

"Beth was right about you."

"Now, remove your jewelry," she demanded. "And your hair is too reprehensive of the twenty-first century free world."

"I wear my hair blunt. How can I change that?"

"Keep it as messed as possible. You wear your hair much too short for a woman of Beowulf's time."

I messed my hair as best I could. It's hard to do when hair is as straight as mine.

I stood in front of the mirror and gasped.

"I look like a barmaid. Yuck! Beowulf will surely send me back."

"I don't have time for this. If you're ready I will now send you to him."

"Will I go directly to him?"

"Maybe yes, maybe no."

"What?"

CHAPTER TWENTY-THREE

A sudden layer of smoke filled the room. Colors flashed on and off. I felt dizzy. I didn't have a clue how long it would take to teleport me to the sixth century. It was cold, damn cold. I stood in front of a Viking long house. People entered and exited constantly. It was definitely the sixth century. I starred at the people, and they starred at me. Some older woman approached me and spewed a few words in what was probably Norse. I nodded as if I understood. She took my hand and pulled me into the long house. There were a few fires going on, thank-God - some warmth. I heard music, some kind of drumming and a flute-like recorder sound. Men were dressed in their fury capes with their long unruly hair hanging in front of their bearded faces. They must have been drinking mead or ale out of a horned flask. They acted like animals where they fondled every woman that passed by them.

I made sure my hair was messed and walked as close to the fire as I could get without jumping into it. I scanned the house looking for Beowulf. It was hard to see with such poor lighting. I sat by the fire warming my cold hands when I realized from my university classes that I was in the middle of a Viking festival, probably *Sigrblot,* the celebration of summer. There were several long wooden tables cluttered with food. I noticed the men were eating some kind of smoked fish. It smelled like hell. I even noticed a head of what looked like a wild boar sitting in the middle of one of the tables. The stench disgusted me. The women were gathered in the center of the house by some kind of metal stove. The place was loaded with smoke, there was a hole in the roof over the stove, but they definitely needed a better ventilation system than that.

Many were dancing whilst they were stinking drunk. Food was smeared all through their hair and clothes. I must admit, I was shaking in my shoes with fear. I felt like I definitely didn't belong.

An unruly-looking man stood in front of me and made a few gestures I didn't understand. He pulled me toward his chest and roughly ran his rough disgusting hands through my hair. He stunk to high hell. He kissed me. I turned away. He kissed me again. Then it happened, he grabbed my breasts. I screamed so loud the music stopped. I tore his hands off of me. "Beowulf!" I called as loud as I could. "Where is Beowulf?"

The crowd talked amongst themselves. Was I a candidate for being burned at a stake, I wondered? The crowd was silent where they didn't move or even flinch. They knew I was different, but they knew what I meant. They knew I was looking for Beowulf.

The man who groped me, groped me again and again. I punched and kicked him as hard as I could. Was this jackass going to rape me? Then he thrashed me to the ground. I bumped my nose and blood poured out, which made my face quite bloody. I found myself in a panicked stupor. I was so winded I couldn't get up. Then the crowd started to howl. I heard a horn blow a few times. I remained on the floor watching the hysterics take place. Two large hands took hold of me from behind and lifted me on my feet. I tried to stand.

"Kyla," he said.

It took me a few seconds to focus on the handsome image that stood before me. "Beowulf, you're timing is impeccable."

He took me in his arms and planted a wet kiss on my lips. The crowd seemed shocked.

"Leave us be; she is my wench," he said, and then repeated himself in Norse.

He approached that jackass who grabbed me. Beowulf blurted a few words to him, drew his sword, and slit the man's arm. The man yelled in pain as his arm bled. Everyone went about their drinking and festivities. I fell into Beowulf's arms with relief and with some sniffles and whimpers. He caressed my face. "So, my love, I hear you're not an expert boar slayer." I kept blubbering in his arms.

"In fact, I rather suck at it. Don't ask me to do that again."

"Suck?"

"Sorry, please excuse my twenty-first century colloquialisms."

He let out a strong deep laugh. I could see how much of a Viking he really was.

He scooped me into his arms and brought me to a large wooden chair, which could have been a throne. He sat in it and placed me on his lap. We were situated at the far end of the long house. I had a great view of the goings on. Some men brawled in the corner; the women shook their bosoms in some of the men's faces. Children were running around unattended. It seemed so savage.

Beowulf tightened his arms around my waist. I think he could feel my heart pounding. I was so nervous. I was terrified to be back in time with the ancient Danes, but I was even more nervous about Beowulf's feelings toward me. He rubbed his big strong hands over my breasts several times in front of everybody. I felt uncomfortable, but no one cared. Then he gathered my skirt and shoved his hands underneath where he plunged his hand into my vagina. I grabbed both his hands.

"No! Not here."

"Why not?" he said, and kissed the back of my neck.

He ran his hands through my hair. I did notice how the women in the room wore their hair long. Their hair looked as if it had never been cut or groomed.

"Oh, yeah, you're a Viking," I said. "I guess you blokes are used to raping and plundering."

Platters and platters heaped with food arrived carried in by the slave women, of course. The men, like African savannah lions, attacked the food while the women and children stood back.

"Come," Beowulf said, standing me up and holding my hand. "Come, my bride, we now will eat."

"Bride?"

116

Maybe I didn't hear correctly. He placed his hands on my face and stroked my cheeks. I think he was having an orgasm. He didn't act like this when he was in the twenty-first century.

He brought me to a large wooden chair, a matching throne? He sat me beside him. We sat in the middle of the long wood table. I scanned the table noticing the Viking cuisine. I saw fruit, seaweed, shellfish, seals, and something I was even afraid to mention – whale parts? In the middle of the table sat the head of a wild boar. Large bowls of honey were passed down the table so everyone could sweeten their meat.

"Now, m'bride, I shall carve the boar," he said, handling what looked like a small machete.

I watched him cut away at the poor pig's face. I looked everywhere in the room, but there. I thought I was going to be sick.

"Beowulf," I said. "I don't eat that." He continued to carve away. I took his arm. "Beowulf, I don't eat that!" I pointed to the pig. "I don't eat wild boar heads, sorry." The dinner guests stopped their feeding frenzy and gazed at Beowulf and me. I fiddled with my tooth necklace. "Everyone is staring at us. Please, tell them to continue their meal."

Beowulf nodded. He stood up.

"Everyone! Eat! Eat now!" he insisted in Norse. They continued to devour their plates. Beowulf sat beside me. "In order to be my bride in this time, you must develop a taste for boar head."

"I think you and I will have to discuss this at another time and place, like twenty-first century London."

"Please, my love, eat."

"I can't do this. If you love me as you say you do, why are you basing so much of our love on me eating that rubbish?"

The dinner guests stopped what they were doing and gave me a good long stare. Beowulf's complexion turned to a shade of red. He tried to act natural, whilst he shoveled a large helping of boar meat into his mouth.

117

"My love, you need to keep your voice down, especially during our feasts."

"Sorry."

"Can you at least eat something?"

"Fruit? Fruit would be good if you have it."

"It isn't the season just now, since we are in a cold spring, but there is some preserved from our warmer months."

He tore away at some grapes. I chewed on the not-so-well-preserved fruit. "It tastes like rubber."

Beowulf was engaged in his animal flesh feast. He tore away at it like a male lion devouring its mate's catch.

"What are you saying, Kyla? Are you not happy here with me?"

"No, no, not at all. I'm very happy to be with you. I can't tell you how much I missed you. I'm just not a product of this time."

"Oh, my love, I'm not a product of your time. I did, however, survive quite well in the twenty-first century."

"Then it's settled. I can't survive in the sixth century. That means you must come to the twenty-first century with me."

"You are my wench. You must give my world a try," he said.

"I'm here, aren't I?" I felt my blood pressure rise. "Isn't this a try?"

"You just arrived, my love. You just began your stay here."

"I'm sitting at a table with a bunch of Vikings who are devouring boar head and whale meat. Isn't this a try?"

"You have a temper. I'm not used to wenches with temperaments like men."

Then I did it. I slammed my fist on the table. The dinner crowd stopped and stared at us. Beowulf turned red with embarrassment. He stopped eating and glared at me.

"Do you wish me to mount you at this time? Do you wish to give me a child now, is that it?"

"Beowulf, you're different here."

118

"This is my home." He cut a piece of boar for me and popped it in my mouth. "Eat!" he grunted.

I moaned with agony. A piece of wild game was in my mouth and there was nothing I could do about it. The stench of it made me want to vomit. His eyes were locked with mine, as he made sure I chewed and swallowed. It seemed like hours before I got the last of it down my throat. I could even detect several of the swine's coarse hairs, which made it difficult to swallow.

"That wasn't so bad now was it, Kyla?" he asked, almost in an orgasmic state of glee.

"I need mouthwash. I must wash this disgusting taste out of my mouth."

An older Viking with long horrible looking hair and the worst teeth I ever saw, approached us. He tapped Beowulf's shoulder. "Who is this wench? She doesn't like boar head?" he asked.

"King Hrothgar, I'm glad you could make it this evening. Please, join our feast," Beowulf said, with a slight bow to his king. I sank into my chair and tried to hide behind Beowulf. "This is my bride. Her name is Kyla. She is from a far land, I must say."

King Hrothgar grunted, and pulled one of the guests from his chair. The king then took over the man's feast. I wasn't too impressed with the ugly bloke.

"What far land is your wench from?" he asked, as he gorged himself with the other man's food.

"She is Geatish, as well," Beowulf lied convincingly.

The king continued to tear away at the slain animal in front of him. Food was caught up in his long stringy hair and his face was oiled with animal flesh. I had to look the other way.

"Beowulf," I said, my voice was getting timid. "Why are we sitting on the bigger chairs, and the king isn't?"

"Because I'm a troll slayer, and you are my wench."

I left a lot of food on my plate. It was too disgusting to eat. The meat was drenched in blood, and those pig hairs were like barbwire. I almost choked several times. I ate fruit and bread and drank some of that overly sweet mead. The women cleared the table for the men to discuss matters. I remained by Beowulf's side. King Hrothgar didn't bother to clean the blood and grease from his face. He looked horrid.

"So, Beowulf, you have been away for some time and so has Grendel."

"I had some matters in Geatland. As for Grendel, only the gods would know."

"Grendel has not made any showings, but recently there has been sightings of him near the coast. What will you do?"

Beowulf chuckled, and said, "I will surely slay him this time."

"When?"

"Tomorrow night. Tonight I must make babies with my bride."

Beowulf and the king nudged each other and laughed. I took a deep breath and noticed the women chatting in the corner pointing and gossiping about me. I reckon they're not too pleased about my arrival.

CHAPTER TWENTY-FOUR

The guests were finally leaving, but not all of them left. I assumed the mead hall belonged to the king, but many parked themselves on the floor and fell asleep.

"Why are these people sleeping on the floor?" I asked Beowulf. "They are my men. They are also troll slayers."

"Of course they are. Why are the women and children sleeping on the floor?"

"They are my men's wenches with their children, and our slaves. Some of the children are also my men's wenches." I nodded not feeling too easy about my new environment.

"You are twenty-three years old?"

"Yes, you know that."

"My people stare, because you are too old for me. My wench should be between twelve and sixteen years."

"Okay, aren't you thirty-eight, in this wonderful century of yours?"

"Yes, I am no longer fourteen hundred years old," he said, with a chuckle. "In my century you would be considered a pedophile," I said.

"I'm sorry, but I don't know what that is. I've never even heard of such a word."

"In the twenty-first century, if an adult man is caught with a twelve year old girl, then he would have to go to the dungeon. Get it?"

"Oh, that's outrageous. Nobody in my time would ever be sent to the dungeon for such an innocent and usual act."

"This is why my time has boxes with talking pictures, and your time does not! Fourteen hundred years is enough time for serious change. Twelve year old girls are children!"

Beowulf smiled at me. "I understand, M'lady, forgive me for my primitive mind."

I rubbed my eyes. "Look, I'm exhausted. I've had enough

of the sixth century for one day. I really must sleep. Where can I do this?"

"Oh, yes, you do require rest after such an exhausting day. I recall when I first entered your time. I was beyond fatigue."

He scooped me into his arms and brought me to a far corner where there were several layers of straw. There were animal hides over-layering the straw. He laid me down. He removed his tunic and then his tights or maybe they were the Viking version of trousers. He was naked. He yelled to his slaves several times in Norse for them to get the fire more active in order to generate more warmth. I was chilled to the bone.

Other people were having sex on the floor. I tried not to look. The fire lessened to a quiet smolder. The light dimmed and I was asleep.

CHAPTER TWENTY-FIVE

A ray of light shone through the long house. I could hear people working, perhaps preparing food. I looked at myself and noticed Beowulf's arms sheltered over me. I felt safe. He smelled better than some of the other Vikings, especially that revolting king.

"Beowulf," I whispered, minding those who were still asleep in the mead hall. "Please, move your arm. I have to go to the loo."

He snorted in a fluster with his hair messed in front of his face. "I really gotta go."

"Where, my love? Where do you need to go?" He asked half asleep.

"The toilet. Remember, I had one at my flat in London. You had a few at your flat, as well."

"Oh, yes. How soon I forget. There are none of that kind in this time."

"I figured that. How about an outhouse?"

"I'm sure we don't have that either. Come, I will take you."

He stood up giving me his hand. He was naked of course, but wrapped a wool shawl around his lower half. He picked me up and wrapped me in another shawl. My teeth chattered from the damp climate. He carried me in his arms outside, because I was bare foot. He took me to a deep hole in the ground.

"This is the best I can do, M'lady. I promise I will build you a *too-let*."

"That boar meat from last night did a number on my stomach."

"Do you think I enjoyed eating that pizza in your time?" he asked, with a laugh. "Yes, in fact, you did. You ate almost an entire box of extra large," I reminded him.

"Oh, yes, what a fine taste it was; such a new experience for me. Now, if you must do your business, this is the time."

I stood there not letting go of his arm.

"Do you have anything like toilet paper?" I asked.

"Paper? Wait here and I will find something that may please you."

And, so he left me there standing by a hole in the ground with a stench that was indescribable. I stood there wrapped in a shawl, watching ugly people walk by. A couple of young women my age stopped in front of me. They conversed with each other in Norse and laughed. I suppose they were laughing at me. The taller one tried to yank the shawl off me. I tugged on it and she ended up falling in the hole. Her friend glared at me, and hollered as if I were Satan. I backed away. The woman in the ground managed to get herself out of the hole. I found it difficult to even look at her for she looked like Medusa with feces in her hair rather than snakes. This episode was surreal. The stench was unbearable. Beth would never believe me if I told her about this.

Beowulf reappeared – thankfully. "What do we have here?"

"Beowulf, they're scaring me," I whined, like a child. He shouted at them in Norse, telling them to leave at once. I liked that. "I feel dirty," I added. "Is there somewhere I can clean up?"

"Yes, my love," he said, and kissed me on the cheek.

CHAPTER TWENTY-SIX

Later that afternoon we sat at the long wood table at Heorot Mead Hall with Beowulf at the center of the table, and me beside him. His men entered and sat around us. The table was covered with large platters of fruit. The Viking men devoured everything - they even ate the fish bones. The female slaves kept filling the horned flasks with mead and the men loved every minute of it. There was some serious buttock-pinching going on. As far as I was concerned, these great Viking warriors were a bunch of sexiest pigs.

I clung to Beowulf, where he knew from his days in twenty-first century London that women are equal. Then King Hrothgar entered. Beowulf's slaves prepared a lavish place setting for him. The slave women dressed me up beautifully – for a Viking woman that is. I had to look good for the king, apparently. What a thought. Why would any woman want to even try to look good for the king? That king? Ugh!

The king took his seat, and a giant horned flask filled with mead was given to him.

"Beowulf, tonight is the night," the king said. The crew of warriors froze in silence.

"Yes, Hrothgar, it is the night."

I poked Beowulf in the ribs. "What's he saying?" I asked.

"Tonight, I will slay Grendel once and for all." Beowulf stood from his throne and pulled his sword to demonstrate to his men and the king that he meant business.

Platters of seafood appeared on the table where I could smell the appetizing aroma. That was the first time anything around this place actually wet my taste buds.

"So much has failed with Grendel, Beowulf. Daneland can no longer afford to have this menacing troll terrorize Village Lejre. You must be rid of the monster, or else."

"Or else, what?" Beowulf asked.

Beowulf's eyes widened. I felt a bit nervous by his expression.

"You and your bride will be banished back to Geatland where you must remain."

"It is my duty to protect the Danes and that is what I shall do." Beowulf declared, and waved his mighty sword.

"You seem anxious to meet your final match with the troll," the king said, and the men giggled like little girls.

Beowulf guzzled his mead. The slave girls hurried to refill his flask. I tapped Beowulf on the shoulder. "What's going on?"

"If Grendel is not put to rest at once, we both will be banished to Geatland."

"Is Geatland similar to Daneland?" I asked.

"Very."

"Is that such a bad thing?" I asked feeling as if I should know the difference. "Kyla, my love, it is my job to protect the people of Daneland. If I am banished back to Geatland, then I am a failed warrior."

"If you really want to defeat Grendel you need a strategy. If you just find him a and blindly fight him, chances are you could lose. You're fighting a troll not a man."

"Strategy, my love?"

"Yes, you need a plan that will not fail."

"I have my sword, Lady Kyla. What else is there?" he asked.

"Round up your men and delegate tasks for each one. Teamwork is the key."

"But I have the strength of thirty men. Do I need so much help?"

"I know. We need to find out what Grendel values most."

Beowulf sat back in his large wooden chair and scratched his bearded chin. "We would have to visit Grendel in his cave of course."

"I guess that would be too difficult to do, huh? What if we lure him out of his cave with food? Does he fancy boar head?" I said, feeling my fingers tremble.

I scanned the men sitting at the table including the king. They were silent as they listened. They didn't understand a damn thing we said, but they still listened. Beowulf took a deep breath and drank me in with his eyes.

"Who wouldn't fancy boar head? That dish is such a delight." I smacked my lips together.

"How can we go about this, M'lady? It sounds risky."

"We can get some of your slaves to cook up the boar head, but they should do it not too far from Grendel's cave. When he smells the aroma he'll surely come running."

"Excellent idea!" Beowulf took me in his arms and planted a wet kiss on my lips. "When he leaves his cave I will enter and take his possessions."

Beowulf's men applauded whilst banging their hands on the table with cheer. "You know, when I spent all that time with Grendel in the London underground he didn't seem so bad. I felt rather sorry for him," I said in a whisper, while the dinner guests had confused expressions on their faces. "He has feelings."

"He's a troll, Kyla. Trolls haven't any feelings. I will inform my slaves at once and get them to work. I will also get some of my men to find the biggest boar possible."

I cuddled in Beowulf's arms. He kissed my neck continuously.

"Beowulf, one more thing. Say all goes well with the slaying of Grendel, what happens after that?"

"I will be noted as Daneland's most fearless warrior." He took my hand and kissed it several times. "And you and I will marry."

"Oh."

"You don't wish to be my wedded maiden?" he asked, as he continued to kiss my hands.

"Of course I want to be your wife. But its this place."

"You don't wish to live in Heorot? This is the king's palace, the most honorable place to live in all of Middle Earth.

"No, I suppose Heorot is as good as things get in the sixth century."

"You don't wish to be in Daneland? We can sail to the west to where the Celts, Saxons, and Gauls reside, if you wish?"

"That wouldn't be too different than here. Couldn't we make a deal with the witch and return to the twenty-first century?"

"Oh, I see, you are not pleased with the sixth century?"

"Are you?"

"Now that you have exposed me to warm shelters with so many luxuries; you have light whenever one desires it. You have a beautiful box with such a large door that has cold food stored in it. I also remember running water whenever one desires it."

"Can't beat it, Beowulf. Would the witch let us return?" He scratched his beard again.

"It's difficult to say, because of her love for Grendel."

"Doesn't she love you?"

"She does."

"So what's the problem?" I asked.

"You," he said. I sat back in my chair and focused on Beowulf's men guzzling the mead. Some of the female slaves began to chant and dance around the fire. I was terrified to ask him why. "My Lady Kyla, the witch is sorry I ever found you. You're in her way. She has never seen me so happily in love. She is astonished that I want to marry someone from the twenty-first century. I feel she is jealous of you."

"Well, that isn't good, is it?"

"No, it isn't."

CHAPTER TWENTY-SEVEN

Some hours had passed. Beowulf's slaves doted on me, they combed my hair and gave me jewelry. They were amazed my hair texture was so smooth and unknotted. They couldn't even fathom that I smelled so much better than them. I shrugged my shoulders. It wasn't my fault I came from the twenty-first century.

Beowulf and his men ate a lot. I suppose troll slayers need their strength before the great attack. They drank a lot as well. I suppose troll slayers also need to be in a drunken stupor before the great troll attack. Then he and his men stepped outside to sharpen their swords.

A wild boar was being hunted somewhere. One of the female slaves took me outside to see Beowulf's collection of horses. They were beautiful, quite stocky looking for horses. The young slave went to fetch food for the animals. I stood beside the most beautiful horse. I felt something come upon me; a presence. I looked in front of me and there was the witch.

"So, now, Beowulf is asking for your hand? How does it feel?" she asked me. "Great. I love him and he loves me. I want to marry him as much as he wants to marry me."

She laughed in a high-pitch cackle.

"You can't marry a Viking warrior from the sixth century. Are you mad?"

"I will marry him."

"Impossible. You're both playing games with my magic. You are abusing your granted wishes. It was never in the cards for you and Beowulf to marry. It wasn't in the cards for you to be in his life at all. None of this was supposed to happen."

"How do you know we were never to meet? You're not God. You're some eccentric woman who levitates and claims to be a sorceress."

I had to take some time to calm down. Her eyes pierced through me like swords. "You can return to your time, but he must remain here without you."

"How can you say this?" I asked.

"I can say whatever I wish. I'm a witch and I have the power," she said, and laughed. "You think you know so much. You think I'm eccentric? Perhaps you should look in a mirror. I find you amusing, Kyla."

I took a deep breath and tried to focus on her with kinder eyes. "You love Grendel, don't you?"

"Yes, but you are helping Beowulf slay him tonight. I will no longer have Grendel, therefore, I must have Beowulf."

"Is the king available?" I suggested, hopefully. "Ugh! I hate the king," she said.

"Who doesn't?"

"The king has been relentless toward Grendel."

"Well, do you blame him?" I asked.

The witch stepped closer to me and raised her arms above her head. "Why does everyone loathe Grendel?"

"Why don't we start with the mere fact that Grendel is a troll? Trolls eat people.

Grendel has been terrorizing Heorot for twelve years."

"The king started this. Now, the king has been cursed ever since."

"You won't catch me siding with the king. He has the worst breath," I said. "Beowulf detests Grendel, and will stop at nothing until he sees him to his death," the witch said. She turned her back to me. "Why am I telling you this? What do you know? You're a wench from the twenty-first century." I looked at her feeling uneasy. She made me nervous. I only felt comfortable with Beowulf. She turned to me and stared me down with the look of vengeance in her eyes. Her black robe blew in the wind. "You must return to your time. You know nothing of Beowulf. Your technology is not required here. You must be off."

"Why can't you understand that Beowulf loves me?"

"He loves me. He constantly mounts me, but you are not aware of this."

I took a few steps back. I felt deflated. Tears ran down my cheeks and I could barely breathe. "He only loves me," I said, trying to be brave. "He would never choose you."

"He mounted me just before your arrival. I may be expecting his child. Beowulf is meant to be with me. He is a brave warrior of this time. He is to marry me and I am to give him a child."

"Says who?"

"Says the Norse scripture."

I didn't know how to respond to that. How would I know what a Norse scripture would even look like? "Beowulf never once mentioned that he was to marry you and have a child with you. You're a liar."

That got her mad. She held her arms above her head and she stared me down.

Some words spewed at me, maybe Norse.

"For the sake of Odin. *Mikill Wotan! Doni langaspjot viti!*"

She waved her hands in the air and repeated the same phrase over and over. A puff of smoke formed around me and I was gone.

***

Beowulf approached the witch.

"I see you are getting acquainted with Kyla. Where is she?"

The witch folded her arms in front of her. "She has gone. She is a difficult girl, Beowulf. You are making a mistake. So, I sent her to Geatland."

"Get her back. I am preparing for battle. I need my wench here," Beowulf demanded.

"She will perish here with you in battle," she insisted. "She will remain in Heorot palace until I come for her."

"Grendel will attack Heorot and slay her."

"No! Hrothgar has granted me eight horses each with golden headgear. I will defeat Grendel and I will take my

131

bride. Bring her back to Lejre."

"She will do fine in Geat. Leave her be."

***

I was banished to Geatland. What an awful place – even
worse than Daneland. I was in some frosty village that was
inhabited by *Homo Hablis* communities, so it seemed. It
didn't appear to be anything like Heorot, not that Heorot is
my idea of *the Grand Hotel*. It just seemed more primitive.
Shit! I didn't think you could get more primitive than
Daneland.

I noticed a few inhabitants scrambling about trying to
make fire. I thought I was going to die of frostbite. I think the
Baltic was the water I was seeing. What a frosty body of
water. Some ugly Neanderthal-looking bloke approached me.
I stood there freezing. He grunted some words at me. I tried
to say hello in Swedish.

"Hej!" I said, feeling desperate. He stared at me and
grunted.

"Good Mórgon?" I said badly, despite the fact it wasn't
morning. He continued to stare me down and grunt even louder.
"God dag?" I tried again, but he didn't seem very cordial.

He grabbed me and threw me over his shoulder like a piece
of meat. Now I knew I was doomed. It was obvious Swedish
wasn't really born yet in Viking times. These blokes were
Vikings not Swedes, or Danes.

I squirmed in his arms and shouted at him. He put me
down roughly. I noticed there weren't too many people
around. There wasn't the hustle and bustle of Lejre in
Daneland. He shook me around a bit and grabbed my arm.
He tugged me over to a small group of homely looking
women. I guessed this *wanker* wanted me to be his slave. I
didn't really care at this point if this was the means of
survival.

The women stared at me even more menacing than Mr.
Neanderthal. This older woman handed me a large clay pot.
She grunted in her Norse tongue. I assumed I had to go
hunting and gathering. I smiled. She shoved me to the

132

ground and kicked me in the stomach. It hurt. I walked blindly to wherever I could find some kind of greenery on the frosty ground. I noticed a group of women allegedly grooming the fields. The soil was like clay, very unfertile. I gingerly kneeled on the ground. I took a few sharp looking rocks and started to pretend I was in the midst of a cultivating frenzy. They didn't seem to bother with me anymore.

My head hung low and my hands kept pushing those rocks into the horrible soil.

I noticed two large feet wrapped in thick leather hide. I stopped. I looked up and Beowulf was peering down at me. I grinned with relief. He scooped me up.

"Finally," I said, with a sigh of relief.

"Forgive me for taking so long, but the witch has been acting strangely. She refused to grant me to Geatland in order to fetch you."

"Does that surprise you?" I asked as Beowulf helped me up. "Let me tell you something: witch rhymes with bitch."

He slowly placed my feet on the ground and smiled. He didn't appear too amused by my humor.

"Has anyone wronged you since your arrival here?" he asked.

"Just the typical Viking greeting, otherwise I can't complain. Nobody even tried to torch me to death."

"That's good to hear. We can settle here in Geatland after we marry if you prefer it to Daneland?"

"Are you asking me to pick my poison?"

"Kyla, this is the sixth century. What do you expect?"

"So, this is as good as it gets?" I said, waving my arm around. "I'm afraid so."

CHAPTER TWENTY-EIGHT

We returned to Daneland and the smell of battle was in the air. The day had ripened and we were behind schedule, but I didn't think I'd be banished to Geatland by that conniving witch. That episode really delayed things. The horses were ready; the swords were sharp. The boar's head was already sitting on a platter ready to lure the beast from its cave.

"This should get Grendel away from his cave, and then I can sneak into his cave and take his possessions," I said, maybe too loudly.

"No," Beowulf said, and grabbed my arm firmly enough where it started to hurt. "You will not enter Grendel's cave. I will do it."

"And what if Grendel pays a surprise visit outside of the cave? You need to be with your men on guard. It's not a big deal for me to enter his cave. I can do this."

Then King Hrothgar approached us. He hears everything.

"Leave her, Beowulf. I think I your wench may be offering her help."

"My Lord," Beowulf bowed his head toward his king. "This silly wench of mine insists she be in the cave to take Grendel's possessions."

"If your wench chooses to do so, then we must leave her be. She may be correct in her dealings with the troll. You and your men must be vigilant in guarding what lies outside of the monster's cave."

I tugged on Beowulf's arm. "What's he saying?"

"You win, my love."

"Is the king saying I can go in the cave?" I asked, feeling a bit edgy.

Beowulf's eyes beamed down at me. He wasn't too enthralled with the king's message.

"Alright, then," he agreed.

The twilight set over the white crystallized ground. Grendel hurdled over the dried brush grunting and groaning. Beowulf and his men remained hidden in the scrub. The horses were held tightly in the woods. Beowulf rode me over to the cave, and the king waited at Heorot Palace with baited breath.

I scurried into the cave. I must admit I was frightened. I no longer felt the sharp damp cold. The cave was dark. I held a lit torch in my hand, but it wasn't easy to maneuver. I saw nothing. I paced around anxiously. I could barely catch my breath.

There was nothing I could take with me. I was about to exit when I noticed a severely decomposed skull of something that could have once been human.

I bent over trying not to throw up. It smelled and it was disgusting. There's no way that thing was a possession. Knowing the likes of Grendel, a troll, would he possess a decomposing skull that smelled like vomit and piss mixed together? Yes, this thing was exactly what Grendel would proudly own. I was delighted that I finally came to terms with this. I had found one of the troll's possessions. But, I would have to pick it up and carry it out of the cave.

Then the cave vibrated with a murmuring rumble. I could hear chaos outside of the cave. I heard men yelling, and I recognized Grendel's grunts. I could hear the horses' screams and I even heard Beowulf throw his voice from time to time. Beowulf and his men were in trouble and I had to get out there.

I held my breath to prevent the disgusting stench to penetrate my nasal passage. I reluctantly picked up the skull and tore myself outside the cave. I witnessed the horses running in all directions, the men were swinging their swords; Beowulf was riding his horse and thrashing his broad sword after Grendel. I could see Grendel swinging from the trees. He was carrying one of Beowulf's men.

"Beowulf!" I shouted.

135

He rode past me and then retreated back.

"Kyla, something terrible has happened," he said, panting. I dropped the skull to the ground.

"Grendel found us and killed one of my men."

I must have fainted then, because I don't remember anything after that.

CHAPTER TWENTY-NINE

The following morning was somber. We ate in silence, not even a single word was spoken. We sat in the brush eating berries and bread. Beowulf wanted us clear from Heorot Palace, the last thing he wanted was to be confronted by King Hrothgar. I looked at him, but he didn't look at me. He ate with his long haggard hair hanging over his face. I tried to get his attention, but it was as if he was in a trance.

"We can try again," I said.

He slowly glanced at me and shut his eyes. Tears ran down his face as I watched him tremble. "I am a failure."

His men guzzled the mead that was packed in their leather sacs. They spoke Norse with a panicked tone. Some of them even prayed to Odin. I had never seen Beowulf fall apart. I didn't know how to comfort a sixth-century Viking warrior who was this upset.

"We will go out tonight and confront this beast face to face," he grunted, whilst clenching his fists. "We will approach this my way. All men will be on their horses and will be vigilant, armed, and guarded with leather armor. No wenches will be allowed."

I tried to suck back my tears. I wasn't sure if he hated me at this point. A lot of good that old skull did for the poor warrior who was killed by the troll.

"Can we go somewhere and discuss this?" I implored.

He ignored me and spewed Norse commands to his men. The men scattered about to bulk themselves with leather protection and chainmail. I sat there beside the skull. I felt helpless. I had let Beowulf down. He looked like a true Viking as I watched him tie up his leather armor. He then kneeled down to me, and kissed my lips in the most erotic way. He and his men rode off as I watched. Then a mist of blue swirls came down from the sky. I knew exactly who was coming to see me. The witch appeared looking as menacing as ever.

"Kyla, you are being invited to the twenty-first century. If I were you, I would accept this invitation."

"Not without Beowulf."

"You are not needed here. Also, I have seen Grendel's mother."

"Grendel has a mother?"

"She can be more dangerous than Grendel. She wants her skull back, Kyla."

"She wants her skull back? Huh?" I questioned in a fluster of confusion. "That skull is her husband. Grendel's father is that skull."

"Oh God, this is getting weirder and weirder."

"King Hrothgar slayed Grendel's father when Grendel was very young. That skull is all they have. You must return it at once."

"This skull that sits beside me is Grendel's father? Oh, my God." I rolled my eyes back. "I can't believe how wrapped up in this I'm getting."

"This is why you must leave for your time at once. Beowulf has a job to do here.

He must protect Daneland. You are but a mere distraction."

"You don't want Beowulf to slay Grendel, because you're bent out of shape for a mere troll."

The witch turned away from me with her flowing black gown whisking in the wind.

"You're a difficult girl. Are all wenches this ill-behaved in the twenty-first century?" The witch walked a few paces away from me. She appeared to be pondering something. Then she whisked back to me. "Kyla, if you continue to refuse the invitation to your time then I will have to banish you to a random time."

"You can do that? Random, huh? Like where?"

"How does the Pleistocene era sound to you?"

"That would be fiendish of you, and Beowulf would hate

138

your guts for it."

"Alright, how about the Crustaceous period? At least you wouldn't have to deal with any people."

"That's right, I'd only have to deal with dinosaurs," I said with my eyes widening. "Maybe I could drop you in the middle of the US Civil War instead. Or, how does the French Revolution sound to you?"

She was making me laugh, but there was a very angry side to her. Then I realized this was no joke and she would probably jeopardize her understanding with Beowulf just so she could abuse her power as a sorceress.

"I need to remain here with this skull until Beowulf returns."

"He will return empty handed. He will have not slain Grendel."

I felt a damp shiver run through me as if the temperature wasn't frigid enough.

Some hours had passed and there was still no sign of Beowulf and his men. I was feeling anxious and worried; however the last thing I wanted to do was let the witch know this.

CHAPTER THIRTY

I had fallen asleep on the snow. Not a brilliant thing to do, since I was so afraid of hypothermia. I can't believe this is their idea of spring. Maybe this is how the world was before global warming. It's not a good idea to fall asleep on the snow in sixth century Daneland. It was the rumble of running horses and men's voices that woke me. I sat up to brush the snow out of my hair. I saw Beowulf's men come toward me, but without Beowulf.

"M'lady, we have had great success," one of his men said, whilst getting off his horse. I wonder if he was aware that he had spoken to me in English. Would the witch have done that, I wonder?

"Success? Where's Beowulf?" I asked, in a panicked state.

"M'lady, our lord is chasing down Grendel and our lord will surely put the beast to rest," the warrior blurted, with a cackle of joy. "He's riding about. You will not catch up to him."

I began to pace as if I was going crazy. I just wanted to see Beowulf in one piece, and safe here with me. The daylight began to dissipate as I watched Beowulf's men set up camp. Thankfully, they had a raging fire going where I could keep warm. They put together some straw and mud and made a little hut for me to sleep in. It was very sweet of them, however, it was disgusting. I couldn't imagine cold mud could keep me warm at night. The moon was out and most of the men retreated to their mud huts. I remained by the crackling fire. One of Beowulf's most respected men noticed that I wasn't budging.

"M'lady," he said. I smiled at him. "You need to be sheltered from the cold and from her."

"Her?"

"Grendel's mother, of course," he stated. "Grendel's mother is on the loose?"

"She is malicious and stops at nothing. She is far worse than Grendel."

"Isn't Grendel also malicious and will stop at nothing?" I asked. While he thought about that, I continued. "Then, they both suck."

He looked at me with a puzzled expression. I had to stop using my twenty-first century slang, but right then I wasn't feeling too culturally and historically friendly.

"You took the skull, M'lady. We just saw Grendel at battle and he is in a sad state, I must say. You took his only cherished possession."

"Wasn't that the plan? Beowulf marveled at the idea. You heard him."

"M'lady, we're dealing with a troll, not a man. He hasn't the ability to reason."

"I noticed that."

That night was long, cold, and haunting. I was entombed in the mud hut again, wrapped up in leather and fur. The strong whistling wind howled so loud that no one could sleep. I heard large animals rustle through the dry branches of the dormant brush. I tried not to cry, because it would make me feel worse. Whenever I'd shut my eyes I'd see Beowulf's strong handsome face.

I could almost feel the hot breath of a stray animal that may have wandered into our camp. I tried not to pay attention to the grunts and faint growls. The poor thing was probably starved. Perhaps it could find some of the food remains that were left by Beowulf's men. I found myself dozing off.

Some hours later, the men scrambled about in a rage shouting in Norse. The loud squeals of some kind of animal thundered through the trees. I didn't hear Beowulf's voice, but I crawled out of the mud hut anyway. Then I saw her.

Hag made Medusa into a raving beauty. She squirmed and raged scratching the men's faces with her long poisonous fingernails. The men were drenched in blood. Her teeth were like swords where I saw her grab at the men's flesh and bite through. She then locked her eyes with mine, as if Lucifer was staring me down. Hag levitated above the men to get to me.

I almost passed out from fear. She hovered above me and blurted something in her language as venom dripped from her decrepit lips. My body was ill, so ill I may have felt an inkling of a heart attack come over me. My fingers tingled and a sharp pain traveled through my arms. She stood before me and continued to scream in her archaic language. She drew closer and closer. I had no idea how to deal with this *she-devil*.

Then I heard the thundering sound of a running horse. I heard the loud calls of a familiar voice. It was Beowulf on his golden horse coming to save me from this nightmare. He rode close behind me, and took me into his arms. He turned his horse around and faced the monster woman. He kissed me and placed me safely to the ground beside one of his best warriors. He rode toward her, and then stopped.

"You!" he shouted, in a deep- throated voice. She snarled at him. "You wretch of a monster! You will now pay for your upheaval of the people of Daneland! You will pay for threatening this damsel! Now, you will die!"

Beowulf sat on his horse with his sword shining before him. Her boney half- decayed feet touched the ground. Her toenails were long and pointed, as well as her fingernails. Her hair was long and knotted in clumps of dirt hanging past her shoulders. Her face was twisted and wrinkled; yet her teeth were sharp fangs.

Beowulf slid off his horse and approached her ready in his guard-of-the-woman sword stance. He swung his sword toward her neck, but her image disappeared and reappeared behind him. He fell forward to the ground and his sword left his hand. She pounced onto his back and bit his neck several times. His power could not buck her off him. Blood poured from his neck. He managed to grab her hair and pin her to the ground. She wailed until her voice cracked. He punched her several times in the face causing her nose to gush blood. She spat in his eyes. It was like acid. Beowulf bent over in agony covering his face with his hands. She continued to bite his neck. He fell to the ground. He might have lost too much blood.

I ran to him, but the she-monster smacked me hard, and I flew into one of Beowulf's right-hand men. I was dazed. His first man helped me up. I looked at them, feeling disgusted from the mother.

"Why don't you help him?"

"This is his battle, M'lady. He is the great warrior of our lands. He must put the troll mother to her death."

She spewed phlegm onto Beowulf, which hardened over him. She danced around him singing an awful tune. Each time one of Beowulf's men tried to approach her she would cast a spell on their swords, which gave them electric shock that ran through their arms. She levitated from the ground with blood dripping off her chin. She levitated Beowulf, who was encased in her rock-hard phlegm, and then they both vanished.

I screamed loud in a horrified cry. The men coddled me. They appeared just as frightened as me. There was one of Beowulf's men, his right-hand man, who always watched over me. He tried to comfort me as much as he could.

"Did she kill Beowulf? Is he still alive?" I yelled, to the men.

"Grendel's mother would never kill Beowulf. She will use him for ransom so she can defeat us all," said Beowulf's main man, as he held me close to him.

"Why wasn't she slain a long time ago?"

"She isn't always one to make an appearance," he said. "She's horrible. I think she's worse than her son, Grendel."

"Oh, yes, M'lady. She has no conscience. It is hard to say whether Grendel does or not."

"Well the witch fancies Grendel," I noted, "so, he must have some redeeming qualities. Not the mother, though, she must just be a continuous horror for the Danes."

"I understand how confusing this must be for you, M'lady, but trolls are not people, they are evil. Grendel and his mother share no difference. The witch is a sorceress; she is a fine one for magic."

I felt awkward and confused, not to mention terrified for my Beowulf. "Our lord and master will find a way out."

"Where is he?" I asked, straining my voice to talk. The men remained silent.

CHAPTER THIRTY-ONE

The mother gathered several small animals and threw them live in a pot of boiling water. She hummed while she stirred her stew. Beowulf lay in the corner of the cave. He managed to roll over, but was stopped by a large row of stalagmites. The hardened phlegm cracked away from him as he moved. She pranced around the cave like a crazed nut hurting his ears with her high pitched shriek. She stopped when she noticed his movements.

"Beowulf, you are now awake!" she shrilled.

"You're just a horrid as everyone describes you." He sat up.

She stood and stared at him. She stepped closer. He consumed himself with trying to pry the hardened substance off his skin.

"Ah, yes, Beowulf. There you are. I must say you still look handsome even if you are distressed," she mumbled.

"I can do without the compliments. Where's Grendel now?"

"I don't know." She continued to stare at him. "My, my, my. I am to eat now. Would you like some?" she said, holding a large wooden spoon dripping with stew.

"It smells awful."

"I made it for you – just for you."

He stood up and gingerly walked to her boiling pot. He tried to glance at it, but he felt himself gag.

"Disgusting! What is this? Animal fur, blood, bones? Mud? Feces? You're a troll!"

"I made this for you," she grunted, and crawled around the cave just as Grendel would do.

Beowulf felt along his thighs for his sword. His eyes widened with panic. "What did you do with my sword?"

She laughed in a high pitch cackle. "My sword now!"

145

"Return my sword. I have the strength of thirty men. Don't make me have to demonstrate to you."

She continued to cackle.

"What are your plans with me, Hag?" She encircled him.

"I like you."

He sighed, "You don't. How could you even? You're a troll mother."

"I would like you." He took a few steps back from her. "I would like you," she repeated, crawling closer to him with her snorting grunts.

She latched onto his leg and licked it. He watched her do it. He tried to shake her off, but she had dug her sharp nails into his thighs.

"You're pathetic," he said. She touched his groin several times, which made him jolt a bit with nervousness. "Don't force me, Hag!"

"Don't force you? Force you to do what?"

"To kill you."

"And how will you do that?"

"I will snap your frail neck right here and now." He pushed her long boney hand away. "Go, troll mother."

"You have something against trolls, or is it the troll mother's you're so prejudice against?"

She continued to wrap herself around his leg. "I loathe the entire lot of you," he asserted.

"Whatever would make a tasty delight like you think such awfulness?"

"Just be gone and let me be."

"I want you, Beowulf."

"Oh, Odin!" he cried. "Please answer my prayer!"

"To pray to Odin will do you no good. You are just a man, and how boring that can be."

"If I am but an ordinary man you need not bother with me. Let me go."

"Oh, I never said ordinary. You are definitely not ordinary. You are a warrior who slays trolls. Not too many ordinary men can do that, can they?"

He bent over her and clasped his hands around her neck. "I'll kill you," he said, grimacing.

"I am not worried. No, no, no – you will never do it."

He tightened his strong hands around her neck. She winched a few times. He tightened even more. She gasped. Her face turned several colors. He released her. He paced around her cave not understanding the danger that surrounded him.

"I will pray to Odin, and you will have no say, troll-mother." She crawled to her boiling pot and began to stir.

"Come, Beowulf. Come and try what I have made for you. You must be hungry."

"Where's my sword?"

She continued to stir so lovingly. He slid his back along side the wall of the cave and plunked himself on the ground with frustration.

"Do not even speak to me, troll-mother."

She held the dripping spoon to his face. The pungent aroma filled the cave.

Beowulf sat on the floor with his head hung down. He tried to ignore the strong smell of her stew. His long hair curled at the ends from the steam from the stew. He leaned against the wall of the cave with his eyes half closed. He turned to her and smiled. She smiled back and crawled to him holding the spoon filled with stew. She sat beside him and caressed his head.

"Come, Beowulf. Eat it all. It's so good for you."

He swallowed the heaping spoonful and continued to inhale the aroma. He smiled at her, his eyes glazed with sudden tranquility. She gently placed the spoon on the floor. Her grin increased with each second. She shifted closer to him. He was oblivious to her actions.

She sat on his lap and caressed his face. He let her do it. Her long gnarly fingers played with his beard. He wore no expression on his face. She gazed at his eyes and lips. She kissed him several times on the cheek, then on the mouth. He tried to pull away from her, but he couldn't. He finally gave in and complied with her. His actions were robotic. He had no feelings for anything or anyone.

She untied his leather vest, where he helped her remove it. He stood up and removed the rest of his clothes. She grunted and roared with excitement, as he stood naked in front of her. She scanned every inch of him. She brushed her fingers along his body. She howled with thundering loudness. His eyes were in a trance. He slowly lay down. She jumped on top of him. She remained on top of him as he entered her. Her sharp shrill yelps penetrated outside the cave.

"You will lay upon me, Beowulf, and mount me so lovingly. Then, when you are finished, I will stuff you into the pot. You should be quite tasty."

Beowulf's eyes were glazed with nothingness.

CHAPTER THIRTY-TWO

My adrenaline kept me warm, while Beowulf's men helped me get through the rugged Scandinavian terrain. A loud high-pitch shrill echoed through the forest. I glanced at Beowulf's men. Beowulf's top man looked at me.

"It sounds like Grendel's mother is pleased of something. She has made her victory."

I tore at his leather vest.

"Victory? What victory? Can you tell where this horrible sound is coming from?" He pointed to a distant cave opening. I was terrified. I had to fight with myself so I didn't think of the worst. We rode on horseback. The howling wind entangled with the loud shrilling of what may have been the troll's mother.

When we arrived to the cave I invited myself in. Beowulf's top man held a torch behind me to give me the light I needed. There I saw a thing caressing Beowulf's bare chest. I fell back with devastation.

"She's quite hideous isn't she?" the warrior said.

I started to cry as I looked at Beowulf with pain in my eyes.

"No, M'lady, shhh. You must not allow the she-devil to upset you so. She is only a troll mother."

"But she's touching him," I said in a slobbering cry. "He is not rational now, M'lady."

"What? Could she harm him if he's not in sound mind?"

"Oh, yes, M'lady. Trolls eat mortals. They find them very tasty."

"Is she planning on eating him?"

"Perhaps. She is aware he is her son's foe. Please keep that in mind."

"Grendel has a gender?" I pulled away from his arms and walked toward Beowulf. "Beowulf, what have you done?" He glanced at me and smiled.

"Kyla, hello. Why don't you sit with us?"

I almost lunged at her, but Beowulf's warrior grabbed me.

"No! Look at M'lord's eyes. The troll mother has conjured a spell upon him."

I stared at Beowulf. He wasn't himself. I stopped myself from going to him, but I continued to look at him. I felt helpless, so I whimpered. Beowulf looked at Grendel's mother.

"Be gone now, troll-mother. I wish to speak with my people," Beowulf ordered. "No, no, no – that will not be necessary, my prince. I must remain here to protect you from their malevolence."

Beowulf chuckled at her. He sat up and grabbed his leather clothing. He stood up and slipped his cloth trousers on. He appeared calm, as he bound up his laced leather footwear. He smiled at me as he calmly laced and tied his vest.

"Kyla!" he said to me. "You are looking beautiful today, despite your salty tears."

"Why are you here with that thing?" I sniffled.

He looked around and scratched his head. "I don't really know why."

"I love you, Beowulf. Will you please come here to me? You have to leave this place. Don't you see that she's a troll?"

Beowulf stepped toward me. His eyes scanned my body several times. He smiled and moved much closer to me.

"Kyla, M'lady," he said, and took my hands. He brought them close to his lips and kissed them several times. He held my hands in his. "Why do you tremble so?"

I pointed to the troll mother. Beowulf's main man reacted and stood in front of the troll mother. Grendel's mother's high-pitch scream was almost deafening. She crawled on the cave floor on all fours. She even crawled along the walls of the cave. I just wanted to leave. Then Beowulf wrapped his arms around me and kissed me several times on the lips. I had one eye on that moronic bitch.

"How I missed you," Beowulf blurted with a struggling sigh, as if he was coming down from a bad trip.

"M'lord!" his main warrior blurted. "We must leave her at once, unless you wish to dispose of her here?"

Beowulf's glassy eyes appeared somewhat coherent.

"Dispose of her? That won't be necessary, Wiglaf. We must find Grendel and dispose of him, as I promised King Hrothgar."

"Why do you spare her? She is a hindrance to our plan of action."

Beowulf appeared groggy. He scratched his head. "I don't really know why I choose to spare her. Perhaps, it is better to go after our true foe and just leave Hag be." The troll mother screamed and screeched even louder. Beowulf looked at her and grimaced. "You can stay here and scream all you wish, troll-mother. Your son must be stopped."

"Hrothgar must die! He must pay for what he did!" the troll mother screeched and grunted.

I looked at Beowulf, "She's got a point. This is all King Hrothgar's fault."

"I was chosen to fulfill the king's demands, therefore I must succeed."

"But Hrothgar murdered Grendel's father. I think that's awful," I said.

"Grendel is a troll, and he must me stopped," Beowulf said, holding his fist in the air.

"Just because he's a troll? That's discrimination. Your king is wrong."

The troll mother crawled to my legs and caressed them as if I were her new-found pet. I was a bit uncomfortable. Beowulf stepped back, and stared at the troll mother.

"Are you siding with the troll mother?" he asked me. "I'm just expressing my opinion. Hrothgar is wrong."

"He is my king, I am in no position to have such an opinion."

"Am I in a position to have such an opinion?" I said, feeling as if I were crossing boundary waters.

"If you are my wench, then the answer is *no*."

I stepped closer to Beowulf, as I tried to shake the she-troll off my leg. "Alright, how about this...if we were in the twenty-first century do I have a right to my opinion?"

"I am in the middle of a troll-slaying operation, and you bring up all of this here and now?"

Wiglaf took a deep breath. He didn't have a clue of what we were talking about. "Beowulf, just answer my question and your troll slaying expedition can begin."

"Would you be my wench in your fine century?" he proposed.

"Of course I would."

"Well, I suppose the answer is *yes*."

"Then, it's settled."

"Nothing is settled, my love, because the troll is still at large. But let me caution you, as you continue to reside in this time. It would be best that you keep your opinions to yourself."

"Got it."

Beowulf swooped me into his strong arms with a stern look on his face. He carried me off with his crew to his horse and we rode off to a place that was not familiar to me. Beowulf's men set up camp. I was ready for a hot shower and a big fuzzy bathrobe – but that wasn't going to happen any time soon.

Night was upon us. I slept in Beowulf's arms wrapped in leather and fur. The cold was sharp and painful at times. Fortunately, we were surrounded by his thirteen warriors and horses, who did their best to keep us warm.

I had no idea what was next on the agenda. Beowulf and his men spoke to each other quite extensively before turning in. I hadn't a clue what they were saying, because they spoke in Norse. It was obvious they wouldn't dare return to Heorot and face Hrothgar if Grendel was still roaming the land.

CHAPTER THIRTY-THREE

It was early dawn. I glanced at the glaze of ice that layered the trees. It was still freezing, even though it was spring. I felt for Beowulf, but he had left our bed of fur and hides. I panicked, and saw him with his warriors and horses. I got up, and threw a leather hide over me. I walked up to him and his men.

"Beowulf? Is something wrong?" I asked, afraid to find out his answer. "I must go and slay Grendel, and I will do it now and I will do it alone."

I glanced at his thirteen men. They appeared disturbed by Beowulf's decision. Beowulf kissed me and rode off on his horse. I began to look a little deeper at myself. I was so burned out from sixth-century Daneland that I questioned what the hell I was doing there in the first place.

I glanced down at the snow and noticed there was some kind of scripture carved on the icy crust. I knelt down to see if I could read it. It was written in English, which amazed me. It said, *Son of Caine.* I glanced at the warriors. They didn't notice it – besides, what would they do with a scripture anyways? If it wasn't about Odin, then nothing else mattered.

***

Beowulf rode through the rugged terrain with not an inch of fear in his veins. He could hear loud cries that resembled Grendel. He continued to ride along greater elevations where his horse showed signs of resistance. He stopped and scanned the land. Grendel's cries grew louder. He slid off his horse and began his climb up the craggy iced rocks. Grendel's howls intensified, as the beast stood before Beowulf.

Beowulf almost lost his grip, but continued to hang onto the iced slope.

"Ah, troll, finally you show yourself." Grendel grunted and

howled. "Come, monster. I will fight you. I will fight you unarmed. This will be a fair duel."

Beowulf slid down the slope and stood in the open ready to fight. The troll leaped down the slope and landed upon Beowulf's shoulders. They grappled and fought. Grendel managed to stay on top. Grendel bit Beowulf many times, but Beowulf punched the troll so much that he stunned him. Beowulf managed to stand up where he kicked Grendel in the head, almost knocking him out cold. Grendel still struggled, but felt himself losing the battle.

"What's troubling you, troll? Stand up, monster!"

Grendel slowly stood up and tried to lunge. The warrior pulled away, but managed to latch onto the troll's arm. Grendel squirmed and jigged. Beowulf refused to let go. Grendel pulled away. Beowulf continued to latch onto the beast's arm. Grendel pulled away with so much force his arm tore of. Then Grendel ran. Beowulf stood in silence holding Grendel's bloody arm.

CHAPTER THIRTY-FOUR

I sat in a circle around the fire with the warriors. I lifted my head when I heard the strong sound of horse hoofs hitting the hard iced ground. I jumped up and felt the cheer from his band of warriors. Beowulf slid of his horse to present us with Grendel's arm. I almost puked. His men cheered. I did puke.

"It won't be long now. That menacing troll will soon come to his death," Beowulf said, planting a kiss on my lips. He then spoke to his men in Norse. I took Beowulf aside to speak with him in private.

"Ah, yes, my love we will make many babies. This is a time of great triumph. Let us all celebrate."

I played with his leather vest.

"Yes, Beowulf, but now we can call the witch and go back to the twenty-first century? Your work is done here. You have given King Hrothgar his wish."

"Not yet, my love. My work isn't yet done."

I stood closely in front of him freezing my butt off. "Is Grendel going to grow another arm?"

"Silly wench, of course not. How does one come up with such craziness? "Beowulf chuckled at me. I felt my blood start to boil with frustration. That made me a bit warmer. I grew concerned.

"Look, Beowulf, I'm standing here wrapped up in a carpet in sixth-century Scandinavia; I've had conversations with witches and trolls, and you're telling me I'm the one who comes up with crazy ideas? What are you talking about?"

"I hear a dragon has made several appearances at our king's mead hall."

"A dragon? Can't we just focus on you slaying Grendel for now?" I said. "Well, of course, my love, if you wish."

I felt that uneasy sick feeling again. "You look as if there really is a dragon that must be dealt with. The expression on your face tells it all, Beowulf."

"Well, yes, M'lady. This is a mystical time, therefore dragons usually creep up every now and again."

"I don't want to even think that you now have to slay a bleeding dragon. Isn't the troll enough?"

"We can discuss this another time, my love," he told me. "I don't wish to upset you. I can tell you are now already getting upset."

"No, we will never discuss this ever again, because Daneland is going to have to slay this dragon on their own. This is all such bullshit."

"Bullshit? No, no it's a dragon, not a bull."

We returned to Heorot Palace. King Hrothgar sat at his large wooden thrown waiting for Beowulf's arrival. I was feeling anxious to leave this century. Panpipes and wooden pipes began to play. Everyone gathered leaving an aisle-way in the middle of the room. Beowulf walked slowly with honor along the aisle-way holding Grendel's arm. When he arrived to King Hrothgar the music stopped. I rolled my eyes back. I couldn't even see a stitch of royalty in Hrothgar's demeanor. He just seemed like a spoiled brat – if that was even possible in the sixth century.

King Hrothgar stood up. Beowulf presented him with Grendel's arm. Beowulf kneeled to the floor. I was growing impatient. King Hrothgar took the arm and held it above his head for all to see. The crowd chanted and cheered. I walked backwards, and made my way out the door. It was so crowded in there I don't think anybody saw me exit. I paced around outside.

"Witch! Witch! Please, answer me!" I called, with desperation in my voice. I continued to pace. Then suddenly I watched her appear.

"Kyla, you should be inside Heorot Palace watching your prince become king."

"Beowulf's not going to be king," I said, with a shrug.

"A great warrior such as Beowulf deserves to be king."

"Beth was wrong. I knew Beowulf would become king."

"Who's Beth?"

"You met her once, briefly. She lives in the twenty-first century. Speaking of the twenty-first century, do you think you can get me and Beowulf back to where we belong – twenty-first century London?"

"Not so fast," she said. "I'm questioning your love for Beowulf. If you truly loved him you would be in that hall right now watching him bask in his glory of triumph."

"I know, but I can't take this century anymore. It's making me sick. I just want a quiet life with Beowulf in his flat in twenty-first century London."

"If he's crowned king, then you will be his queen. You cannot leave if you're the queen of Daneland."

"Daneland can do just fine without Beowulf and me. The troll has been slain. What else is there to do around here?" I asked.

"Well, you see there's this dragon."

"Don't talk to me about that fucking dragon! I don't want to hear about it!"

"Also, Grendel's mother won't be too forgiving when she discovers her son is dead. She'll be back with a vengeance," the witch said. "Go inside the hall and watch your prince reap his awards – after all, he does deserve it."

"Okay, just tell me one more thing before you go. When will we go back to twenty-first century London?"

Her image was starting to fade, as she said, "That is up to Beowulf."

She was gone. I walked back into the mead hall. Beowulf's top man, Wiglaf, noticed me. He took my arm and led me to his master. Beowulf stood beside King Hrothgar looking pleased. He took me in his arms and kissed me. The crowd roared, so I forced a smile.

That evening the king prepared an endless feast served on the long wood table.

I was getting used to seeing boar head displayed as the main course. The king had given Beowulf several gold gifts. He had made it known to his people that Beowulf would soon be taking his throne.

After a long evening of music, dancing, drinking, eating, and lovemaking the warriors, slaves, and royals finally got to sleep. I slept tightly beside Beowulf. In the middle of the night the blowing wind woke me. I heard a sound, as if one of the doors opened. The howling winds intensified. I was so exhausted I fell back to sleep. Then a crashing noise, and yelling woke up all of us. I noticed one of the doors was open.

King Hrothgar was in a panic. He kept shouting at his warriors that an intruder had entered Heorot. Beowulf sprung from beside me and fetched his sword. The king's men were in an outrage when they discovered the king's most loyal advisor, Eschere, was gone. I ran to Beowulf.

"Is someone missing? What happened here?"

"Something unthinkable has happened," he said, and kissed me on the mouth. I watched the king run around the mead hall in a panic.

"Why is Hrothgar so upset? What happened? "Eschere has been abducted from us."

"Who did this? Was it the dragon?"

Beowulf glanced at me and held in his laughter.

"Silly wench. Dragons don't abduct people. Everyone knows that. Look, my love, this is not the time to be poking fun of our situation. All men know dragons breathe fire, tenderize their victims, and eat them."

"Yeah, of course they wouldn't abduct anyone. That's just not what dragons do.

How the hell would I know what dragons do?"

Beowulf took me and brought me to the far corner of the hall. "Kyla, I know who did this."

"Grendel's mother?" I guessed.

"You are precise. She wants revenge and that would mean she demands compensation. We took Grendel from her. She wants compensation."

"I don't know who is the bigger pain in the ass, Grendel or his mother."

"Both. But now I must find her. Her hiding place is known to be aquatic. She lays low under water, and when she sees a long boat sail by she will attack."

"So, you're going to find her somewhere in the icy water?"

"I have no choice, my love."

"Can you get the witch to help you?" I asked.

"The witch's purpose is not to forever grant me wishes," he answered. "I bet she would if I weren't around."

"Perhaps."

CHAPTER THIRTY-FIVE

That afternoon Beowulf took me out on his long boat. This was not my idea of a romantic outing. The cold sleet was relentless, and I just couldn't get warm. The water was icy and somber. Beowulf's long boat was half the size of some of the other's I saw. We were alone.

"Kyla," Beowulf said, as he rowed through the choppy Baltic waves. "I'm sorry for what I'm putting you through. This isn't fair. Do you wish me to ask the witch to return you to your time?"

"Don't you love me?" I asked in a panic.

"I love you enough to not watch you suffer in this century. Of course, without you I couldn't go on. You are my everything, my love."

I watched him row. He didn't seem the least bit frozen like me. His hair was very long and so unruly it often blew in front of his face. He rowed with strength and confidence. Then he appeared somewhat fed up. He slowed down his rigorous rowing. I was hoping that he didn't regret asking me to join him. I was bundled only in leather hide and fur. Only my eyes were exposed to this horrible climate. I caught Beowulf staring at me from time to time.

"Is something the matter?" I inquired.

"Forgive me, my love, but sometimes I can't get over your beauty."

"Beauty? I look like a fur ball. All you can see is my eyes."

"And what enchanting eyes you have, my love."

I took a deep breath and started to relax. It was only a few minutes later, but it seemed like hours. We were in the middle of nowhere. The water seemed a bit calmer than usual. Beowulf stopped rowing. I perked up, and stared at him with my lips half parted.

"We must park the ship here. She will come soon."

"I can't wait," I muttered, a little surly.

"You see, my love, you do wish to be back in your time. This is torture for you."

"No, I want to be in my time with you."

"This isn't possible at the moment. My work isn't finished here. You know this."

"You know," I said, and paused with a slight snicker. "I have friends who are in love with chartered accountants, construction workers, and computer programmers, but lucky me, I'm in love with a sixth century troll slayer."

He laughed but then an expression of seriousness wore on his face again. He stared at something far in the horizon.

"What is it?" I asked, not wanting to know the answer. "Grendel's mother?" He extended his arm in front of him pointing his finger.

"You see, there it is; the sea monster that lives in these waters. I remember it as a boy. I would come go on my father's boat. We would see these images of this creature's greatness."

I squinted my eyes to see what it was he was seeing. "I see something, but I don't think it's a sea monster."

"Oh, yes, you must look exactly to where my finger points. There it is. I've seen some of its body parts before. It has a tail that I cannot even describe. Its grandness is overwhelming. That is a sea monster."

I sat and waited. Beowulf was mesmerized by it. "Has this sea monster ever tried to harm you?"

"Not to my knowledge. I don't even think my father was ever in a threatening situation with the great beast," he recounted. I took another long look at this creature. And then I laughed. Beowulf pulled in the oars. "What is this? Laughter I hear? What a strange time you come from. How can one laugh at such a great beast?"

I scooched a little closer to him and I took his hand. "Darling, this is not a sea monster. I just noticed it's humped back and its tail. I kid you not, my dear, this is a whale."

"Call it as you may, but it is still a sea monster," he said. I kissed him on the cheek.

"Tell me, how would you know of such things if you are not a wench of the sea?"

"In my time everyone knows about whales. They're, in many ways, similar to us."

He chuckled. "Not a chance, my dear Lady Kyla, it is so obvious that they are monstrous fish of the cold seas."

I nodded my head. "Beowulf, they aren't fish, they're mammals like us."

"Mammals? What's that?"

I scratched my head and paused. "On second thought, I don't think I'll even go there. Yes, yes, it's a sea monster."

The boat then lifted and splashed back on the water. I screamed and leaped into Beowulf's arms.

"Is this not your whale, my love?"

"Whales are very aware animals. This was no whale. Was that her?"

"No, she hasn't the strength to lift an entire boat."

"If it wasn't her, and Grendel is dead – was that the dragon?" I shook with fear, which warmed my frigid state.

"No, no, my love. It is known by all, that dragons are not famous swimmers. It most certainly wasn't a dragon."

"Okay, then, what the hell was it?"

My panic made me rude and aggressive. He paddled the boat about a meter away. He looked at me and smiled. I sank down in my seat and tightened the hides around me. I stared into the horizon and noticed that sea monster was diving in and out of the water.

"You are the expert of these whales," he said. "Would a whale do this or would a sea monster?"

"Well, I'm looking at the whale out in the horizon, and it's still there. It could have a mate. Whales don't usually bother with people, because they have bigger fish to find. They don't usually waste their time. Now you've got me thinking there is another creature, and could very well be your sea monster. What do they look like?"

"They can be any size or shape. Some have large teeth and some even breathe fire."

"I can't understand your world," I said, with a sigh. "It's a mystical world, my love."

In the distance there was a loud splash in the water. Then the crashing waves got closer to us. I felt the cold water on my face. It didn't feel very comfortable. "What's that?"

"That is a sea monster, no doubt."

"How do you know it isn't Grendel's mother?"

"Grendel's mother would have made a more explicit showing by now. This is definitely a sea monster," he said, as he pulled the oars into the boat.

Something that looked like a gigantic tail splashed several times causing our boat to rise and fall onto the crashing waves. This tail bore no resemblance to a whale. The still water was now chaotic. The large tail got so close to our boat that it brushed against my shoulder. I winched.

"Shhh, my love. Don't react with so much fear. I am here with you."

Beowulf acted as if this was his daily routine, similar to hitting rush hour traffic each morning. I watched the gigantic tail encircle us, but further away I saw something else rise from the turbulent waves. It was a scaly comb that sat on top of a large snakehead. It had one eye in the middle of its hideous face. It opened its jaws to expose its teeth.

I tried to keep my winching and gasps to a minimum. Beowulf sat in the boat and watched. He calmly pulled his sword in front of him and reached for his shield. The monster lifted its head from the water. I found myself dripping in my own sweat, despite the frigid temperature. It made a loud vibrating tone with a few menacing snarls.

Beowulf scratched his beard as he watched. It swayed its tail to create unruly waves.

The water was so turbulent I thought our boat would definitely capsize. Its tail pressed against our boat and tipped us into the cold water. I almost passed out from the shock of the icy water as I tried to swim vigorously to keep warm.

Beowulf lunged for me and held me above his shoulders. He managed to swim to the boat. As I sat on his shoulders, I witnessed him struggle with tilting the boat right side up. It wasn't easy, because the water was continuously turbulent from the frequent swaying of the sea serpent's tail. He managed to kick the boat with his legs, which astonished me. The boat turned, he grabbed it with one hand, and it fell into place. He safely placed me in the boat.

"Your strength," I said, trying to catch my breath, "is remarkable."

The monster roared several times exposing its pointed fangs. Beowulf remained in the water holding his sword in front of him. The monster's jaws drew closer to him. It roared its loud vibrating tone, which stirred the waters even more. Beowulf continued to hold his sword up to the monster, not flinching or even gasping for breath.

Its jaws slowly wrapped around Beowulf, bearing its sharp fangs into his armor, but Beowulf swung his sword a few times and pierced its mouth. It dropped Beowulf in the water. The water turned red with the monster's blood. Sea monsters bleed red? Sea monsters bleed?

Its tail swayed from side to side, causing the boat to rock up and down, as it rode the unruly waves. I was in a cold sweat with my fingernails digging into the sobbing wet leather. Its tail hit Beowulf hard and knocked him out. Beowulf was still bobbing in the water, but he was sinking fast.

I jumped into the water and swam to him. The sea monster brooded over its wounded mouth. I tried to get Beowulf to come to and did my best not to let him sink. My adrenaline kept me going, so I didn't die from hypothermia. It was difficult for me to maneuver when the water was so turbulent. My exhaustion almost got the best of me, however, I was more focused on Beowulf.

I dunked his face in the water several times. He coughed and gagged, but thankfully came to. I wanted to cry; I had never felt this cold in my life, but I was so glad Beowulf survived. He continued to cough whilst I kept his head above water.

"Beowulf, we've got a problem!"

"My love, why aren't you in the boat?"

"Guess," I said.

"Thank-you, my love, for saving my life."

"We're going to die of hypothermia before this big snake does us in. You're sword has floated over there somewhere. I can't believe your magic sword floats."

"Of course it does. It wouldn't be so magical then if it didn't, wouldn't you think?"

"It's cold! I can't take this anymore!"

"Can you swim to the boat? I need to fetch my sword."

He had to swim directly in front of the serpent. The monster noticed Beowulf as it gushed blood from the mouth. It tried to smack him with its tail again. I was trying to reach the boat, but then the brutal waves started up again with the swaying of the monster's tail. Beowulf reached his sword and waved it at the monster. He thrust his sword at the serpent's tail and wounded it. Blood poured out, as the monster screeched with agony. Beowulf made his way to the boat and climbed in. The sea monster slowly descended back into the water. I couldn't stop panting with fear.

"Beowulf, is it going to come back?"

"It could. I'll just pierce it with my sword again."

"I can't live like this," I said, shivering.

He chuckled, as he positioned the oars and began to row. He paddled unbelievably fast to get us out of the sea serpent's view. I looked back, where I could see the monster struggle with its wounds.

"It's in pain," I said, as Beowulf rowed like a mad man. "The water is still red with blood. That could attract a fleet of sharks. Sharks are attracted to blood in the water, because they think it's an easy kill."

"Oh, really?" he said.

"Yes, sharks do that sort of thing."

"Sharks?" Beowulf slowed down his rowing and smiled at me. "Have you ever seen a shark?"

"Just on television. Have you?"

Beowulf appeared winded as he continued to smile at me. "If you haven't seen a shark would it be so astonishing that I haven't either?"

"I don't know what you've seen in the sixth century," I had to admit. "I can't get my head around it."

"You're in the sixth century now. Can you not get your head around that?"

"Yes. I ask myself everyday what I'm doing here."

"Does it feel right to you to be in my arms?" he asked, pointedly. "Of course it does."

"Then you must stop asking yourself so many questions. Perhaps this has nothing to do with the sixth century after all."

"I guess."

He belted out a hard loud laugh. "My lovely Kyla, this is what I love about you."

He picked up the pace of his rowing. I smiled at him knowing he was probably poking fun at me. There was a tug at the other end of one of the oars, and it fell into the water. Beowulf didn't appear too startled by it. He took the other paddle into the boat with him.

"Where did it go?" I inquired. "She has it now."

"Who? Grendel's mother?"

The boat rocked, but the water was calm. I felt nervous.

"She's upon us," he said, as he looked around the boat for her. "I don't see her."

"Of course not. She thrives in the water most of the time," he said, standing up to search for her.

I noticed a dark shadow behind Beowulf. There was something crawling onto the boat. I pointed. Beowulf turned around, and Grendel's mother was on the boat with us.

"Ah, troll-mother. What is it you want?" Beowulf asked ready with his sword in *boar's-tooth* stance.

"I deserve payment for my loss," she demanded, looking more disgusting than the last time I saw her.

"You deserve nothing. Go! Leave Daneland and never return."

"I deserve compensation. You took Grendel from me. Hrothgar took so much from me. Now you all must pay!"

"You're a family of trolls. You eat our people and terrorize those whom you don't eat. You must die."

She stood on all fours and crawled to his leg.

"You must give me compensation for your sins, Beowulf. I am to give you your child." I was sickened by her request. Beowulf laughed in her face. His response to her was indifferent. He was in control at all times, which amazed me. She stopped crawling. "We must have a child...together."

"Leave here! Be gone, troll mother!"

She leaped onto Beowulf, and sank her fangs into his neck. He grabbed her and forced her to the floor of the boat. He slapped her around and punched her quite hard in the jaw. I could barely watch. She howled and screamed so loud it was deafening.

Beowulf battled with her as if he had done this many times before. She kept lunging for his throat. His strength was too overbearing for her to conquer. He pinned her to the floor.

"You leave us! All of us in Daneland! If I catch you here again, I will kill you." She hacked and coughed as she rubbed her hands along her throat.

"You will never kill me."

"Don't push me," he warned.

"You will never kill me. You spare me, because you love me."

Beowulf pulled away from her. He watched her squirm in her own blood. She tried to wipe the blood from her disheveled face.

"What have you done with Eschere? Bring him to me at once," he demanded. "Eschere is no business of yours."

She made her way to the edge of the boat and dove into the water. Beowulf leaped at her, but she was already gone. He dove off the boat and into the water. I sat and watched. He must have swum under the boat, because I couldn't see him. A few seconds passed and I still saw no sign of him. I hung over the edge.

"Beowulf!" I screamed, at the top of my lungs. "Beowulf!"

Did she finally get her way with him? I kept telling myself not to panic. I searched all sides of the boat and there was no sign of him. I sat there gasping with panic. What was I going to do if something had happened to him? I felt very alone. Suddenly, he appeared from behind me. He clutched onto the boat and climbed in.

"Oh Beowulf, thank-God. I thought the worst."

"You waste too much time on the worst, my love," he said, and gave me a kiss. He felt cold and wet, but that never seemed to bother him.

"Now what are we going to do?" I asked, feeling numb from the cold and from what I had just witnessed.

"I will go to her lair and fight her there."

"You were there already, and things didn't work out too well."

"She poisoned me with her potion. This time I will learn not to receive anything from her."

I was getting frustrated with him.

"Don't you think you should have known a long ago not to trust anyone of troll nature?"

I then sat back. I had raised my voice at him. He's a sixth-century man. I needed to understand this.

He looked at me in silence. His long golden hair blew in the wind. His deep blue eyes glistened off the sunlight. He really did look like a king. He started to row back to the shore. He didn't say a word to me the entire time. I felt my heart pump with angst. Did I blow it with him? Maybe he would prefer a sixth-century damsel who doesn't talk back.

We finally reached land. He carried me in his arms to where his men had set up camp. Then he kissed me on the lips and smiled. He walked to his men and spoke to them in Norse. I watched him converse with his team. I wondered what life would be like if he and I married, had children, and remained here. Oh, my God, such a cruel blissful thought.

Beowulf approached me.

"My loving Kyla, I must finish the troll mother. I am asking you if you would like to accompany me, since women of your time are so courageous."

"Of course I wish to accompany you. You gave her another chance and let her get away."

He looked at me and chuckled.

"I told her that, yes, but what I have in mind is to destroy her."

"You lied to her."

"Kyla, she's a troll mother."

He didn't seem too amused. I followed him to his favorite horse, where he gathered his equipment.

"Beowulf, can I ask you a question?"

"Of course, M'lady," he said as he fascined his gold weapons securely on his horse.

" After you slay the troll mother, would it be possible for you to beg the witch to appear, and ask her if she could grant you and I back to twenty-first century London?"

"What about the dragon, Kyla? I cannot leave this time with so much yet to do."

"Fuck the dragon!" I sputtered.

"Oh my, I don't think that would be a pleasant sight, my love." He took my hands and kissed each finger. "When the she-devil is gone from my Daneland, then I will call for the witch. We will leave here soon enough."

I immersed myself in his arms. We kissed.

CHAPTER THIRTY-SIX

We rode our horses to the troll-mother's cave. I felt a bit nervous, because I've learned that trolls can be unpredictable. We stopped by her lair and slid off our horses. We walked toward the cave opening. Beowulf briskly stormed into her cave.

"Troll mother! Come forth so I can see your haggard face!" he called out.

I stuck behind him as tightly as possible. She appeared. She crawled along the ground floor on all fours.

"I see you are here for me. Lay bare! I will tenderize you and put you in my pot." I couldn't believe this. He walked closer to her.

"I want you gone from Daneland and never to return, or I will slay you now!"

"I am just a mere old troll mother who is very lonely. Why do you come here to disturb me? You are just like your King Hrothgar," she accused.

"You are not to be trusted, just as Grendel was not to be trusted."

"Ah, you do the dirty work for your king. I want to see your king here with us. He is the root to all evil."

"He is my lord, and is to be respected as king of the land," he said.

"You're a stupid warrior. Are you doing this, because you wish to be king?"

"I am doing this, because trolls must be stopped. Why am I wasting my time with you?"

"You entered my premises uninvited. You must be gone or you will be my dinner."

Beowulf noticed a fantastic sword sitting beside Grendel's decaying body. He swooped down to grab it, and cut off Grendel's head in the process. Grendel's mother screamed that shrilling screech again. I held my hands to my ears. Beowulf swung his sword at her. He lunged at her and pinned her to the wall.

"Where is Eschere?"

"You see my stew sitting in that pot. He was very tasty I must say."

Beowulf swung his sword at her and sliced her arm, then cutting her legs. She moaned and howled. He thrust his sword into her belly and stuck it in deep enough to impale her. I stood back, feeling nauseated. I couldn't believe what I had just witnessed.

"Beowulf!" I began to cry. "What was all this just now? Did you have to kill her like that?"

"Like what, my love?"

"You impaled her."

"How else? Do you, perhaps, have another method?"

"I know she's a troll, but this entire scenario really sucks," I moaned with anguish.

"Yes, it does, I'm afraid. You were feeling some sorrow for Grendel. Are you by any chance feeling the same way for his mother?"

"She was just missing Grendel. I don't get any of this. Why'd you cut off his head?"

He took me into his arms whilst holding Grendel's head. "Come, we must go to King Hrothgar and show off this trophy."

We rode off. It was a long bumpy ride. We had to stop a few times, so I could vomit.

***

We entered Heorot. King Hrothgar sat in his large wooden throne. Hrothgar's subjects noticed Beowulf holding Grendel's severed head. The crowd hollered with delight. The horn was sounded to gather the subjects of Heorot, and the people of Daneland. King Hrothgar stood up.

An aisle was formed in the middle of the room for Beowulf to walk with his trophy. The horns sounded loudly. Some of the female slaves took me, and dressed me in some

171

long flowing gown. It was still ugly, but to a Viking woman this was their *Versace*. Beowulf walked along the aisle way, he stopped at the king, and kneeled to the ground. He then held up Grendel's head, as he continued to kneel.

The king took the head. He spoke in Norse to the crowd and the people cheered. The king presented Beowulf with a gold necklace. He placed it around Beowulf's neck. Then he gave Beowulf five gold coins.

"Beowulf, you will soon be king of Daneland. You have almost fulfilled your tasks of showing great bravery, strength, and royalty. Your final and most challenging task will be the slaying of the dragon."

Beowulf stood up and faced the roaring crowd. "I will not stray from this challenge, M'lord."

One of the slave women brought me to Beowulf. He took my hand, bowed and kissed it. The crowd chanted. The king coaxed the crowd to settle down.

"Our future king Beowulf has selected his queen. She will be known to all of Daneland as Queen Kyla."

The crowd roared. I tugged on Wiglaf's arm.

He looked at me and smiled. "Wiglaf, what did the king just say?"

"M'lord, Beowulf will be king and you will be his queen, M'lady."

I felt sick to my stomach. This didn't look like we had a ticket out. That night, Beowulf and I snuggled by the large burning fire at Heorot Palace. He was very frisky I must say. He planted himself on top of me and thrust it into me several times. It didn't matter to these sixth-century men who watched and who didn't. I wasn't used to people walking around me during sexual intercourse.

He was very sexy. His heavy breathing was quite the turn on. He made sure my hand never left his penis. He had saturated his veins with mead that night to celebrate his successful slayings, which left me with a very drunk, horny Viking. If he weren't so damn gorgeous I'd probably tell him to get a real job. He poured himself another flask of mead.

"My love, soon we'll be married and you will be my queen."

"I'm so glad for you," I said. "I love you more than anything. I've never known love like this."

He forced his tongue down my throat and planted a very wet sloppy kiss on my lips.

"I love you with all my heart, my loving queen."

"Beowulf, we need to discuss matters."

I tried to push him back. The music in the mead hall was so loud I could barely hear myself. He gave me a blank stare. "You wish to return to your time."

"Forgive me always pressing the subject, dear, but I don't think I could live here another day."

"I don't understand your strong dislike. We are to be royalty. We will live it up."

"No, the sixth century is not living it up. Even though we are royalty, I don't consider this the high life. I can't deal with these slaves either."

"Are they not doing a suitable job for you, my love?"

"Slavery is wrong! Where I come from, nobody owns slaves."

"You wish to do all your chores yourself?"

"You're not getting it, are you?" I said.

"I understand you long to be back in your time. I will call for the witch, and she will cast us back to your time."

"That was easy."

Beowulf stood up. He was naked. He helped me up. I covered myself with that hideous gown.

"Come outside the hall with me, and we will call for the witch."

"Aren't you forgetting something? Aren't you going to get dressed?"

"I'm quite warmed from the fire." He took my hand and held it tight. We walked outside the hall. A very nude Beowulf called, "Witch! Witch! Please, come upon my request!"

We waited a few minutes. He wanted me to focus on him.

173

His hands were everywhere. There were people walking around.

"Beowulf, please, I can't do this anymore tonight. You need to calm down. I never saw you like this."

He smiled at me, but kept a serious expression as if his behavior was part of the usual courtship of his time.

The air looked dense and swirls of color formed in front of us. The witch appeared.

"Ah, Beowulf, you look marvelous tonight," she said, primping her breasts. "You know I have slain Grendel and his mother?"

"I know. What do you need from me?"

"You must send Kyla and I to twenty-first-century London."

"That could be difficult. I wasn't prepared for such a large request in the middle of the night."

"It seemed easy enough for you before, you bitch!" I said, losing my temper with her. "What's with this middle of the night shit? Aren't you on-call twenty-four-seven?"

"Maybe you need to look in a mirror to see who the real bitch is here," she responded, with evil in her eyes.

"Ladies, please. Don't spoil my evening of grandeur," he pleaded.

"First, Beowulf, you must put something on. You're making it difficult for me to concentrate," she said, with half laughter.

"Yes, my dear, please get dressed. I can't understand how you can tolerate this climate without your hides."

He rushed into the mead hall to fetch some clothing. The witch's eyes were closed so she could concentrate.

"Kyla, I can get you to London, but a thousand years to the future from this time. Is that good enough?"

"That would be the sixteenth century," I blurted with anger.

"There's a castle, and I'm sure that would be suitable. I can banish you from sixth-century Daneland and get you to England, but the century would be different. Is this fine with you?"

"Of course it's not fine with me!"

"The sixteenth-century is not such a big difference from the twenty-first century. If I were you I'd take it."

"Take what?"

"Take London in the 1500s."

"This is getting more and more fucked up. You could place be back in my time if you wished. The problem is that you won't."

"There's a castle. It's the most renowned castle in London. It was in the sixteenth century and it continued to be a spectacle. I say you should go. This is a wonderful opportunity for you."

"To do what? I don't want to live in a castle with royalty."

"You're a very rude girl, Kyla."

I yawned, and said, "Yup, so I am."

"Just think of the fun you will have there."

"With who? The king? Not that king."

"Think of all that you will learn."

"All I'll get from that time is decapitated. Can't you do better that that?" Beowulf returned wearing tights and a leather vest.

"Well, are all things settled, Kyla?"

"No! She's fucking us around, that bitch."

"You really need to wash this girl's mouth out with soap," she told Beowulf. "Are we going to twenty-first century London?" he asked.

"Well, it's sixteenth-century London. Shouldn't that be good enough?" The witch instilled.

"Sixteenth century? What would that be like?" Beowulf asked.

"She refuses to grant our request," I told him. Beowulf looked puzzled. "She's doing this on purpose. We don't want to live in sixteenth-century London, Beowulf."

"But it would be so much more modern than this time, my love," he said not really knowing what the hell he was saying.

"No, no, no."

"Just think, Kyla, it was a vibrant time of great explorers. Think of all the trading routes that were just beginning," the witch said, as she tried to suppress her laughter.

"I could read a book if I wanted to engross myself in the sixteenth century," I said, feeling defeated.

Beowulf slid his arm around me.

"Perhaps, London wasn't as great a city in the sixteenth century as it is in the twenty-first century. Witch, tell me, could you send us to sixteenth-century America? That may be more suitable for my queen."

I pulled away from Beowulf. "That's even worse!"

"Why, Kyla? I don't understand why this upsets you so. Isn't America the land of plenty?"

"Sixteenth century America? I need more time to explain this to you, but now is not the time."

The witch hovered over Beowulf.

"Please, obey her request. Do it now," Beowulf pleaded, in his cordial style. He looked at me. The poor man often hadn't a clue of what I was talking about, because so much had happened, on a time-line, after the sixth century. He took my hand. "We must get to the twenty-first century."

"Tell her," I said, pointing to the witch.

"Beowulf," the witch said, as she descended to the ground. "You will never survive in the twenty-first century."

"The twenty-first century is where you first placed me. Why do you object now?"

"I am not objecting. I cannot conjure enough mystic energy to get you and Kyla there, because she is not of a mystical world."

"Excuses," I said. "She's making things up as she goes along. She's lying about that mystical world rubbish."

"Oh, my love, I don't think she's making anything up."

I leaned my head on Beowulf's chest. "Beowulf, I can't live another day in your time. It's making me sick! I hate it here!"

"Tell me, Beowulf, was the twenty-first century too confusing for you?" The witch asked trying to act composed.

"I liked it very much. I quite liked the idea of having so much done for you. Imagine that a machine can wash clothes. But, most of all, I liked the people."

"Us twenty-first century types must bore you to tears. What do you like about the people of my time?"

"They know so much, my love."

"But none of them know how to slay a troll."

"This is true. You and I must rid ourselves of this time and return to your time.

Would it be possible for us to be married in your time?" He kissed me several times on the lips.

"Yes! Yes! I would love to marry you, especially in the twenty-first century."

"Witch, send us to twenty-first century, London," he requested, politely but stern.

She closed her eyes and tried to concentrate. We watched her concentrate for a good five minutes. She actually spoke in tongues, which sounded quite eerie. She waved her arms several times above her head. Then when I reached for Beowulf he was gone. I gave the witch a strong stare.

"Where's Beowulf?"

"I'm sorry, Kyla. I told you this wasn't the right time for such a large request." I stepped closer to her and glared.

"Step back. You're making me angry. He's in Greenland and you're not."

"Oh my God, Greenland! What century?"

"I think it's the tenth."

"The tenth century? Why? Send me there, as well," I demanded. "Why are you so interested in tenth-century Greenland?" she teased. "Because Beowulf is there, why else?"

"Yet you can't digest sixteenth-century England?"

"You want to separate us, that's what you want."

"I'm tiring of your insults."

"Send me to Beowulf...now!" I said, lunging for her neck.

"Get away from me, you shrew!" she said, pushing me away. "Besides, you wouldn't be able to survive the voyage to Greenland, especially with Erik the Red in charge."

"Erik the Red? Shit! Are you mad?"

"He'll do fine with Erik, trust me."

"Erik the Red was an outlaw!" I shrieked. "So is Beowulf."

"Beowulf is a troll slayer. He was ordered by the king to slay trolls."

"There's no difference. Beowulf will do just fine with Erik."

"Bollocks!"

"You're an awful woman" she told me. "I can't do any more tonight. Stop bothering me."

"I'll kill you!" I screamed, but she was gone. "What the hell am I going to do in sixth-century Daneland without Beowulf? I'll perish here. He'll perish there.

"Kyla, if it makes you feel any more at ease you can watch Beowulf's whereabouts in my crystal lens," the witch said holding up a beautiful crystal medallion.

"Crystal lens? That sounds ridiculous."

"It's magical, it's mystical, what more do you want, Kyla?"

Kyla reluctantly took the lens and held it close to her eyes. She could see Beowulf in the image. "He's on a boat? He's rowing the boat?"

"Yes, Kyla, this lens helps me keep aware of where Beowulf and others are at all times."

"Is he a slave?"

"Yes, Kyla."

"Oh, my God! Who's in charge?"

"Guess?"

"I think I'm going to pass out."

CHAPTER THIRTY-SEVEN

The strong winds hindered the sails of the long boats that sailed the choppy Atlantic. Beowulf found himself on the chief long ship joined with several other men in a rigorous rowing expedition. He scanned his surroundings several times. Some of the other rowers stared at Beowulf from time to time.

He stopped rowing, which caused the ship to slow down. He quickly grabbed hold of the oar and continued to row. The vessel picked up speed and power. He glanced at the slaves, who were situated in rows. Their job was lighter when Beowulf kept his hands on the oar.

He noticed someone standing at the bow of the vessel. He stared at the man who was obviously in command. He stopped rowing and the ship slowed down considerably. The slaves moaned and complained in Norse. He stood up, but realized he could not move his feet. He looked to find that there were heavy chains around his ankles that linked to the side of the ship. He sat down to it again, and the ship picked up power. Several of the slaves grimaced at him. Beowulf pretended he didn't notice.

When the time was right, he slowly dropped his hands to his ankles and tugged at the chains a few times. He broke the link, but continued to row. He focused on the man in charge at the front. This man appeared aggressive. The leader drank a flask of water and the slaves watched. Just as the commander turned his back to the crew Beowulf stood up.

The commander paced a bit at the bow of the ship with his back to them.

Beowulf slowly walked through the center aisle of rowing slaves. Each one of them focused on Beowulf, but continued to row. The man who stood at the front had bright red hair and a long red beard. Beowulf tapped him on the shoulder.

"Who are you?" Beowulf asked.

The man turned to Beowulf in shock. He drew his broadsword and sliced Beowulf's arm. Beowulf grappled for the man's sword and knocked him to the floor pressing the point of the sword to his throat.

"Who are you?" repeated Beowulf.

Beowulf withdrew the sword into *left tail* position. He watched the red-bearded man stand up, where he kept his focus on Beowulf. Beowulf glanced at the slaves and looked beyond the ship to see that there were several long ships following from behind. Beowulf stood in front of the man face to face.

"I suppose you haven't a name. Tell me where we are going."

"Greenland," the man grunted.

"Greenland?" Beowulf paused for a few seconds to scratch his bearded chin. "Where is Greenland?"

"Beyond Iceland. We move westward,' he explained to Beowulf. "All I know to the west is Britannia. Is there more beyond?"

"There has to be. So, you know the riches of Britannia?"

"Yes. I have been there."

The red bearded man's eyes widened. He fussed with his sword and held it in front of himself as if he were ready to thrust. "What did you trade?"

"I was not there to trade. I was there for a wench."

"You go to Britannia for a wench? You have the brains of an ox."

The man laughed. Beowulf smiled, and slouched his posture. He pretended to yawn, which caught the commander's attention. Beowulf stepped closer to the man and pulled his hair. The man grunted as he waved his sword in front of Beowulf.

"You must return to your post."

"I don't fear you. You should fear me, therefore, I am

180

warning you."

"I will slit your throat, stranger," the commander said. "I will slit yours far sooner."

The commander tried to step back, but there wasn't any space. He gazed at Beowulf.

"We travel west," the man said. Beowulf stepped closer to him. "Tell me who youare."

"I am but a slave on your ship," Beowulf answered. The man laughed in Beowulf's face.

"Yes, you are a slave, and I am a great explorer. I have seen Greenland before. It is the new world."

"Who inhabits there?"

"Us. I discovered it; it belongs to me."

Beowulf felt baffled by the man. "How will you live?"

The man abruptly waved his sword. Beowulf didn't flinch with even a glimmer of threat. The red-bearded man waved his sword with conviction in front of Beowulf.

"We will trade with Norway."

"I see. What does this Greenland have to offer?"

"Much."

Beowulf stepped very close to the man, pushing the sword away.

"Much lumber?" Beowulf asked. The man shook his head, and looked away. "That doesn't sound very promising. If there are no trees, what will you trade?"

"Everything. Many Norse will live there and create a new world."

"You must make it like Britannia."

"I can see that you know Britannia well. When were you there?"

"It was a different time," Beowulf said, looking everywhere but at the man.

"When?" the man asked loudly.

"Tell me who you are first," Beowulf pressed. The man clenched his fists and struck Beowulf on the arm with his sword. Beowulf grappled for the man's sword; he sat on the man and cut his face. "The next time you swing your sword at me, you will be sorry."

The slaves continued to row, but were entertained by the newcomer's boldness. "Release me!" the commander demanded. Beowulf stood up holding the man's sword. The commander sprung up, and then stepped back. "Where are you from?"

"I am from Geatland, but I live in Daneland. I am Beowulf."

"You are very strong. I can use you for many of our missions to the new world. I am Erik, I am known as Erik the Red."

"Erik, I will do what I can to help you." Erik nodded to him. Beowulf glanced at rowers. "Where I come from I had slaves of my own, now you have made me a slave."

"You row so well, and I am the mightiest Norse chieftain in all of Iceland and now my Greenland."

"I don't mind helping your slaves, but I am a great warrior just as you are a great explorer."

"It is obvious that you are a warrior. You can help me conquer those who do not wish to comply."

Beowulf gave a slight bow to Erik, as he walked somewhat backwards to his seat. He sat down and noticed several eyes focused on him. He began to row and the ship picked up power. The ships continued to ride the treacherous waves until they reached Greenland's eastern shores.

It was dark. The slaves were released from the long ships. Beowulf helped carry their belongings onto land. Beowulf scanned the large island. Erik walked beside him and smiled. Beowulf returned the gesture.

"There are no settlers here?"

"I am the first. But soon many Norsemen will settle here and establish this great land. This is why I have named it Greenland. I want all to think this is of a green land, just like Britannia is green."

"Green it is not. You will be fooling your people," Beowulf said with seriousness in his voice.

"No. My people will make it green."

182

"I'm sure they will. It will take a great deal of work to make this land green. How does one even start?"

"This is all mine and I will think of a way." Erik said, waving his arms over his head. Beowulf took a deep breath of frustration. "Do you know what time we are in?"

Erik stayed focused on his slaves boarding onto the island. "You don't know?" he asked. "The year is 982. Why did I not see you board my vessel in Iceland?"

Beowulf's eyes dropped to the ground. "It's as if you just appeared on my ship."

"The year is 982?" Beowulf slapped his hands over his face. "I can't believe it."

"You are acting strangely," Erik said, appearing nervous. "You do behave different than the rest, that is for sure."

"Oh, that's so far from where I came from. I'm missing my loved one just now."

"More of my ships are coming. There will be wenches, lots of wenches."

"I'm not interested. I can only see my own love."

"Is she a slave? If it's beautiful slaves you wish, I can arrange that for you." Erik said.

"I suppose she will feel that way now that I am not with her."

Beowulf gave a slight bow to the great chieftain and offered to help the slaves with their belongings and livestock. As Beowulf worked with Erik's slaves he heard them speaking amongst themselves in Norse. They were very curious about him. There were already a few Viking dwellings built from Erik's last visit. Beowulf did his best to help the new settlers orient themselves on the island.

Erik approached Beowulf. "Build several fires to keep my people warm," he ordered.

"With what?"

"Go to the women. They brought animal fat from our old world. We can build fire from that."

"Yes, of course," Beowulf said, and bowed his head to the great chieftain.

183

That night they sat around several burning fires to stay warm and cooked their food. Several female slaves gathered around Beowulf. Erik offered Beowulf a flask of mead.

"Come and drink with me and my men. We will have food, wine, and wenches to celebrate this new land of mine."

Beowulf took a deep breath as he guzzled down the mead. He gave a slight bow to the women as he continued to stand. He sat beside some of the female slaves and they passed him some bread. One woman sat very close to him. She passed him some meat. He smiled at her and took the food. Beowulf noticed how Erik kept his eyes on him.

"What's the matter, newcomer? You're not indulging in my hospitality?" Erik wondered.

"I feel out of place," he answered. The woman sitting very close, leaned against him to give him a kiss on the cheek. Beowulf pulled away from her. "I'm sorry, but I already have someone." She stared at the ground. Beowulf stood up. "Thank you for your kindness, but I must walk a bit and think about things, if you don't mind."

"Think about what? You're a warrior? Do warriors think?" Erik blurted, into a snort of laughter.

Beowulf turned from him and walked toward the docked long ships. He could hear the festivities of Erik and his people. He walked along the shore and gazed at the damp Atlantic. He kept his eyes on Erik and his people in the distance.

"Witch!"

Brilliant colors appeared and a petite image of the witch formed in front of him. "Beowulf, I see you have become acquainted with Erik the Red."

"I don't trust this man. Who is he?"

"He's an explorer," she explained.

"No, I doubt he is only that, He is also something else."

"He will someday go on a further journey to the west and discover great lands."

"I don't care, because I feel in my blood that he is not to be trusted," he insisted. "What do you care? You're a troll

184

slayer."

"Who is this man, witch?"

"He was exiled from Iceland, because he is a murderer."

"A murderer! I knew it! This man cannot be trusted. Every time I speak with him there is a confrontation."

"Of course, he feels inferior to you. You dropped out of nowhere and you have the strength of thirty men. What do you expect?"

"Are you defending him? Just like you have always defended Grendel." Beowulf asked.

The witch became agitated.

"No, I'm not. But it is acceptable for you to murder trolls, is it not?"

"They're trolls!" He folded his arms. "You defend trolls and you defend this man, Erik. Why do you do this? You claim to have feelings for me, you don't."

"Beowulf, now you're acting like a child. Where is it written that I must feel exactly what you feel?"

Beowulf paused and tried to gather his thoughts. "How is Kyla?"

"She ails for you, unlike you ail for her," the witch observed.

"That's not true. I have been placed here, because of you. I need to survive, because I know you too well. I have to be civil with Erik the Red."

"You appear to be very comfortable in your new century and country."

"I do not wish to be here with that explorer. I wish to be with Kyla in her time."

"I love you, you know," the witch said.

He threw his hands in the air. "No, you don't! Please place me in twenty-first century London with the wench I love and wish to wed."

"I don't understand what you see in her. I'm confused as to why you have chosen her to be your bride."

"Look, it's not my concern to sway you to approve of Kyla. I would just like it if you could put us both back in her time and place. That is not such a large request."

"I am still having trouble," she said.

"I'm growing tired of this. Please, adhere to my request."
Her face turned red with fury.

"Not so fast. You seem to think this is such an easy
conjure for me. Your wench is not of the mystical world, and
you know this."

"She was correct about you."

"You have lost yourself within this wench, Beowulf.
What has happened to you?

You used to be so different."

"I have come to my senses, that's what. She and her
world have taught me a great deal."

"Yes, you have learned the destructive outcome of the
Industrial Revolution. At least the sixth century is pure and
original. Her time period is dreadful."

"Think as you wish. Just grant me this last wish, and I will
never ask of you again," he said. "You need to do this for me."

"I understand that."

He began to pace. He peered at the Vikings in the
distance by the fire. "Look, they will suspect something. I
need to return to them now. Please, just honor my request and
all will be well. I can't go on another minute without Kyla."

"Oh, yes you can. You are stronger than you think,
Beowulf."

"Kyla is living in sixth century Daneland without me. It
would be as if I were in twenty-first century London without
her."

"The plan was to have you in twenty-first century
London without her. Somehow this plan has not added up
correctly," she said, scratching her head.

Beowulf threw his hands in the air with frustration.

"According to you this has not worked out, but now I must
join this band of explorers."

He turned away from her and walked toward the Vikings
by the fire. He stood and watched them eat their roasted
meat. Erik sat with several women.

186

"Come join us, newcomer. Eat," He said. Several female slaves huddled around Beowulf, and gestured for him to sit with them. He remained standing. Erik's smile dissipated. "Eat! Eat now, newcomer."

Beowulf remained standing. The most attractive female slave approached him. She took his hand and kissed it several times. Beowulf smiled at her, but pulled away. She offered him bread. Beowulf took it and bowed to her showing his gratitude. She took his hand and brought him away from the burning fires.

"Am I not beautiful to you, newcomer?" she cooed. "Yes, you are, but I already have someone else."

"Then where is she?"

"Far from here, too far," he said, sadly.

"If she is truly yours, then why isn't she at your arm now?" He took a deep breath and shook his head. "Would you like to be with me tonight?"

"I can't. I'm sorry."

"She is so far from here, so why can't you? I think if I tempt you enough I will be yours tonight."

"Please, don't waste your evening on me. There are so many others you could spend your time with."

"But you're so strong," she said, caressing his arm. "There are other strong men here."

"Not like you."

"You're very kind, but don't waste your time. You won't see me around much longer anyway," he said, removing her hand from his arm.

"You just got here."

"I'm drifting through this time, that's all."

"A warrior needs to be in one place. So, why are you going to many different places?"

"I don't know."

"You should know, shouldn't you?" she asked. He shrugged. She took his hand inside both her hands and squeezed. "You are a mystery, newcomer."

"I suppose I am." He tried to break his hand away from

hers, but she refused to let go. "Please, don't bother with me any more tonight."

"Maybe tomorrow night?" she inquired.

"I hope not to be here tomorrow night."

"Where will you be?"

"Hopefully, the right place with the woman I love."

"Is there a chance you will be with us tomorrow night?" Again, all he could do was shrug.

"Then you will be with me tomorrow night."

"That's not possible."

"Tomorrow is another day."

"Yes, it is," Beowulf said, glancing back at Erik.

"Why won't you sit and eat with us, newcomer?" Erik shouted, and grunted. Beowulf smiled. He stepped away from the woman.

"I'm not well, I'm afraid. I think I may have to leave."

"Newcomer! Why do you refuse such a beautiful wench?"

"I'm misplaced. I don't belong here."

"Why do you keep saying you are misplaced? I don't understand your dilemma," Erik said, looking confused.

"I don't expect you to understand. I don't even understand. But I bid you good luck in your explorations. I know you will soon discover some other great lands. You are sure to make Greenland prosperous."

"Greenland has all the riches a man could want. But I will continue my explorations westward."

"Please do. The world awaits your discoveries."

"I'm starting to like you, newcomer," Erik said, and lifted his cup.

Beowulf gave a slight bow and walked toward the shore. It was dark and cold.

He could barely see the ocean that stood before him. He could hear the crashing waves and feel the cold sprinkles, but the darkness was too great. There seemed to be no inhabitants on the mysterious island. He continued to walk until he could feel something happening to him. The colors of the witch appeared and encircled him. He was gone.

I sat in the mead hall crouched in the corner. I was wrapped in Beowulf's furs and hides. King Hrothgar would glare at me from time to time. He was probably wondering where Beowulf was. I felt so uncomfortable I wanted to scream. One of Beowulf's men, Wiglaf, came and sat beside me.

"M'lady? Where is m'lord?"

"I think he had to go somewhere. He better get back soon or I'll shit myself. Oh, pardon me. I'm just saying that he needs to get back here."

He took my hand and kissed it. He bowed as he inched away from me. Hrothgar was still giving me dirty looks. What was even worse than Hrothgar's dirty stares; it was getting dark and Beowulf wasn't here. The thought of sleeping in this disgusting mead hall without Beowulf was unthinkable.

A few hours passed and everyone was asleep in Heorot. I curled up in the furs and tried to imagine myself with Beowulf. I felt so empty and alone that I started to cry. I had to concentrate on sucking back my tears, because I didn't want anyone in the mead hall to hear me. Amazing enough, I finally fell asleep. All was quiet.

Then it happened. I heard the horses cry and scream. The wind howled louder than usual. Hrothgar's subjects ran in a panic, and Beowulf's band of men drew their swords. I sprung up to see what was the commotion. I looked and saw nothing. Then I ran to the door, because whatever it was, it was definitely outside Heorot. I stood in the doorway and had to catch myself from fainting.

What was this thing that stood before us? It spewed several ground shaking sounds. I had to cover my ears. I felt the mead hall shake. I felt myself tremble, but continued to peer at this beast. Was this the dragon? Was I staring at a fire-breathing dragon? Did this beast have two heads? Was I just having a nightmare?

Hrothgar kept calling for Beowulf, but no reply. It snorted with stringy drool dripping from its mouth. Then the king glanced at me. I knew what he was thinking. If I had the power to bring Beowulf back I definitely would. Beowulf's men and the king's subjects worked together showing no fear, as they kept the beast from going any further.

This beast was two-headed. It had a pair of over-powering curled horns on each of its heads. Large horny plates of armor outlined its jawbones; with long sharp needles that protruded from its chin like a beard. It's nostrils flared and snorted with oozing liquid and steam. Its tongues were long and forked. And, its fangs were so enormous that they jetted outward from its mouth. Its red eyes were enflamed. Its necks were long and scaly with horny spikes along its backside. It had webbed bat-wings with tiny claws at each end. The tail was thick and scaled; it looked as if most of this beast's power was in its tail. It did seem to have keen eyesight. I could tell by the way it observed what was going on.

I remained in the Heorot doorway too frozen from fear to even move. Then the beast stopped its actions. It let Beowulf's men sling arrows at its leathery skin, but it didn't flinch or react. It slithered its tongues around and back in its mouths. It focused on me. It gazed and focused on me. I was sickened with fear. I could hear Beowulf's right- hand man call to me. He told me to get inside the mead hall. So I did.

***

Beowulf walked the land feeling disoriented. He noticed the shoreline, which looked familiar to him. He noticed the small village; the people, their style of dress. A group of men passed by him as they bowed their heads to him. Beowulf bowed back to them as well.

"I'm home? In Geatland?" Beowulf walked to the shore and stared at the menacing waters. "This is sixth century Geatland, I know." He gazed at the Oresund Strait and smiled. He suddenly wiped the smile from his face. "I'm not in Daneland. Oh, dear Odin, help me get to my queen. Witch! Witch! Come before me!" He looked around to make sure none of the villagers were watching. "I must know how Kyla

190

is. Tell me.

Do you hear my call?" Vibrant colors appeared in front of him. He knew the witch had heard his call. "Witch, come before me now."

Her petite frame manifested in front of him.

"You guessed correctly; you are in sixth century Geatland. How does it feel to be home?"

"I want none of this. Take me to Kyla. I know she's in trouble," he said.

"But she is with your band of men, and Hrothgar's subjects. She will be fine."

"They all need me to be there. Why did you put me here?"

"Get on your ship and go," she said. "My ship is in Daneland."

"Your land of Geat is well aware of who you are. Go to a ship builder and get a boat."

"Can't you send me to Heorot?" he asked.

"I won't do that, I'm afraid. I have given you all too much already," she said, with a demonic stare.

"Has the dragon made its appearance to her yet?"

"Oh, yes."

"Oh, my Odin! No!" he shouted, and clenched his fists.

"You can pray to Odin as often as you like. This is your mess that you got your sweet love into. Who pleaded to be sent to another century when the troll was about to defeat you?"

"I didn't think I would have such a price to pay."

"Be careful what you wish for, Beowulf."

Beowulf stepped back. His eyes dropped to the cold sand. He paced along the beach, and then he looked at the witch again.

"I need to get a boat," he said. "Yes, you do."

CHAPTER THIRTY-EIGHT

Things were getting shaky at Heorot. The king kept questioning me in Norse. He was damn mad, I could see. I didn't understand a thing he blurted to me but he was damn mad. I think he was demanding Beowulf's whereabouts from me. What the hell was I supposed to say to him? Even if I had an answer for him, my Norse is not up to snuff.

The dragon had made another appearance the previous night. I was terrified with every second that passed. I couldn't understand why Beowulf's men couldn't just slay the damn thing. It's like they were paralyzed without him. One cool crispy morning I was trying to use their disgusting facilities when a puff of smoke appeared before me.

"I see you are adapting well as a Viking mistress," the witch said, whilst hovering over a tree.

"Adapting? I'd rather say I'm existing," I said, whilst in a squatting position. "You appear rather chilled. Use Beowulf's hides."

"I can't. Somebody vomited on them."

"Oh."

"Where's Beowulf?" I asked her.

I stood up and tried to wash myself using a water-filled barrel. I was getting used to being frozen to the bone when I washed.

"Your good warrior is on his way. He shall be with you shortly. He is upon the Strait now."

"What's he doing there?"

"He is trying to reach you, of course," she said.

"So, you put the effort into getting him out of the tenth century with Erik the Red, and you couldn't place him here in Daneland?"

"What are you insinuating, Kyla?"

I took a deep breath and tried my hardest to be cordial to

192

her. "You see; this proves it. You are abusing your power as a sorceress."

"I'm growing tired of your childish behavior. It is not written that it is my job to continue granting warriors a series of wishes. He initially made the choice to be taken from his time and placed in another. He made the choice to fall in love with you. It is not my responsibility to constantly open the golden door of prosperity for him."

"So, that is why you cast him near here, but not exactly here?" I said. "He was sent to Geatland. It is his homeland. What is wrong with that?"

"Everything! It's not here."

"He will always cherish his time with Erik. This was a special time for him. He gained a world of experience being placed with Erik. I'm sure he wouldn't trade that for anything."

"I think you're wrong. What do you think he would gain hanging about with a savage like Erik the Red?"

"Erik was a great explorer."

"Look, I really don't have time to chat. There's a fucking dragon who keeps crashing this party, and Beowulf is sailing the Strait right now."

"Don't worry, Kyla, he will reach you in due time."

"Can't you just bring him here to me, and send us both to twenty-first century London?" I pressed.

"No, no, no. I can't do that. You're not part of our mystical world. You are an outsider; it just isn't that simple for a sorceress like me to conjure such. You are not making an ordinary request."

"So what's an ordinary request? Isn't this entire episode out of the ordinary?"

"Kyla, part of your problem is you are in constant resistance of Beowulf's mystical world. What kind of lover are you to him, when you refuse to understand him?"

"Go to hell!"

The witch continued to hover over Kyla in silence. She paused as if she was telling herself to be nice to me. Bitch!

193

"He will reach you in due time," she finally said. "If you want someone to blame, blame Beowulf for this mess. He's a sixth-century warrior who thinks he can give you a fruitful life in the twenty-first century. Now, that is out of the ordinary, don't you think?" she said with a devilish grin.

"I think you're lying to me about this mystical world bunk. Send us back to the twenty-first century now, so I can be with Beowulf under normal circumstances."

"To the man you love, these are normal circumstances."

"I'm sure he's not too used to hanging about with Erik the Red in the tenth century."

"I really don't understand what Beowulf sees in a shrew like you," she spat.

I had to collect myself and get a grip. "He is on his way to you. When he arrives I will do what I can to get you both to your time. However, the dragon must be slain beforehand. He cannot leave here until he fulfills his duty to the king and all of Daneland. If you deny Beowulf from his passion, then you are denying who he really is."

"I saw that dragon. Did you know it has two heads?" I exclaimed. "Did you know that thing saw me? It gave me a dirty look. What did that mean?"

"It most likely can sense that you are the warrior's queen."

"Oh great! Not only does that thing have two heads, it's also intuitive."

"This is a very sly dragon, Kyla."

"I'm afraid for Beowulf. I don't want him slaying any more monsters. Frankly, I've had enough of this rubbish."

"He obviously has not."

"What if?" I said, and put my hands to my face and began to cry. "What if the dragon slays him instead?"

"Beowulf is very aware that the dragon could easily take him. This is a very different situation from the slaying of Grendel."

"I don't think I could bare it."

"You have to. He's a warrior. He understands all too well that the life of a mighty warrior means that some day he may

194

lose the fight."

I stepped closer to her.

"You know something about his destiny, don't you?"

"I use to know more. Now, that you entered his life, his destiny may have changed." The witch fluttered around me and began to sob. "You were not in the cards. Why did you appear?"

"He knocked on my door. I was minding my own business in my wee little flat."

"I don't understand how he ended up at your door."

"I had nothing to do with where he ended up when you cast your spell," I said, looking down at the ground.

"I suppose its just one of those things. Now that you are in his life it may have changed everything. The mystical world plays strange tricks."

"I don't understand this mystical world. Tell me this, has my entering his life put his destiny in danger?"

"I can't answer that question."

"Alright then, has my entering his life put my destiny in any danger?"

"You? You're not from the mystical world. You're not part of any of this."

"So, then you answered my question."

She rolled her eyes back and sighed with frustration. "You are not part of the equation. You were never ever supposed to be part of the equation."

"But here I am speaking to a bloody witch in sixth-century Daneland. So, I guess I must matter."

"Oh, Kyla, I don't really understand what Beowulf sees in you."

"Tell me. Has my entering his life changed his destiny?" I asked. "I don't really know, but it's possible."

"What would his destiny have been if I had never entered." Her body language suddenly displayed great lament.

"I can't tell you that," she whimpered. She turned away from me and levitated way above the ground. She wept and wept. "Kyla, you know how the story ends."

A blend of colors appeared, then smoke. She was gone.

CHAPTER THIRTY-NINE

I layer in a pile of hides and fur. I felt a large warm hand caress my back. Who was doing this? Could it have been one of Beowulf's men? An even worse thought – could it even be King Hrothgar? I was afraid to turn my head. Whoever it was, his touch seemed very intimate and familiar. I felt several wet kisses along the side of my neck. He pressed against me. I turned, and it was Beowulf.

"You're back! I'm so glad, my love," I blurted, with tears.

"I have returned for you, for I could not bare this part, my love."

"I'm glad you're here, but we both need to be in the twenty-first century." He kissed along the side of my neck.

"I can't tell you how I've missed you. I can only imagine the horror of you here without me," he murmured.

"Well, you're timing couldn't be better. I met your mate, the dragon."

"So, he has made his fearsome appearance, has he?" He caressed my shoulder and smothered me with several more kisses. "I will slay him at once."

"Not so fast. He's a much bigger deal than Grendel was. He breathes fire. Can you top that?"

"I'm aware of this, my queen."

"It has two heads. Tell me, what dragon has two heads?" I said. "A two-headed dragon is quite usual, my queen."

"You say this like you're trying to convince me that it's quite usual to get a parking ticket when parked too long on the street."

Beowulf chuckled.

I kissed his fingers because it was so nice to see him laugh again. "Have you spoken with the witch?"

"In fact, I have. This is how I have managed my return. She claims she is trying her best to fulfill our request, but not all can be easy, I'm afraid."

"She's a liar, don't trust her."

"She is working very hard in trying to meet our needs, Kyla."

"No, she's not," I said, firmly.

"She's having difficulty, because you are not part of our world."

I glanced at something else, trying to refrain from sounding like a dirty barmaid. "She's making this shit up, Beowulf. She's very capable of placing you and I together in twenty-first century London."

"My love, you don't understand sorcery," he said, caressing my face. "You come from such a modern age that I do not understand your world. I will, however, live with you in your world. I will do what I can to impress you in your modern utopia. It will not be an easy challenge for me, but I will do what it takes in order to keep you in my life."

"I think a much bigger challenge is that dragon, don't you think?"

"Oh, the dragon is not the challenge you speak of," he said, with a nervous chuckle. "I understand I will never be the king of the Danes, but to have you as my very own queen is the biggest reward any warrior could ever imagine."

I never had a man speak these words to me. My love for Beowulf was growing so intensely, it was as if I had known him for centuries.

"Beowulf, please get the witch to bring us back to the twenty-first century."

"She knows I have a mission, my love."

"Mission?" I asked.

"My mission is to slay the dragon. I didn't warn you about this earlier, because I thought there was a chance the dragon would have changed its course. Now, it has made its appearance at Heorot."

"Okay, so you slay the dragon. Then, what other creepy-crawlers will come out of the woodwork?"

He laughed, "No other creepy-crawlers will show up, I

assure you."

"Well, this troll and dragon slaying is not your everyday routine."

"The sixth century is a mystical time, my love."

"Aren't trolls and dragons mythical?"

"Not in my time. As you can see, trolls and dragons are very real."

King Hrothgar glanced at us from across the mead hall. He looked as disgusting as usual. He always had particles of food hanging from his shabby, dirty hair.

"Hrothgar keeps looking over here," I said with a whisper.

"Of course, he is," he said, glancing at the king. "I hope all was well between you and the king?"

"As good as could be expected. He was a little agitated with me, because you weren't here."

"My poor love," Beowulf said, and kissed my hands.

I noticed in the corner of my eye the king slowly made his way to us.

"Beowulf! Ah, good Beowulf, you have returned to Heorot Palace. My kingdom needs your protection from the dragon," Hrothgar said.

Beowulf turned to the king. He kneeled to the floor with his head down. "Forgive me for my absence. I had to tend to a serious matter in Geatland."

"I'm sorry to hear that, Lord Beowulf."

"It was out of my control, my king."

"We have a serious matter here. The dragon keeps showing itself. It has been flying through the sky setting most of the village on fire. Your queen was without you. Tell me, what is your plan? How do you intend to slay this beast?" the king asked.

"I intend to strike it in its lair, of course."

"What are you two saying?" I cut in.

Beowulf placed his arm around me and smiled at his king. "Dear Kyla, my king is asking me how I want to slay the dragon."

"Okay, how?"

199

"I told him, I intend to slay it in its lair."

The king grit his decayed teeth and blurted with a snort of laughter. I wanted to vomit. Beowulf glanced at me. I couldn't believe he said that. I had to start setting myself up for something really terrible, now that I understood what this dragon was all about.

"Good, good. When will you do this?" the king continued with an idiotic smirk on his face.

"I must lay out a thorough plan with Wiglaf and the rest of my men, and then you can consider it done, m'lord," Beowulf said, bowing even lower.

"That will be all, Beowulf," the king said.

Beowulf turned to me. "Well, the king is pleased with my plan of action, Kyla."

"Why the dragon's den? Isn't that the most dangerous place to knock him off?"

"It is the best way to catch him off guard, my queen," he said, rubbing my shoulders. "Where is Wiglaf? Have you seen him? He is the main warrior, my top man."

"He's always talking to me and making sure I'm comfortable. Despite the fact it's utterly impossible to ever feel comfortable in the sixth century."

"Yes, that sounds like Wiglaf."

"I think he's at the other end of the mead hall with his wife."

"How have you faired with her?"

"Not great. She's like a cave woman, as far as I'm concerned."

"Cave woman? A woman who resides in caves?"

"No, more like Neanderthal."

"I did read about that in your time. She's a pleasant sole, is she not?"

"Not."

"I'm sorry to hear that you aren't getting on with her. She would've been my first pick as a friend to you."

"I guess if she's what Wiglaf fancies then – hey, who am I to say?"

I caught Beowulf chuckle. He always laughs at my sarcasm and gestures.

"I must now gather my men, and we must put forth a plan of action on how to enter the dragon's lair."

"I'm not in favor of you barging into some mythical two-headed, winged lizard's den. Can't you meet up with that thing somewhere else?"

"Why is this idea bothering you so?" he asked me. "You do understand me, don't you, Kyla?"

"I understand you, Beowulf, but I'm still not in favor of you entering the dragon's den."

"I don't understand. Why would you feel this way? I'm a warrior."

"If you get stuck in his den, you may never come out," I said, as I started to cry. "I will come out, my love."

He embraced me firmly in his arms and kissed me on my head. He kissed me on the lips and took me in his arms.

***

It must have been around midday when Wiglaf came rushing over to Beowulf.

They spoke in Norse together. I stood there and tried not to look interested. I liked Wiglaf and I came to trust him.

Beowulf then took me aside. "Come, my queen. We must sit by this tree and talk a little." I could tell by his facial expression that something was wrong.

"What is it now?" I asked, feeling nervous. "One of the king's slaves has run away."

"Oh, well, that just goes to show you Hrothgar treats people like rubbish."

"The slave returned." He took my hand. "He told us that he had come across the dragon's treasure. Ancient treasures that may have belonged to a tribe of warriors who appear to have been killed in battle three hundred years ago is what the dragon holds. King Hrothgar is pleased. He has upgraded this slave to join my band of men."

"Oh, no, I know where this is leading."

I closed my eyes and tried to remain calm.

"The treasure is encased in a tall stone mound."

"Well, tell Hrothgar to find his own treasure. You and I have got to get out of here."

"No, my love, the king's slave has stolen some of the treasure, and the dragon is out of its mind with vengeance. It's coming this way, because it senses the slave is here."

"And Hrothgar thinks this is a good thing?"

"Yes, in fact, he does."

I paced in a feverish stomp. "I hate that king!"

"Shhh, Kyla. Please."

"It's not like anyone here understands me. And my Norse is rather rusty."

"My love, please. This is what King Hrothgar has been hoping for."

Beowulf took me in his arms and caressed me. We kissed for a good while. "Beowulf, I'm not in favor of you slaying this dragon. Can't we just leave the sixth century and return to my time?"

"I'm a warrior, Kyla, therefore, I have an obligation to the king and his people."

"Yes, of course."

"Of course, because we were meant to be, my love. You are my damsel and it is your duty to wait for me to slay the beast. Now, what is so wrong with that?" he seemed as if he was getting frustrated with me.

"Did I upset you? I'm sorry if I did. Try and understand, I don't come from a magical mystical world. I've had enough of the troll family and now suddenly this disgusting dragon appears out of nowhere."

"We were so consumed with Grendel and his mother that I forgot to tell you that there was a dragon."

I sighed with frustration. "Beowulf, how can you forget to mention that their is a dragon?"

Wiglaf returned to us. He was holding an iron shield. He said a few words to Beowulf in Norse. Then he looked at me and forced a smile.

"M'lady, this shield is for m'lord. He has chosen to

202

fight the dragon alone." Wiglaf bowed as low as he could go, and crept away from me still in a low bow.

"What's this?" I cried, hysterical. "Why are you doing this?"

"This is my allegiance to Odin, to the king and the people of Daneland."

"I should be your priority, Beowulf, not them."

"This is who I am, my queen. I cannot change that."

"Can't you call the witch? She needs to get us out of here." I broke into such an uncontrolled cry that I started to hack phlegm, then blood.

"Come, my queen," he said, as he took my hands. "You must calm yourself.

There is nothing to worry about. How I wish you could relax about this."

He wiped tears from my face. I tried to breathe normal and get a grip.

"We must begin our family. Come to me. I want to express my deepest love to you. There's no need for tears."

He dried my tears and took me to his mound of hides and fur. He made sure the fire in the middle of the room was well kindled. He slowly removed my dress, where he carefully undid every tie. I lay there naked, as he undressed himself. He came upon me. I could feel the intense energy from his chiseled body. He came into me with every thrust. I moaned, expressing the intense ecstasy.

We lay in each other's arms. He called for his slave to fetch us some flasks of wine. We sat by the fire sipping and fondling each other. Thankfully, the furs and hides were so heaped up that if anyone walked by us in the mead hall, they wouldn't notice us. Or so I thought.

CHAPTER FORTY

The sunlight dissipated and dusk set in. I was asleep in his arms. Beowulf tried not to wake me as he crawled out of the hide bed. I opened one eye, noticing how he gingerly tried to make his way out of the mead hall.

I rose and quietly followed his footsteps. I stood outside freezing. I stood behind a pile of chopped wood. He didn't see me. I watched him gear his horse with his magic sword and magic iron shield. Wiglaf helped him. Then I watched Beowulf ride off. I sneaked around Wiglaf, because I knew he would obey Beowulf's orders and forbid me to follow him. Wiglaf spotted me, as I knew he would. I played dumb and pretended I knew nothing of Beowulf's whereabouts.

"M'lady? Shouldn't you be asleep?" Wiglaf asked.

"Oh, yes, I was just looking for that disgusting hole in the ground." I faked a yawn. He took me by the arm and escorted me to the potty hole. "Uh, thank you. One more thing; Beowulf was not in bed with me. Perhaps you know his whereabouts?"

"Oh, m'lady, I don't think I can say, forgive me."

"Are you keeping secrets from me? I'm Beowulf's queen. How can you do this?" He bowed as low as he could go. "I understand."

"By the way, I haven't seen your horse lately, Wiglaf. Is he alright?"

"Yes, m'lady. He is just there." Wiglaf pointed behind a cluster of bushes. It was dark, but thank God the snow brightened things up.

"Oh, yes, he is looking well," I said, with a smile. "Perhaps after morning you would like to ride him again?"

"I would like that very much."

He continued to bow. I gestured a thank you to him, and made my way to the poop hole. Wiglaf smiled at me and walked away. I squatted down as if I really meant to use it, but made sure nobody noticed me.

I kept close to the ground. Wiglaf was preparing for something, obviously a battle with the dragon. I kept low to the ground and inched toward the horse. Wiglaf appeared engrossed in what he was doing. He appeared to be sharpening several swords and daggers. I was almost crawling in the spring snow. I stopped a few feet beside his horse. Just as he turned away from me I leaped onto the horse and rode off. I'm not the world's greatest rider, but thanks to my parents who spent loads of quid on riding lessons. Wiglaf's horse was the most obedient.

I was nervous as hell, but I couldn't imagine not following him to the Dragon's den. I followed the fresh tracks of Beowulf's horse. This was very difficult to do. It was almost impossible. I didn't know my way. I was terrified of getting lost. Wiglaf's horse picked up the scent of Beowulf's horse, which made my escapade worth doing.

I saw a man on a horse several meters before me. It was so hard to see, I assumed it was Beowulf. He was trotting much faster than Wiglaf's horse, but he must have slowed down at some point in order for me to even trail behind him. As much as I wanted to race up to Beowulf I made sure to keep my distance. Wiglaf's horse skidded on the icy snow from time to time, where I almost fainted with fear. I held onto the reins for dear life. I wasn't used to conditions like this. There were no roads, or paths; it was icy cold, untouched wilderness.

The scenery was creepy. I was terrified of those mystical creatures like trolls and dragons. I felt vulnerable. All I could see was eerie cragged rock, which looked frightening in the dark. Chunks of ice had fallen making the foot-printed path difficult to travel. I followed Beowulf up a winding hill. He had slowed down. Wiglaf's horse was having trouble with the traction on the icy slope. I was gentle with her as she was with me. Wiglaf is a gentle sole, figures his horse would share the same characteristics. I could see Beowulf enter a cave. The closer I got, the more I wanted to turn back. I couldn't see him anymore. He was inside and I was still outside.

I parked Wiglaf's horse beside Beowulf's. Wiglaf's horse appeared edgy, but she was familiar with Beowulf's horse. I took a deep breath and gingerly walked toward the cave. My adrenalin was racing and I realized I no longer felt the damp cold. I entered the cave. It was so dark I couldn't see a thing. I made a quick exit. I stood outside the cave opening feeling so nervous and afraid I could feel my knees buckle. I also knew all too well that Beowulf was dead against be following him to any of his battles. I tend to get in the way, so he thinks. All I knew was that Beowulf was in there, but I couldn't hear or see him. Where was that dragon?

Beowulf was in the cave for almost an hour, I wanted to call his name, but that would only make things worse. I wished I had guidance from someone, maybe even the witch. The witch hates my guts, why would she want to help me in a time like this? I truly think she's part of the problem.

I stepped away from the outer walls of the cave. "Witch, this is a time of desperation, can you appear?" I called softly, hoping Beowulf wouldn't hear me.

A puff of colorful smoke formed in front of me and the witch appeared. "Kyla? What is it?" she asked sternly.

"Can't you see Beowulf has been in that cave for over and hour and only God knows where are the dragon's whereabouts?"

"So?"

She amazed me, how rude and thoughtless she was. I had no respect for this alleged sorceress. "How is it you are so uncaring of Beowulf?"

"Beowulf and I had our times together. He has decided to make his life with a twenty-first century woman who is of not a magical mystical world. He's on his own. He has informed me countless times, that he will, for now on, do things his way. I no longer have control over Beowulf."

"I'm afraid of the dragon and I'm afraid of Beowulf."

"So."

"You're a terrible sorceress. I don't really think you're doing your job."

The witch crossed her arms in front of her and took a big sigh. "Kyla, what do you want me to do right now?"

"Can't you seize the dragon?"

"I'm not a warrior, Beowulf is. That's his job."

"I don't want him to know I followed him but I also want him out of that cave."

"The dragon can't be in there, because if it was, you would've known by now."

"Why is Beowulf still in there?"

"He's waiting for it."

"Oh."

"Kyla, you're wasting my time here. Let your man do what he knows best. He's a warrior."

"I can't do that."

"Then, you're not the right one for him. Let me leave you, now." She lifted her arms and spoke a few Norse verses of something and she was gone.

Then, I heard tree branches break, and the icy ground rumbled like an earthquake tremor. I was still, too afraid to even wince. This couldn't be the witch pulling one of her selfish pranks, could it? I looked up and saw the dragon flying through the air. The gigantic reptile was flying like a bat, and it was coming in for a landing.

Beowulf exited the cave. He held his torch in front of him.

He called out to me. "Kyla? I didn't want you here! You must leave at once!"

"I don't think I can do that. Look up!"

Beowulf stepped back and gazed at the beast coming in for a landing. "It's magnificent, isn't it?"

"I don't know if I'd describe it that way. Why are we standing here?"

Beowulf grabbed me and jumped onto his horse. He rode so fast I almost fell off.

The dragon spotted us and tried to swoop down to snatch us. It made several loud roars and snarls. It even

207

breathed fire at us. Beowulf rode like a mad man, and parried off the fire beams with his magical shield. I held onto him as tight as possible, and tried not to keep my eyes opened. We rode along the craggy cliffs where his horse managed to stay focused and managed not to slip on the icy ground.

"Look, Kyla. A cave."

"It's too small for the dragon to enter, isn't it?"

"That it is, my love." *

He leaped off the horse, carried me in his arms, and we bolted into the cavity. It was so damp I couldn't stop shivering. We waited and heard nothing. Maybe twenty minutes passed.

"Beowulf, do you think we lost the dragon?"

"No, m'lady. It knows exactly where we are." He said, with a chuckle. "It's a bloody reptile. They're not the brightest lights, you know."

"Oh, that's where you're wrong. It's a dragon. It's very difficult to out smart."

"Dragons have intelligence?" I said. "I find that hard to believe."

"You'll see, my love."

I was so tired, but I dared not sit down. The cave floor was an inch deep in cold water. There was also some kind of movement in the water. I couldn't tell what it was. I would hear a splash, and then some other noises that I couldn't really decipher. I was so exhausted that it hurt. Whatever was swimming around my frostbitten ankles, it didn't seem to have teeth. I just didn't dare sit.

"Beowulf, I'm so tired and cold."

"This is our spring, my love."

"This is not my idea of spring," I said, with a grimace. "I fancy the cold. I'm surprised you don't."

"Why would you be so surprised? I hate the cold. I guess you've never been to Spain? You know, the land of great food, the guitar, and Picasso."

"The home of the Barbarians?

"Barbarians? You don't know much about Spain."

"I do know it's occupied by Barbarians. What is your fascination with this land?"

"It's warmer than England. It's sunny. I've always wanted to visit, but I could never get enough quid to vacation there."

"Well, then, when we return to your time we will visit Spain first thing."

"That would be wonderful."

I smiled at him. I got all excited, but then remembered the dragon. Then we heard a loud shuffling noise come from outside the cave. The sound of heavy breathing and grunting became louder and louder."

"Shhh, my love. It is the beast. It has come for us."

"What do we do?"

"Wait."

"For how long?"

"For as long as it takes."

I tried to compose myself, which was a challenge. I could hear that thing grunting and snorting outside the cave. I could feel its hot breath, which made my skin curdle. An hour must have passed. It seemed as if it was gone.

"Can we go outside now, Beowulf? This cave is too depressing for me."

"Why would you make such an odd request, my love?"

"I'm cold and miserable, that's why."

"That's not enough, my queen. If I know that beast – it is still out there."

"I haven't heard anything in quite a while now. Is it walking on its tip-toes?" Beowulf glanced at me and sighed. "It's a dragon, my love."

Then we heard a loud cracking noise outside the cave. The dragging sound of large claws entered our premises. I yelped, but Beowulf grabbed me and held my mouth shut from screaming. The claws felt around for us. Beowulf placed me on his shoulders and stepped up on an elevated part of the cave: we were lucky the ceilings of the cave were quite high. The claws could only reach so far. I was so terrified I no longer felt the damp cold. Then the claws dragged out of the cave. I felt relieved.

Maybe a half hour passed. Everything was silent. Beowulf and I held each other.

The claws abruptly returned; they were dragging something that we couldn't quite decipher. Then, I tried to focus my eyes. I stepped a bit closer, but not too close. What I saw was two half eaten and decomposed human bodies. I fell back gasping for air. I stood on all fours to vomit. I cried in a hysterical stupor. Beowulf seemed more consumed with my reaction rather than what evil tactics the dragon was up to. He held me in his arms and kissed me on the head several times.

"My love, we're dealing with a dragon here. They are not of any valued substance, nor do they have manners."

"Beowulf, I've been quite tolerable until now. I've lived with trolls in sewers and underground stations; I was attacked by a wild boar; I've argued with a witch; I've had to deal with that king's lack of table manners. I've done it all, but this is below the belt."

"I agree, M'lady."

"I'm so glad you understand my feelings," I said taking a deep breath, so I wouldn't hyperventilate.

"What's even more upsetting is these two half eaten cadavers that lay here in this cave, are in fact, two of King Hrothgar's subjects."

I began to cry harder and louder. "How awful!"

"One of them is the fool who stole from the dragon. The other one, I'm not too sure of. It's difficult to tell. He no longer wears his head, but I recognize his armor. He was one of us."

"I never told my mother any of this!" I said, crying harder.

"Spare your mother if me, M'lady. She is sure to dislike a troll-dragon-slaying Viking warrior like I."

"You're right about that. She always set me up with doctors, accountants, you know, somebody reliable. It's just, well, you know, I'm having an awful time with this dragon thing."

"Yes, of course you are, my love."

"I really wanted to introduce you to my mother. She helped me sew that tunic for you. Did you know that?"

I was so whispery at this point that I couldn't stop babbling.

"I'm sure as soon as this beast is put to rest we will have a splendid time with your mother."

"How can this be?" I said, and burst into another crying fit again. He caressed my head. "What will be my mother's response when she finds out what you do for a living?"

"Oh, that. I'm really not sure what I could say to your mother. Perhaps the truth may work." He smiled and held me tight. "The truth will work, my queen. I'm sure your mother will figure me out sooner or later."

He made me laugh; I don't know how. The dragon made some kind of roar that shook the cave so much that parts of the cave's ceiling crumbled to the ground. I realized that I had to compose myself or I would crumble along with the cave. The dragon's claws entered the cave again searching for us. We stayed as far as possible from the opening.

It must have been an hour. I was asleep on Beowulf's chest as we both rested on one of the more elevated parts of the cave. It was difficult to sleep with half mutilated bodies in the cave with us. I was so exhausted I didn't even care anymore. I woke up to the sound of silence. I looked at Beowulf, who was sleeping quite soundly. There seemed to be some light creeping in through the cavity. Beowulf woke when he felt me moving about him.

"Did you manage to rest, my Kyla?"

"I wasn't in deep REM if that's what you mean?"

"I'm sorry, my love, but I'm not sure what you mean."

"That's okay, you're a dragon slaying warrior. You don't have to know." He kissed my forehead.

"Things have got a bit quiet in dragon world, don't you think?"

"It seems so. Now could be our chance." He stood up and

211

clutched my hand. We crept to the cave opening. He poked his head out of the cave and then retracted back to me. "All looks well. We need to find my horse and be gone."

"Are you going to call for the witch to get us back to my time?"

"I need to slay the beast first," he reminded me.

"I know, I just wanted to see if you changed your mind."

He chuckled and clutched my hand even harder. He led me outside the cave. It was morning and the daylight felt good. He led me to where he had left his horse. He looked behind a cluster of pines. The horse wasn't there.

"Search the snow for horse tracks. It's not like this horse to wander off." I searched and searched, but the snow was fresh and untouched.

"Maybe it snowed whilst we were in the cave, and your horse wandered off before that?"

"I don't even see his dung anywhere. This is odd. Or is it? I just had a grizzly thought, Kyla. I think the dragon may have taken him."

I sat down in the snow and cried. "I liked your horse."

"My horse was very special. But there is no time for tears, my love. We must leave. How did you get here?"

"Wiglaf's horse."

"Ah, I see. Wiglaf lent you his horse."

"No, no, I took his horse. I don't think Wiglaf would have lent me his horse in the middle of the night when you had dragon slaying on the brain."

"Where did you leave his horse?" he asked me.

"Shit!" I said, brushing the snow off my dress. "I left him by the dragon's den."

"Perfect."

"Not if you're a horse."

"Let's hope the dragon is still doing its rounds and hasn't made it back to its lair yet."

"Rounds?" I asked. "The dragon has rounds? What the hell does that mean?"

"Breathing fire on Heorot could be considered one of

212

the beast's rounds."

He took my hand and led me toward the dragon's den. We had only been walking for a short time when we heard noises from above. We looked up and the dragon was tearing up the sky with its menacing bat wings and grumbling roar. It spotted us and encircled to descend toward us. "It sees us!" I cried, panicking.

Beowulf took my arm and ran so incredibly fast that we were back in that disgusting cave. I glanced at the cadavers by mistake and almost vomited. Then a rat scurried about my feet.

"Beowulf, I really hate this cave."

"I understand, my love. I'm not fond of it either, but it's the only way for our safety. I really must stop running from the beast, and confront it."

"Can't we just leave the sixth century?"

"I can't just yet. Perhaps, I could ask the witch to send you to your time and I can come later after I have slain the dragon."

"I'm not going anywhere without you."

"It might be what is best, my love." He stepped toward me and embraced me.

He brought my hands to his lips and kissed them. "I love you, my queen." We heard the dragon's heavy breathing outside the cave. "Kyla," Beowulf whispered. "It's here."

"Oh, shit."

Its slimy claws dragged their way back in leaving body parts of Beowulf's horse. I stood by the slimy cave wall and whimpered. Beowulf's horse was an amazing animal. He was beautiful. Now all that remained were chewed up limbs.

"I've had enough of this beast! It must be stopped at once!" Beowulf shouted, as he adjusted his armor and weaponry for the bloody battle.

Beowulf charged out of the cave to the stench of fresh flesh. The sound of heavy breathing saturated his ears. He glanced to the side and saw the beast's sharp fangs. He backed up to return to the cave. I ran to Beowulf.

"Why are you back so soon?" I said, in disbelief.

"Whatever you do, do not, and I mean do not leave this

213

cave until I tell you to."

"What did you just see?"

"The jaws of the dragon await us on the other side of the cave opening. I will cut its mouth now."

"Is there another way you could do this?"

"This is the only way."

"Why isn't your band of men included in this?"

"This is something I must do alone."

He exited the cave to discover that the dragon had changed positions. It was asleep beside the cave opening. Beowulf re-entered the cave.

"Kyla," he said, extending his hand to me. "Come with me now."

I took his hand and did everything I could to keep quiet. We walked outside, and there was the sleeping dragon. It was very close to the cave.

"We will have to climb over it," he said, in a faint whisper with his finger over his lips. "I will help you. Please, not to worry."

We were about to climb over a sleeping dragon; why would I worry? We crept along its nose, which was moist and slimy. We found it difficult to keep steady. I thought I was definitely going to slip and fall right in its mouth. Then Beowulf held my hand and led me onto its back.

The dragon flinched from time to time as we walked on its body. This was another difficult task, because it had so many scales and bones jetting from its backside that it was difficult to remain on our feet. I was so nervous I almost lost it. We had to somehow slide down its arm. Beowulf took me and held me close to him and he slid down. I yelped and the dragon opened its eyes.

Beowulf seemed glad that it woke up. Me, on the other hand, didn't feel so encouraged. We had reached the ground. Beowulf pushed me away from him.

"Go! Go as far from here as possible!"

"No! I can't do that!"

The dragon slowly lifted its spiky heads. It fixed its

inflamed eyes on Beowulf.

Beowulf held up his sword with his magic shield. "Fight me, you beast!"

It opened its enormous jaws and breathed fire at Beowulf. Beowulf was fast enough to move out of the way, but some of his hair was singed. Beowulf swung his sword several times and then thrust it into the dragon's belly only to understand that the dragon's scaly body could not allow any penetration of a sword. He then swung his sword five times at the dragon in *guard of the woman* stance. He blurted something in Norse to the beast.

"Blot! Brusi! Ormstunga!"

He continued to swing his sword. Whatever Beowulf said, the dragon didn't like it. It snorted and snarled at him. It breathed fire again. Beowulf wasn't fast enough to move out of the way in time and his shoulder caught fire.

I screamed, feeling helpless. Beowulf was calm and managed to stomp out his burning shoulder by rolling on the ground. The dragon charged at Beowulf while he was stomping out his enflamed shoulder. He tried to stand up quick enough, which caused him to fall backwards and lose his sword for good. He then held his shield in front of him each time the dragon enraged itself to spew fire.

"Shall I call the witch?" I shouted, out of desperation, as I stood behind a tree. "What for?" he responded, lying on his backside behind his shield.

"This isn't going so well! I don't want to lose you!"

He gave me a quick glance, but turned his attention back to the dragon. The dragon was even more agitated with me being present. Out of its anger it tried to bite through Beowulf's corselet. I closed my eyes; it was too horrid to watch. The dragon's tail had moved and I ran like hell to get out of the way. I stood by a cluster of trees. I got a hold of myself and concentrated on calling for the witch.

"Witch! Please appear! This is an emergency!" A puff of smoke festered where the witch appeared. "Please help. Beowulf won't survive this one."

"Do you have no faith in your great warrior, Kyla?" she asked, calmly. "Of course I do."

"Then you must let him be who he is."

I turned to Beowulf and the dragon still had its jaws wrapped around his torso.

His shield would be of no help at this point. I focused on the witch.

"Can't you do something?" I squinted my eyes to look at her. "And you claim to love Beowulf more than me."

"If you love him the way you claim to, you would allow him to be the man he is."

"I don't want anything to harm him. Look at that thing. Its teeth are piercing right through his corselet."

"Oh, Kyla, you are such a silly girl. Let your warrior be," she said, with a chuckle. "I can't believe it. You're supposed to be a sorceress."

"Yes, I'm a sorceress, I'm not God."

"But you have the power. Can't you at least fetch his sword?"

"I won't do that, Kyla. Aren't you forgetting how the story goes?" I was silent while I stopped to think a bit.

"In fact, he is supposed to die here, you know this already, don't you? This is his destiny."

"No! Please!" I shouted, with a dire cry.

The witch whisked around me. She looked troubled.

"I am at a loss. I love Beowulf, just as you claim your feelings for him as well. He will die of a mortal wound. You know this."

"No, he won't!"

"You know this is when he is supposed to die," she reminded me.

"He's the mighty warrior. He's going to slay the dragon." I could feel my eyes fill up with tears. "He fears nothing and he will win this battle, just like the other battles."

"Oh, Kyla, stop this silliness. He will lose this battle."

"Destiny can change its course."

"Not in this mystical world. It cannot change; no, I'm so

216

sorry," the witch said, with a tremor in her voice. "If you love him the way you say you do, then you would help him."

"You and I both know Beowulf would never accept my help," she said. "Yes, he would, because he wants to have a life with me."

"He may love you, but he is a warrior, first. He is a sixth-century Viking, who only knows one thing and that's to please his king and show the people of Daneland that he is the mightiest warrior of all."

I could hear Beowulf cursing at the dragon, while the thundering sounds of the dragon's roars penetrated the land.

The witch began to cry. "I don't wish to see Beowulf die." She paused and wept. "Wait, there is a way!"

"Can you do something to the dragon?" I asked.

"No, of course not. But if we transform Beowulf from mystical to ordinary, we could perhaps save him. He would no longer be of the mystical world."

"It's what's mystical about him that makes him powerful though, right?"

"If he were to travel to twenty-first century England could a doctor cure his mortal wounds?" she asked me.

"Yes, even if the wounds are from a dragon, I suppose."

"Then he must become ordinary in order to be transported to your time with you at his side."

"Can you get him to my time at this very instant?"

"No, we must watch the dragon have its way with him first."

"That's no good! Who makes up these rules of sorcery? I mean, it appears to me that you don't know what the hell you're doing. You're just making things up as you go along."

"How dare you, Kyla! You immature little child! What does Beowulf see in you?

If I were you I would stop these bursts of silliness, and would start acting like an adult woman."

"Why was it all so easy when you sent Beowulf to the twenty-first century and now it's impossible?"

"Because you are now in the picture," she said. "You

217

have to face up to what is."

"I don't believe in that rubbish," I answered back. "What if the dragon kills him? "Then there wouldn't be a twenty-first century doctor who could save him."

"So now, you're finally capable of sending us back to the twenty-first century?"

"I would have thought in your precious twenty-first century there would be a way to have mortals dodge their mortality."

"No, that hasn't happened yet. Maybe that's for the twenty-second century."

I knew she was being condescending, but I was too exhausted to fight her. The witch held up her arms and appeared to be conjuring some kind of spell.

"Then mystical he will no longer be."

"Wait! You can't do this whilst he's being devoured by that thing."

"When would you like me to do it? When he's already dead? He has to be ordinary just now. There is no other time, Kyla."

I bit every fingernail down to nubs. The witch held her arms to the sky. "Alright then, Beowulf will no longer have the strength of thirty men, he will be an ordinary man. He will no longer be a warrior, no more band of men, special horses, special armor and weapons, and not even Wiglaf. Is that suitable for you?"

I stood there in silence.

"Either way, he gets the mortal wound."

"I don't want him harmed."

"He will be harmed no matter what, but if he becomes ordinary he has a chance for survival."

"He will be completely out of your life if you do this, right?" I noticed the witch started to shake. I gathered she didn't like this any more than me.

The witch looked at me with tears in her eyes. "Why are you doing this?" I asked.

I watched her levitate much higher than her usual hover.

"Because true love, Kyla, is unconditional."

Beowulf managed to fend off the beast for a short time by bucking it off him with his shield. Beowulf stood erect holding his shield before him as he faced the beast eye to eye. The dragon slithered its long slimy tongues around its gnarly jaws. I looked around the dense brush for Beowulf's sword. I got on my hands and knees to sift the icy ground. I couldn't find it. The dragon drew its jaws closer and closer to Beowulf.

Beowulf's shield did deter the beast from charging at him. It had to be somewhat careful when it approached Beowulf for the shield was too powerful. Beowulf was engrossed in winning over the dragon. He was fast on his feet as he watched every move the dragon made.

Then I heard the witch's voice blurt some phrases. I couldn't understand her; she may have spoken in Norse. Then the dragon got too close to Beowulf. He held his shield above his head, but the dragon continued to get closer. It managed to knock the shield from Beowulf's hand with its tail. The beast was terrified to be so close to Beowulf's shield. It drew its jaws toward Beowulf and wrapped its teeth around his torso. I stood there and watched, feeling helpless.

I fell to the ground and wept. His corselet failed to protect him. Blood streamed out of his punctured wounds, and the dragon's venom entered his body. The dragon spewed fire at Beowulf. As I cried, I noticed to the side of me, sat Beowulf's sword. I knew his magical powers were gone, but it could give him the last bit of strength to survive. I crawled to his sword and slid it over to him on the icy ground.

Beowulf struggled to reach his sword. He took his sword and managed to stand up, despite being drenched in his own blood. Just as the dragon turned toward him Beowulf thrust his sword deep into the dragon's abdomen, where there must have been a non-scaled area. The dragon gasped and wailed. It's tail swung from side to side. I continued to sit and watch. The dragon fell on its side and died.

I ran to Beowulf. He had fallen to the ground drenched in

blood. I cried as I held his hand to my cheek.

"Beowulf, please hold on!"

He looked at me and slowly shut his eyes.

CHAPTER FORTY-ONE

I sat just outside the operating room, biting my nails and pacing the halls. One of the doctors entered the waiting room to meet with me. I looked like hell dressed in my sixth-century rags. I took a deep breath.

"Please, tell it to me straight. Will he make it?"

The doctor removed his glasses and wore a serious expression. "Can you tell me what animal has done this to him. The authorities need to know."

"I don't think that's important. What is his prognosis?" I asked.

"I can't really tell at this stage. We're all astonished at the size of this man's wounds."

"Is he conscious?"

"Good heavens, no."

"When can I see him?"

"Not tonight," the doctor said, and looked at me with an expression of bewilderment. "Was he attacked?"

"You could say that. I really need to see him."

"He won't even know you're in the room. It's best if you come back in the morning."

"No," I stated, shaking my head.

"He has giant teeth marks in his torso. What animal did this to him?"

"You wouldn't believe me if I told you."

"If you know the animal that did this you must notify the authorities at once so it can be stopped. I've never seen anything like it. This man has severe wounds." He paused, and scanned what I was wearing. "Are you two actors?"

I paused. I really didn't know how to answer. "Yes! "I see."

"We're stunt people."

"Stunt people. Well, that explains it. That's a very

221

dangerous job."

"It's a job," I answered, feeling like an idiot.

"Then, what did this to him?" the doctor pressed, scratching his head.

"A dragon." Fuck! Why did I say that? I'm going to be admitted to the loony bin.

"A mechanical dragon, perhaps, used in a film? Komodo dragon? They can be quite dangerous. Were you in Borneo?"

"Uh, sure," I said, lying my ass off.

"Is this man your husband? Boyfriend?"

"Fiancée. Yes, he's my fiancée.

"Oh, I'm so sorry this has happened to the man you plan to marry. Please, come back tomorrow morning. I'm sure we will have more answers."

"Will he make the night?"

"He's somewhat stable. I suppose he may. I'm not really sure."

The doctor forced a smile and walked off. I stood in the hall feeling very alone, but glad to be rid of sixth-century Daneland. I walked over to the main desk at the Emergency entrance. The receptionist glanced at me. She motioned to one of the nurses to join her. They both examined my attire. I tried not to let what I was wearing intimidate me.

"May I help you?" the nurse said. "Can I use your phone?"

"This phone is strictly for emergencies, ma'am."

"I don't have my cellular with me. I really need to ring my friend, so she can pick me up."

"I'm sorry. You'll have to use a pay phone," the nurse said.

"I don't even have any change. Please, I really must use your phone." The receptionist glanced at my clothes again. "I'm an actress, okay."

"Why are you penniless?"

"Because I'm a starving actress. What kind of question is that?" I glanced at some of the people sitting in the waiting room. "I was attacked by a mugger."

"How awful," the receptionist said.

222

"Please, I really must ring my friend. I have no other way of getting home."

The receptionist and nurse stepped aside to discuss my situation. I couldn't believe there was so much red tape over whether or not I should be allowed to use their bleeding phone. Then finally the nurse took me aside.

"Young woman, we will allow you to make one phone call. It can be no longer than two minutes. This phone is for emergencies only."

"Thank you." I rang Beth, who answered the phone. "Beth!"

"Kyla? Oh, my God! It's really you."

"I'm at the hospital. It's Beowulf, he's not doing well."

I started to cry. The nurse and receptionist glanced at me from time to time. "Was it that fucking troll?"

"Much worse."

"I can barely hear you. Can you speak up?"

"Not really. I'm not supposed to be using the emergency phone at the admitting desk in the hospital."

"What happened?"

"I can't really say just now. Just get here."

"Alright, I'll be fast," Beth said, and hung up.

The nurse and receptionist couldn't stop staring at me. "Be thankful it was only a mugging," the receptionist said.

"My fiancée was beaten by that terrible mugger and now he's in the OR," I said. "Anyway, thank you for letting me use the phone."

I was standing in the front foyer when I noticed Beth approach. We embraced as I cried in her arms.

"Kyla, just look at you. What the hell happened?"

"I can't even begin to tell you. I thought I'd never see civilization again."

"Why are you crying? Shouldn't you be thrilled to be back?"

"Beowulf is in the O.R. A fire-breathing dragon attacked him. I don't know if he's going to make it." I started to weep again. "I wish the witch could help."

223

"Oh, yes, that witch. Well, come along. I'll get you home and into some normal clothes."

We sat in the taxi. I didn't say a word. Beth came with me to my dorm. The first thing I did when I arrived home was to jump in the shower. I must have showered for an hour. Beth sat patiently in my room, until I came out.

"I feel clean, finally," I said, wrapping myself in my fluffy robe. "So, maybe you need to get that witch. You may need her help."

"I can't do that. Beowulf is no longer magical. He is now an ordinary man."

"I never knew that he wasn't an ordinary man. What's so unordinary about him?"

"He's a Viking warrior, who is constant battle with trolls and dragons. How many men do you know do that for a living? Does that sound ordinary to you?"

"Yeah, okay, I get it, but is there something else that makes him extraordinary? "Beth, my fiancée is a fourteen hundred year-old Viking warrior, isn't that enough?"

"I always thought he looked smashing for his age," she said, with a girlish grin. "And, You're engaged. How wonderful."

I felt a little teary-eyed. "Yes, it is wonderful, isn't it? However, there are liabilities when your fiancée is a fourteen hundred year-old troll and dragon slaying warrior."

"I suppose so. Age shouldn't really matter, though. What matters is true love."

"Yeah, you're right. Who cares that there's an age gap between us."

"Who would ever know there's an age difference, Kyla. He looks like he's in his late thirties…and, surely, he doesn't act as if he is fourteen hundred years old. He has loads of energy."

"Yes, you're right. Who would ever know?" I paused. "But, I would know."

"So?"

"Don't you think marrying an ancient Viking warrior would have its share of liabilities, Beth?"

"I dated a bloke last year who definitely had his share of liabilities, remember?"

"Oh, yeah, he was spending all your money. What a loser he was."

"Exactly my point."

"But, Beowulf eats, drinks and breathes what he does. He would be happy to know that he would die as a warrior. He's cut from a different cloth. I'm just wondering if I'm crossing boundary water, here."

She looked at me as if she was overwhelmed from the conversation. "Kyla?

How about that witch? I never liked her."

"She's out of the picture. The deal is that she steps out of Beowulf's life when he becomes ordinary. He is just a man now. He must heal like an ordinary man."

"Wait. That doesn't mean some morning you'll wake up and he'll actually look his age, does it?"

"Shit, I hope not," I said.

"Didn't he have special powers or something?" Beth asked.

"He was a magical warrior with the strength of thirty men, a magical sword and shield, a special horse with a golden headdress, and a band of men."

"Wow, if you would have told me this a year ago I would have said bollocks to you, but since I know Beowulf, and I've met the troll and the witch, I believe you."

"I know it all seems so surreal, doesn't it?" I said with a sigh.

"But he doesn't need to be magical any longer. He no longer lives with trolls and dragons. He now lives here in your world with you."

"You're right. He doesn't need to be magical. He is now ordinary."

"Yes. There's nothing wrong with that. You both can tell your children someday how their father was once a mighty troll slayer in a magical world. Imagine, you can tell your children that their father was a Viking warrior from the sixth century.

225

How thrilling."

"Yeah, I guess we could," I chuckled. "But you know what? I never once bothered to think what this would do to Beowulf. What if he doesn't want to be ordinary?"

"He loves you, doesn't he? Of course he'll be ordinary."

"I saw him differently in the sixth century. He really is a true warrior. What if being an ordinary man just breaks him in two?"

"He survived that fucking dragon, didn't he? He'll be glad to be ordinary and living in your world with you."

"You're right. If the witch didn't send him here to our time the dragon would have surely killed him."

"Oh, well, then you see, you did him a big favor. You saved his life," she said. "You're right. I did the right thing. Anyway, I better get some rest. I have to get to the hospital bright and early tomorrow."

Beth smiled as she started to leave my dorm. "When will you tell him?" she asked.

I stared at her not knowing how to respond.

"Kyla, you fool, when are you going to tell Beowulf that he is an ordinary man?" I felt my nerves jump.

"He is going to have to know, won't he?"

"I haven't really given it much thought. I'm very consumed with him surviving the night. I'm so worried that he won't make it."

"Of course he'll make it. Even though he's not a magical warrior anymore, he'll still fight like hell to survive."

Beth and I embraced, and she left.

CHAPTER FORTY-TWO

It was 7:00 AM. I made it to the hospital to discover that Beowulf was in ICU. Thank God! I entered the room. He was hooked up to machines, and was unconscious. His body was wrapped in bandages. His beard was shaved and his hair, tied back. I sat beside him the entire day. He didn't wake. The following day I entered ICU again. That same doctor I spoke to before was there.

"He's no longer here. He's been moved to a room," the doctor told me. "When did that happen?"

"Early this morning. He's conscious now."

I was so delirious with glee that I had to catch my breath. I raced to his room to see him lying in bed.

"Beowulf!"

I leaped into his arms and kissed him. He stared at me. "Kyla, please tell me where I am."

"We're in the twenty-first century."

"I figured that much, however, what is this place?"

"It's a hospital. You've been badly wounded."

"By the dragon? Of course." He focused on something else in the room. "You managed to call the witch, did you?"

"Yeah, she did come when I called her."

He tried to turn around in bed, but winced with pain.

"She sent us both here to your time. Interesting. Did she experience any difficulty? She did claim that there were complications, because you are not part of the mystical world," he questioned, lifting one eyebrow.

"She didn't have too many obstacles this time. I don't really understand your world, Beowulf. I'm just so glad that you're alive and well. I'm so glad that you're here with me. I love you," I said, taking his hand and holding it to my face.

"Oh, my Kyla," he forced out.

He tried to catch his breath from the exhaustion of talking.

"I'm so glad. I am still your queen?"

"My queen?" He tried to move. "Yes, always."

"So, you're my king?"

"King?" He tried to breath without hurting his ribs. His eyes shifted from one side of the room to the other. "Please, Kyla, I'm no king. I'll never be king."

"I'll call the nurse. Maybe you need more pain killers."

"Yes, the doctor has me on something called morphine."

I ran outside his room to fetch a nurse. She was very prompt.

"His pain is getting the best of him is it?" the nurse said, as she hooked up an I.V. to his arm. "He wasn't feeling too bad about an hour ago, when I removed his I.V."

"Perhaps my presence has upset him."

"I'm exhausted. Please, don't think that," he said, with a gasp as if it hurt to talk. "I think it's best you let him rest," said the nurse. "He's lost quite a bit of blood."

"Beowulf, my love, you're going to pull out of this. You'll be fine."

He forced a smile and squeezed my hand. I reluctantly went home.

***

That afternoon I sat in a café with Beth.

"I don't understand why you're not with him now," she said to me.

"He needs to heal with no distractions. I think I remind him of what he could have had. I think I stripped him of who he is."

"Then go to him. He's here in our time, because of his love for you."

"No, he's not. He's here because I forced him here. I know who he really is. I saw him in action as a true sixth-century Viking warrior," I said, and began to cry.

"Kyla, get a grip. You're not handling this well at all."

"The witch is gone forever. She will never return," I explained. "Isn't that a good thing?"

"I don't know what the hell is a good thing."

228

"Maybe you need to see a professional about this. You've experienced the unthinkable. This isn't normal everyday stuff."

"I don't care about that. I love him so much that I can't stand it. He's so banged up still. He looks rough."

"He was attacked by a fire-breathing dragon. How do you want him to look?"

"I don't think I can have it both ways," I said, crying. "He seems so unhappy. He would have been king if he was still there."

"He would have been dead. That dragon would've finished him," Beth said. "You should never speak this way to Beowulf, because he's a fearless warrior with the strength of thirty men."

"He's an ordinary man of the twenty-first century. You better tell him soon that his mystical world of magic is over."

"You're so blunt about this. Do I really need to tell him?"

"If you don't, he'll hate you." Beth sipped her coffee. "You're jerking this bloke around."

"So, you think I need to tell him he is now an ordinary man?"

"As soon as possible. What if he tries to lift a building and realizes he can't?"

I sipped my coffee and fell almost into a trance as I pondered it. "Shit, yeah, I never thought of that. I think he's so depressed in the hospital right now, because he doesn't understand why his mystical powers aren't healing him. I'll go first thing in the morning and I'll tell him."

"Why wait? Go to him now. Visiting hours don't end 'till half past nine."

"Nah, I think it's best I let him rest. I'll do it tomorrow."

It was a typical rainy morning. I got to the hospital as early as I could. When I arrived at his room he wasn't there. I went to the nurses' station feeling panicked.

"Excuse me, he's not in his room."

"Oh, yes, Wolfgang was discharged about an hour ago," the nurse said. "Reception rung a taxi for him."

"Where did he go?"

"Home, I think. He really didn't say much. We rung him a taxi and he left. "Okay, I'll try him at home."

I dashed out of the hospital and hailed a taxi. I was feeling like shit. Maybe he lost interest in me. This wasn't like him. I got to his flat and knocked on the door. I wiped my sweaty palms on my coat. I was so nervous I had a few pangs of nausea. He opened the door holding himself up with crutches. I stormed into his flat.

"Why didn't you ring me? I would have helped you to get home."

"Home for me is sixth-century Daneland. This is not home for me. I'll be in these crutches for a good while says the doctor. Large bandages cover my wounded abdomen. It hurts when I talk; it hurts when I breathe. Eating isn't what it used to be."

"It takes time to heal, Beowulf."

"Heal? Warriors don't heal. They either strike with a winning victory or die."

"This is the twenty-first century. We have doctors. Doctors heal people."

He hobbled around the room appearing as if he was anxious about something.

"Please sit, Kyla. You must be so pleased to be back in your time."

"Flush toilets. You can't beat them," I said, making conversation. I watched him struggle to sit down. He was awkward with the crutches. He grit his teeth as he dealt with the pain. "Why don't you let me help you?" I rushed to his side, but he pushed me away. "It will take a few weeks to get back on your feet."

"I sit here like a useless swine. I am of no use to anyone."

"Please, don't say that. You're just a little depressed right now. Soon enough you'll be back on your feet. Isn't it important that you and I love each other?" I asked. He stared at the floor; then he glanced at me. He nodded. "I understand you're feeling awful right now, but this will pass."

"Why doesn't the witch answer my calls?" he wondered aloud. "Why are you calling her?" I asked, starting to panic.

"I need to speak with her. I don't understand why she couldn't send you and I to twenty-first century London, because you are not part of our mystical world, and then all of a sudden she could. I find this to be all too baffling."

"Are you upset with her?"

"Yes, I am."

"Don't be," I advised.

"I'm surprised at you, Kyla. You always had a strong dislike for her."

"She makes things up as she goes along. If this is what sorcery is then it's pretty shoddy, don't you think?"

"However, I was given the opportunity to confront the dragon, but then she sends us to this time in the middle of our battle."

"Maybe she wanted to save your life."

"She did that once before, when I asked her to rid me of Grendel and she conjured a way to get me to this time and place. Why would she do this again, especially when I did not make a request?" he asked.

"She claims that she loves you. Maybe she didn't want to see you killed."

"She knows my destiny. She has always known the day of my demise." He was raising his voice. He rubbed his stomach to sooth his pain. "She knew I was to have a victory over the troll. That's why she agreed to send me to this century in the first place."

"She didn't want to see you get harmed by the dragon, Beowulf."

"How do you know this? Why is it, you are not part of our mystical world, and yet you have the power to call the witch?"

I sat beside him on the couch. I took his hand and held it.

"I love you more than anything. Please, try and understand something for me.

You are also not part of the mystical world anymore."

231

"I am a great warrior with the strength of thirty men. I should be healing myself right now."

"No, you're healing the way any ordinary mortal man would heal. You will never speak with the witch again, because she is no longer part of your world. You are in the twenty-first century with me. You are now ordinary. You no longer have the strength of thirty men. You are a very well built man with incredible strength of your own. You don't need the strength of thirty men in this time."

He tried to get up but he couldn't. He dropped his crutches to the floor. I picked them up and handed them to him.

"This was your request to the witch?"

"Yes, because I didn't want to see you die." I started to cry. "I love you. I didn't want to see the dragon devour you."

"If you love me then you must love all of me," he said.

"I do love all of you."

"I'm a Viking warrior. You must be able to accept that."

"Haven't I always?" I said, dabbing at my eyes.

"No, you have not been able to do so. I am so angry right now!"

"Angry at what? I saved your life by getting the witch to bring you to my time."

"I never asked you to save my life. How could you do such a thing to me?"

He managed to stand up. He walked clumsily around his flat. He couldn't face me no matter how hard I cried.

"I love you, Beowulf. I've gone through hell to keep you in my life, and this is your fucking reaction?"

He turned to me with a stone-face expression.

"Why didn't you let me die? You pitied me. I'm a warrior. I am not to be pitied.

Why didn't you let me die?"

"I could never do that."

He couldn't look at me. He hobbled to the bedroom and shut the door. I sat on the couch and cried. I waited in his flat for an hour; he didn't leave his bedroom, so I left.

I rode the tube for hours going from one part of London

232

to the next. I never left the station. I'd never felt so miserable. After a few hours I finally climbed the stairs of Russell Station and got back on street level. I walked to the university campus and looked for Beth. She was sitting in our favorite café with a few of our classmates. I waved to her. She came to me.

"Kyla? You look dreadful. Have you been crying?"

I tried to compose myself, so I could get a word out without falling apart. "He doesn't love me anymore."

"Did he say that to you?" Beth asked.

"Not in so many words, but if you saw him you'd understand. He hates me."

"I can't imagine Beowulf hating you. I think you're going off the deep end here. Did you tell him he's no longer mystical?"

"Yes," I admitted.

"I guess that must have put him over a bit. He'll get over it."

"He's shattered from this, Beth," I said, being emphatic. "He's a sixth-century Viking warrior. How in the hell is he going to get over this?"

"Did you tell him he no longer has the strength of thirty men, and that he'll have to heal on his own?" she asked. I nodded. "The man has a tremendous physique. He probably has the strength of ten men. I'd say that's rather good, wouldn't you?"

"He doesn't think the way we do. He would have preferred to die from the dragon wounds, than to have me save him."

"Oh, I see. He's one of those. It's that warrior thing. He's like a knight or something. He probably feels you've offended his honor."

"I most certainly did. I think I'm going to lay low for a while. I won't see him. I'll give him time to think things through."

"Yeah," Beth said, "I would. Once he starts feeling better, he'll ring you."

"I hope so."

"By the way, did the dragon die?"

"Oh, yes. Beowulf jabbed his sword in its gut. I saw it fall to its death."

"Was he and his sword magical at the time?"

"No, he was ordinary at that point."

"So he slew the dragon as an ordinary warrior? With an ordinary sword?"

"Yes," I said, catching on to her point.

"Does he know this?"

"No."

"Why?"

"'Cause I'm an idiot."

"Yes, you are. Go and tell him. That will change everything. He doesn't need magic. He can do the job on his own wits and strength. He has a brilliant body. His eyes are mesmerizing…I'd do him."

"Can you fuck off?"

Beth and I embraced, and I ran off to fetch a double-decker. I arrived at Beowulf's building. As I stepped off the bus. Beowulf was sitting on the front step reading a book.

"It's nice to see you out and about," I said, with a smile. He slowly reached for his crutches and held himself up.

"I wouldn't say I'm out and about, Kyla. I needed fresh air."

"London isn't going to give you fresh, but it will give you air," I said, chuckling at my own bad humor.

He wasn't at all amused, when he said, "Kyla, we need to talk."

"Oh, shit. About what?"

"Us."

"Double shit."

"I think it would be wise if I were to make my own way in this time and place. I mean, without your guidance." I felt my heart drop. "I've burdened you enough. It's time I act like a true warrior and venture through this century and country on my own. I can no longer do this to you."

"What are you doing to me? You're not a burden. How

234

can you think this?"

"I have let down so many people, including you. I am not deserving of you." He straightened his posture with the use of his crutches, where his eyes only looked down at me, and his head remained straight. "I have given this a great deal of thought.

Please, don't make this more difficult than it already is."

"I thought I was your queen."

"I don't deserve a queen like you," he said, with a monotone voice. "This can't be happening," I said, trembling with stark panic.

"Please," he said, standing straighter farther from me. "We need a separation of some sort. I don't think I can bear to be with someone so fair as you. Forgive me."

"Beowulf, please, get a hold of yourself. This isn't like you."

"Oh, no, Kyla, this is very much like me. I am a fallen warrior."

Tears poured out of my eyes. I choked on my own saliva I cried so hard. He turned away from me.

"I love you. Don't you love me anymore?"

"This is the problem. Just, please, do as I ask of you. Do not ring me; do not try to see me. I will come for you if my situation changes."

"Situation? What situation?"

"I must try to regain my honor."

He hobbled up the stone stairs that led to his flat. He didn't even turn around to give me a last look. He walked from me until I could no longer see him. I stood on the sidewalk and cried. It started to rain, of course. I hadn't an umbrella, but I could no longer feel wet or dry, hot, nor cold.

CHAPTER FORTY-THREE

One year passed since I last saw Beowulf. I cried a lot, but never let on to anyone what kind of pain I was undergoing. As long as I stayed focused I could get through the day. I couldn't believe how much he meant what he said. He really wanted me out of his life. We had gone through so much together. We experienced something that no other being would ever experience, and we were in love. Maybe he never loved me in the first place. Maybe this is the way Vikings did things.

I tucked away all the photos of us together, all his Norse warrior tools that he had left behind, and even the Viking jewelry he gave me. I had to find a way to stay sane. I tried to get on with my studies and achieve high grades. I started jogging, and I even tried to date other blokes, which wasn't easy.

"Kyla! Wait up!" called Beth, as she stepped off the bus. "Where do you want to do lunch today?"

"Whoa, you cut your hair."

"Yes, it's too short isn't it?"

"It's rather ugly, wouldn't you say? Where did you go to get it done?"

"Don't rub it in," I said, and shrugged. "Hair grows."

We went to a tiny café in the basement of a larger restaurant. We seated ourselves, and ordered tea. Beth sat back and stared at me.

"Didn't you go out with Duncan the other night?"

"It was awful; never again. He's such a yawn. He's also not the most handsome." We received our tea and scanned the menus. "I used to go here with Beowulf, you know."

"Now, now, none of that. We made a pact. This is the new you. You're no longer living your historic world with Beowulf, the dragon slayer. Those days are done for."

"It's only been a year. It will take a good long time for me to get over someone like him, don't you think?"

"A year is too long. Get that man out of your thoughts. You begged me to not let you sway in his direction," Beth reminded me.

"I know, but I can't help it. I still love him."

"You'll some day meet someone who is much more interesting than Beowulf."

"You've got to be kidding," I said, and started to laugh.

Beth buried herself in her menu. "This restaurant is too fattening."

"Oh, Kyla, I went to see that latest flick at the downtown cinema last night."

"What flick? If it didn't gain its acclaim from Cannes then I'm not interested."

"You're such a die hard, Kyla. Beowulf quite fancied it."

I spewed the tea out of my mouth. "You went to see a film with Beowulf?"

"Yeah, I think it was the second or third film we saw together."

"Why didn't you tell me?" I asked.

She stirred her tea a few too many times.

I had to catch my breath. "Well, how is he?"

"He's doing okay, I suppose."

"How did he look? Is he well?"

"Very well. He's gained a bit of weight. He looks marvelous."

"Did his wounds heal?"

"Oh, yes."

"Is he seeing anybody?" I inquired, not able to help myself another second.

"I'm really not sure. Well, I mean, I don't live with him. I don't know if he's seeing anybody. He might, um, or he may not."

"Are you good friends?"

"I'd say, but just friends."

237

"Nothing like what I had with him?"

"Oh, Kyla, get a grip. You went separate ways a year ago. You've been doing quite well on your own, I would say."

"Thanks, but I don't think so. I do what I have to do to survive. Does he ever speak of me?"

"All the time."

I smiled stupidly. "Really? Do you think he misses me?"

"I'm not going to get into any more of this. He still thinks you should have let him die."

"Well, I strongly disagree. You would have done the same as me."

"He feels he's offended the rules of a great Norse warrior. I try not to get him started on this, because he makes me crazy with this ancient rubbish. Then he starts to pray to Odin for strength. Why is he so hung up on having so much strength? Doesn't he have enough?"

"He's not from our time. He's never going to get it, no matter what. Strength is everything to a sixth-century Viking warrior. He feels he didn't fulfill his king's wishes, therefore he'd much rather be dead," I said, and started to whimper. "The dragon was supposed to kill him."

"King's wishes? Did you meet the king?"

"What a loser."

"If he's such a loser, why does Beowulf go on about him so much?' "He was king of the Danes; a high ranker."

"Why didn't you fancy him?"

"Because he was disgusting. Everybody in the sixth century was disgusting.

They smelled too."

"Oooh, how awful."

I tried to laugh, but tears ran down my cheeks instead. I lowered my head so nobody would see that I was crying in a café. Beth scanned the room with her eyes feeling a bit uncomfortable.

"Lets not discuss that silly dragon bit. Did I tell you that he's been improving his English? He's doing quite well with his courses."

238

"Courses? He's going to school?"

"Yes, he's on the campus and he's taking English courses. He's doing well."

"I'm so glad. I must say he never ceases to impress me."

"Oh, yes, impressive is definitely what he is."

"How come I never see him around?"

"It's a big university. What's the population of London?" I gave a fake snicker.

"Oh, yes, you're right. Anyways, I really must pay attention to the time. I have another class in just fifteen minutes."

I stood up and pushed in my chair.

"Don't go around looking for him," Beth advised. "He needs this time to venture on his own."

"Of course he does." I said, and smiled. She smiled back at me.

"Beth, do you think he'll ever reconsider and come back to me?" I asked with a sniffle.

"I don't know the answer to that. He needs more time to be amongst the modern world. He just needs time, I guess."

CHAPTER FORTY-FOUR

The university year was finally over and I had completed my Bachelor of Arts degree in Ancient English Literature. Beth did not finish, however she was just a few courses short. Convocation day had finally arrived and I was damn glad. I never thought I would see this day, especially with so many interferences like trolls and dragons. My parents sat in Convocation Hall, whilst I was situated elsewhere getting fitted with a graduation gown.

Before I put on my gown, I took a peek at the seated area just to get a glimpse of the turn out. I noticed my parents managed to get their seats near the front. It was easy to spot them, because my mother wore a bright orange dress. The crowd was getting immense. It was an exciting time.

I stood in a line with the graduating undergraduate students dressed in our black gowns exposing the university's colors around the collar. The bagpipes began and the chancellor of the institution walked down the aisle. I stood in the back with everyone else. The long speeches were quite boring. I sighed and yawned a few times, but always wore a smile. Then they called upon the undergraduates of English – one by one, we stood on the stage to accept our diploma and received several handshakes from the dean and the chancellor, as well as other university officials.

"Kyla Brookes has received her Bachelor of Arts Degree in English," the announcer said, over the microphone.

I stepped onto the stage and received my diploma. I shook hands with all the V.I.Ps and stood on the stage with the chancellor and the dean for photos. As I stood there with cameras flashing in my face I looked to the audience, so I could see my parents. My mother and father applauded me, as if I was responsible for discovering the theory of relativity. This was a grand moment for them. I could see my mother pulling out a hanky to wipe her sobbing eyes.

Then I noticed someone standing in one of the aisles. Someone without a camera was standing in the middle of one of the aisles? How rude. How uncouth. I focused on this person, a man in a tweed blazer. Why would I care what this bloke was wearing? Oh, shit! It was Beowulf.

I froze, rather than smiled for the camera. He noticed that I spotted him. My heart raced with panic. He turned away and started to exit the hall. My heart sank. I wished someone could tell me what to do next. There were so much applause and so many people. If I didn't take advantage of this moment I may never see him again.

I ran to the edge of the stage and jumped down. The audience stopped applauding. I fell to the floor, because I got tangled in my gown. My diploma went flying. Some of the ushers helped me up. I smiled at them and started to run. I ran past my parents.

"Kyla! What are you doing?" shouted my parents.

I had to ignore them, because I had no time to waste. I dashed out of Convocation Hall. I ran like I never ran before, I saw him in the distance.

"Beowulf!" I called out, but he didn't even turn his head. He was walking faster than I was running. "Beowulf! Stop!" He crossed the busy street and left me at a red light, because the traffic was too dense. "Beowulf! Please, wait!"

He turned and saw me. He waited on the other side of the street. When the light changed he crossed the street to me.

"Kyla, you're still wearing your convocation gown." I was winded, and out of breath.

"Why didn't you wait for me?" I asked. "I just heard you calling now. I'm sorry."

"Beowulf, why?" He tried to smile.

"I haven't seen you in so long," I said, desperately trying to suck in my tears. "So, why did you show up at my convocation?"

"I see. Well, I wanted to see you convocate. I felt it was important."

"To me?"

"To you and to me."

A tear trickled down my face.

"I haven't seen or heard from you in a year. Why?"

"Well, I still love you very much, that's why? But I am not worthy of you, m'lady."

"Yes, you are!" I shouted, hoping this time he would believe me.

"I made a terrible blunder. I don't really think I can face you any longer."

"You can face me as long as you want."

"No, I don't think I can."

"But you went to my convocation to see me graduate?"

"I couldn't bare not to. You see, I've been suffering since our last meeting."

"Your wounds seem to have mended."

"Oh, yes, of course, my physical wounds are very much mended, thanks to modern medicine. Physically I feel very well, thank you."

"So, what do you mean when you say you've been suffering?" I heard my name being called from a distance. I turned my head to see both my parents coming my way. "Shit, my parents are coming."

"Oh, how nice that you're parents are here," he said, with a smile.

"Yes, parents usually show up at convocations. Please, before my parents get here, what do you mean that you've been suffering?"

"Suffering greatly, yes, because I no longer have you." He appeared nervous and awkward at the same time.

"But you do have me. You never lost me. I have also had a rough year without you. Beowulf, I don't think I can stand another day without you in my life."

"Why would you want a broken down inferior warrior like myself?"

"Because you're not a broken down inferior warrior."

"My very own bride to be had to rescue me from the

242

fire breathing dragon," he said. He gasped as he tried to catch his breath. "I was supposed to do it on my own without help from my damsel. I am only a memory of a warrior. I can only depend on my magical strength, and without that I am no longer a great warrior."

I stepped closer to him.

"You're wrong. You don't need any of that witch's magic." I tried to focus. I took his hand and held it to my lips. "Beowulf, listen to me."

"Kyla!" called my mother, in the background.

"Yes, m'lady." He stared at my hand. "I have forgotten how beautiful your hands are. The mere touch from your delicate hands sends me to places I cannot even describe."

"It has been too long. But there is something that you don't understand." I kissed his hands several times. He pulled them from me.

"Unfortunately, I do understand all very well. I am a failed and fallen warrior."

"Stop saying that!" I tugged on his blazer. "Listen to me for a minute." He was still and silent. "The witch could only send you to the twenty-first century with me if you were to have your magical powers stripped from you in the middle of your battle with the dragon."

Beowulf stepped back. "That witch. She always takes the long way, doesn't she? I'm surprised. I mean, wouldn't that entail that she would also be banished from my life?"

"Yes, how would you know this?"

"I am from a magical mystical world, m'lady. If I no longer have the magic, then I am of no interest to a sorceress."

My parents were getting closer.

"Kyla!" my father called, as they approached us. "What has got into you? What is this sort of rubbish you're pulling on us on this very special day? You jumped off the stage and ran out of the hall."

"You killed the dragon before you came to this time and place," I said, ignoring my father for the time being.

My parents stood beside us looking flustered.

"Kyla? Who is this man?" my mother asked, pointing at Beowulf.

"I slew the beast?" Beowulf said, with wide eyes filled with surprise. "Is that even possible?"

"Yes. You jabbed it somewhere around its belly; perhaps this was an area of no scales. You thrust your sword into its gut and it fell to the ground. I saw it fall to its death. You saved the people of Daneland. You are king of the Danes."

"Kyla, what are you talking about with this man?" my mother demanded.

"I slew it without magic?" Beowulf asked with a look of bewilderment on his face. "Yes, you have the strength to be a warrior on your own. You don't need magic.

You are the finest warrior who ever lived."

"But how? If you saw the beast fall to its death -- why didn't I see the same?"

"You had lost too much blood. You were passed out."

"But I must have had my magic still if I were losing blood from being wounded. How could this be?"

"Yes, you suffered a mortal wound and you still managed to slay the dragon. This means you are the truest and the finest of all warriors."

He took me in his arms and kissed me passionately in front of my parents. I slid my arms around his neck. He engulfed me into his arms and mauled me with kisses.

"What is all this absurd talk about dragons?" my father demanded, as he glanced at my mother.

Beowulf stopped kissing me when he acknowledged my parents' presence. "Kyla, my love, I no longer have the strength of thirty men, so why would you be here with me in my arms?"

"You have the strength of maybe ten ordinary men, but that's all you need for this century. The men in the twenty-first century have the strength of one man. You have a tremendous amount of strength, even for the sixth century."

Beowulf turned to my father.

"M'lord, would you say the strength of ten men is

244

sufficient for the twenty-first century?"

My poor father had such a confused expression on his face. "M'lord? You have the strength of ten men? Kyla, who is this?" my father asked.

"Hello, my name is Beowulf," he said, bowed and took my mother's hand and kissed it.

"M'lady, forgive me," he said as he continued to kiss my mother's hand. "You're name is Beowulf?" my father asked, with a puzzled expression on his face. "If you have the strength of ten men, that is very impressive."

"Is it?" Beowulf asked, as he rose from his bowing stance. My parents glanced at each other and they both nodded. "And, m'lord, I plan to marry your daughter, Lady Kyla. I will make her my queen. If this is suitable to you?"

"All of a sudden you're getting married?" my mother said, looking joyous and nervous at the same time. "Queen? Who is this man? Is he affiliated with the royals?"

"No, he's not. And it's not all of a sudden. Beowulf and I have been through loads together. He is definitely the man I want to marry." Beowulf and I kissed.

My father looked at my mother. "I suppose we have a wedding to plan, don't we?" he said.

"But, tell me, my queen," Beowulf said, smiling at me. "Would it be too much to ask for us to move to Denmark?"

"Maybe we should visit there first. None of Denmark would even come close to resemble what you once knew."

"Denmark? Kyla, you're moving to Denmark?" my mother asked, alarmed. Beowulf and I embraced. Beowulf smiled at my parents and bowed his head. "Wherever we choose to live wouldn't matter, because I know that I lived up to King Hrothgar's request."

"You are king of the Danes!" I cheered, and lifted my arms above my head.

THE END

www.ingramcontent.com/pod-product-compliance
Lightning Source LLC
Chambersburg PA
CBHW011459170626
46814CB00008B/2968